FALSE FLAGS

HENRY PHILIPS

CATALINA PRESS, LLC

Catalina Press, LLC
Tucson, Arizona
www.catalinabookpress.com
books@catalinabookpress.com

Follow us and our authors on:
Twitter: @CatalinaPress
Facebook: @CatalinaBookPress
Instagram: #CatalinaBookPress

Cover design by A2

Art Direction by Bob Ciano

First paperback edition published 2020

This book is a work of fiction. All characters and events in this book are fictitious. Any resemblance to real persons or occurrences is strictly coincidental.

ISBN: 978-1-953721-00-6

Printed in the United States of America

1

José slowly tugged the bundle along the floor of the tunnel. His breathing punctuated the *corrido* he sang quietly, almost imperceptibly, as he struggled. He had a few hundred yards to cover from the entrance in the storage-room floor of a disused auto repair shop on the edge of Nogales, Sonora, to the opening cut in the concrete slab of a ramshackle bungalow close to the border fence in Nogales, Arizona. Unlike the better-maintained and busier tunnels used by the cartels, this tunnel had no electric lights and no ventilation, a forgotten antique from an earlier age of smuggling when the Border Patrol was less sophisticated with their surveillance.

While the desert above broiled at a dry 105 degrees, José soaked through his rayon shirt in the damp, funky air below ground, the moisture a remnant of last night's July monsoon thunderstorm. Dust caked his face and hair and slid on droplets down the wet canyon of his spine. He wore a hiker's headlamp on his forehead, and his perspiration made him stop every minute or so to curse and slide the lamp back into position above his sweat-beaded eyebrows. Just 50 more yards and he would emerge from the opening in the floor of what had been the master bedroom closet but was now the base of a pyramid of debris. Looters had long ago ripped the plaster and lathe from the walls in search of copper pipe and wire, so the walls that once hid the comings and goings of a household now only cast threadlike shadows against the light seeping into the house through stained roller shades.

As he dragged the bundle the last few yards, José started again at the beginning of his song,

"El dia tres de noviembre / que dia da tran senaldo / matron tres de Guerrero / esto rinches desdichados."

He stopped as he reached the end of the tunnel on the Arizona side, pausing for a moment, willing his breath to slow so he could listen for the faintest indication of someone, anyone, at the tunnel exit. He heard nothing. He waited a bit more. Still nothing. José grasped the length of rope he had tied to the straps of the bundle and used it to draw the bundle northward behind him as he slowly, quietly ascended the crude wooden ladder staked to the wall of the tunnel.

At the top the stench of rodents assaulted him, their decomposing bodies in the pile of debris above the trap door effective at keeping any interlopers from picking through the pile and uncovering the tunnel. José dropped back down, took a deep breath of the damp, slightly foul air below, and pushed himself up and against the plywood that covered the top of the tunnel opening. He emerged into a fetid room, the light a dark amber as it leaked around and through the tattered shades partially covering the dirty windows. He took a breath and pulled the bundle up through the closet and into the center of the room. It joined five other bundles he had already dragged between the two countries over the course of the day.

Each bundle was shaped like a medium-sized duffle bag, smaller than a soldier's but larger than a gym bag. They were heavy. José did not know what made them so dense. They were too heavy to be meth, oxy, or weed, and dollars never moved north in such quantity. Dollars always found their way south in the great, organic exchange of what each side of the border valued from the other. He could see that the bundles were lined and sealed with plastic sheeting. He thought maybe they held gold or some other precious metal, but he could not imagine he would be trusted with something so valuable. On the other hand, he had been told by the narco who had given him the bundles that if he tried to open them, he and his family would be dealt with in the usual, brutal way. His curiosity could not compete with the certainty of gruesome murder, so he simply piled the bundles in the center of the room, as he had been told to do.

José reached into the pocket of his shirt, which had already dried in the heat of the room to a burgundy-brown of fabric and dust, and pulled out a pack of Marlboros. He opened the carton, extracted the last cigarette from its red-and-white refuge, and tossed the empty carton onto the floor. He flicked open his lighter and lit the end of the cigarette, drawing the smoke deep into his lungs and expelling the first breath with a cough. He absently picked a speck of tobacco from his lower lip and looked around the room.

When he finished the cigarette, he dropped it to the ripped linoleum floor and snuffed it with the heal of his boot. He stepped away and idly watched the last threads of smoke rise from the crushed butt. Then he sighed and walked back toward the tunnel opening, absorbing the increasing rat stink as he approached the closet. Just four more bundles to go.

JOSÉ SHIFTED his perch on the bar stool and used the mirror behind the bottles of tequila and gin to search for the narco. Looking back at him was a sea of semi-drunks, men with cowboy shirts open midway down their chests, their arms cradling young women bursting from the tops and sides of their dresses. Pounding music drove a weak, rhythmic motion in the crowd that periodically bumped José on his stool. A short girl in a blue dress squeezed next to him on his right. She had the round face and baby-fat middle of a teenager from the south. The girl smiled tentatively but Jose ignored her. He looked down at his cigarette, the dwindling pile of pesos on the bar, and the almost empty bottle of Pacifico. Fuck! Why did the narco want to meet in this place? José hated the noise and the heat, preferring to meet at one of the narco's places of business, or in the street, or in his car. He knew he was just a small part of the organization, but he was tired and did not want to be there.

José sighed and took a drag from his cigarette, then the last swallow of his beer. When the bartender worked his way back down to his end of the bar, José pushed a bill toward him and told him to save his seat. He stepped down from the stool and waded into the ocean of sweaty bodies.

At the back of the room a crowd stood waiting for the one bathroom, so José squeezed past the men and women and through the back door. He stepped into the alley and welcomed the relative cool of the night. Looking up and through the weak streetlights, he saw a hint of stars. *No rain tonight*, he thought. He turned to his left and walked to a slight indentation where two buildings met. He unzipped his jeans and had just begun to water the side of the building when he heard footsteps approaching from the direction of the door. He turned his head slightly and saw the narco. He was not embarrassed as he stood exposed, facing the building, but he felt unprofessional. He finished quickly and zipped, absently rubbing his hands on the legs of his jeans before turning to face the narco.

"Is it complete?" the narco asked.

"Si," Jose answered, looking down respectfully. The two men stood without speaking for a moment and then Jose heard soft steps behind him. Before he could turn, he saw a glint below his chin and felt the blade enter the left side of his neck and cross to the right, a hand on his left shoulder gripping him for leverage.

The narco stepped back to avoid the crimson spray and watched José's eyes grow wide, his jaw silently flapping, before his head flopped to the side and he collapsed to the pavement.

2

Eric West did not want to wake up. He did not want the sun to be intruding into his bedroom from behind what were supposed to be blackout curtains. He did not want the incessant electronic wail of his alarm clock pounding into his brain. He did not want to be this hungover. But he also did not want to feel the bite of his Supervisory Special Agent (SSA). So he fumbled for the alarm and punched it, rubbing his eyes and the bridge of his nose with his other hand. He pressed harder across the bridge and then above his nose, trying to force the pain from the front of his cranium, through his brain, and out through his hair into the pillow, but he was unsuccessful. "Tylenol," he mumbled,

He rolled onto his side then sat up, hunched over his knees. Eric willed his legs to lift him erect and he shuffled into the bathroom. The mirror reflected unshaven cheeks supporting bloodshot eyes, the stubble lending a particular melancholy to the picture. He opened the medicine cabinet and grabbed the plastic bottle of Extra-Strength Tylenol, flipped off the non-childproof cap, fished two tablets from the bottle, and popped them into his mouth. He tried to swallow them, but his mouth was dry and he gagged. *Shit!* He slowly walked to the kitchen, and a glass of water later, the pills were on their way, he hoped, to easing the throbbing in his head.

A shower, a shave, and a protein shake later, Eric was drinking black coffee in his government-issue Malibu on his way to the FBI Resident Agency in Tucson. He pulled into the lot and used his ID card to enter the building through the side door. As he walked into the room of cubicles that was his home away from home, he noticed an unusual hum of activity in the corner near the SSA's office.

Spotting Eric, the SSA called through the crowd, "West, you're heading down to Nogales with Montez, pronto."

Eric started toward the SSA's office door and the small crowd gathered there. "What's up, chief?"

"A Border Patrol agent was shot and killed there, close to the border," the SSA replied. "Get going before the locals contaminate the crime scene."

Great, Eric thought. While the FBI had exclusive jurisdiction whenever a federal employee was killed in the line of duty, local law enforcement—in this case either the Nogales Police Department or the Santa Cruz County Sheriff's Department—usually resented it when the bureau rode in and took away their murder. He hated the over-the-shoulder glances from the local cops when the feds arrived. His father had been a small-town cop, and long before Eric had gone to the academy, his dad had occasionally come home to Eric and his mother and complained about the heavy-handed feds as he slipped off his service weapon and slid it onto the top of the kitchen cabinet, out of reach of Eric and his brother. When Eric graduated from Quantico, he promised his dad he would not be the kind of FBI agent his father resented, but there was no escaping the sense of superiority that came from representing not just a few thousand—even 10,000 or 100,000 local citizens—but the federal government and the power that it carried.

Montez looked over at Eric. He walked from the SSA's office to his desk and pulled his Glock 19-M service weapon from the top drawer, inserting the pistol into the holster at his waist and covering the distance to where Eric was standing in a few steps. "You look like shit," he snickered.

"Better than I feel," was the reply as they turned for the door.

LESS THAN AN HOUR'S drive down Interstate 19 to the Mariposa Port of Entry exit, and less than a mile from there, they reached the house. Four white-and-green Border Patrol SUVs were parked in front, two with their lights flashing, along with a half dozen Nogales PD marked cars and an unmarked Crown Vic or two. Yellow police tape stretched diagonally from the passenger-side mirror of one of the Border Patrol Tahoes to a stringy bush next to the house. The house looked abandoned, its stucco cracked and the paint peeling from its siding like the bark of an old birch tree. Another line of tape stretched from the rear windshield wiper of the Tahoe to a dented drainpipe at a corner of the house. At the feet of a knot of officers inside the tape, he could see the green-trousered legs of the agent, the dusty, tan, lace-up boots pointing left and right toward the sky.

Before he and Montez reached the tape, he stopped and looked around, rotating his body 360 degrees to try to gain some appreciation for what the crime scene had been before being overrun with law enforcement. The houses surrounding the house where the agent met his end spoke of modest circumstances but not necessarily criminality. One house had a small pink tricycle on the concrete walkway a few feet from the front door. Another had a cardboard sign advocating for a local political candidate poked into the parched lawn. Eric turned back toward the tape, looked at Montez, and stepped forward and underneath, holding the tape high enough so that when he pitched forward to clear it, his still-sensitive head did not pound too badly.

The two FBI agents introduced themselves to the local PD and Border Patrol agents. Eric and Montez had worked a case involving the murder of migrants on federal land the year before, but they did not recognize any of the agents. With a few words they expressed their condolences for the loss of one of their own. The group opened to admit the FBI agents to the inner sanctum of the scene, the nearly final resting place of the person on the ground who, it turned out, was a woman, not a man. The Border Patrol agent had three tears in her uniform blouse, denoting shots that had been stopped by her bullet-proof vest but which had probably stunned her and perhaps broken a rib. Unfortunately, the shooter or shooters had also fired at what had been a tanned, pretty face, and the damage there was more obvious.

"Did she report her stop?" Montez asked.

"Agent Walsh called in suspicious activity around the house. This area was part of her regular patrol," replied a tall, husky man in a green uniform. "Next we heard was a local PD report of shots fired. We were here with Nogales PD in two or three minutes"

"You see any vehicles leaving the scene?" Eric asked.

Silence.

The two walked toward the front door of the house, which was ajar and opened to darkness inside. They slipped on disposable booties and went in. Eric pulled a small, LED flashlight from his pocket and played the beam around the room. Someone had already found the pile of debris covering the entrance to the tunnel, probably drawn by the stench, which had hinted to them of another murder to be discovered. They looked down the tunnel then turned back to the room. Border Patrol would explore the tunnel and seal it up after the investigation. The dust on the floor might have displayed footprints, although those were probably lost now. Eric noticed what looked like drag marks on the floor, pointing from the tunnel to the center of the main room.

A Border Patrol agent noticed his interest and volunteered, "Yeah, we saw that. Looks like someone dragged marijuana bundles out of the tunnel."

"Do pot smugglers kill Border Patrol agents?" Eric asked, which drew a sour look from the man in green. Something brighter and cleaner than the rest of the tableau drew Eric's attention and he pointed it out to his partner.

Montez slipped a plastic evidence bag from his pocket and, using the bag like a glove, picked up a crushed Marlboro box, its cellophane wrapper intact. The two exchanged glances as Montez made a notation on the evidence bag with a sharpie and slipped the find into his pocket.

3

S outh-Central Phoenix is a tangle of highways, gridded roads, and industrial buildings. In one sand-colored concrete building a few blocks north of Interstate 17, a man received a trailer load of empty 55-gallon polyethylene drums, mostly blue in color but a few in white and a handful in black. The barrels were surplus from a pickle company, and even though they had been washed and rinsed, they still emitted a vinegary, pickle smell. That did not bother the man. He liked strong spices, and the vinegar smell helped cover the sharp body odor of his colleague, who was sweeping past every few minutes driving a forklift stacked with a dozen barrels in two layers. The driver of the forklift added each load to the hundreds already accumulated inside the building. This truckload was the last.

A hundred miles to the south, in the Tucson FBI office, a technician had easily obtained a few good fingerprints off the Marlboro carton's surface and electronically sent a high-resolution picture of them to the FBI laboratory in Quantico, Virginia, saving the originals as evidence. At Quantico a technician painstakingly untangled the jumble of whorl lines from one another to capture a complete print of a right-hand index finger, as well as partials of the next two. There were some indications of a thumbprint on the opposite side of the carton, but those were sufficiently smeared to be less useful than the others. Another technician would then use the characteristics to search the FBI's national fingerprint database and try to get a match. That, of course, presumed that the owner of the print was in the database. That was not always a good assumption when it came to smugglers, if that was who had satisfied his nicotine habit inside the house.

Eric and Montez had recovered a crushed cigarette butt, but it was even less likely that any recoverable DNA would be in the database. Twenty-first century professional law enforcement rolled its collective eyes at the image of a universal catalogue of bad guys' DNA, so that the least speck of a smidgen of a morsel of something a criminal had eaten, smoked, held, or excreted could solve a crime in 55 minutes. It just was not that television-easy.

Eric was at his desk, looking over photos of the crime scene, when Montez walked over with a match for the fingerprints. "José Rodriguez-Marquez, DOB nine April, nineteen sixty-nine. Veracruz, Mexico. Served two years eight months for smuggling two women and a load of pot across the border. Deported back to Mexico in two thousand eight after serving his sentence."

"Looks like he came back for a visit," Eric said, his brow slightly furrowed. "I'm assuming with that light sentence there was no weapon involved."

"None in his record. That was his only hit in the system. What's bothering you?"

Eric leaned back in his chair, which gave a muted squeak. He put his arms behind his head and asked, "Dope smugglers don't carry guns, not small fry. Why'd he shoot her?"

"Maybe he didn't," Montez replied and let the comment hang.

ABOUT THREE HOURS LATER, Eric was on a stool at Maloney's Bar, nursing a beer. Summer is hard on a college bar, with the usual flood of ebullient students replaced by loners, hard-core drinkers, and bored staff waiting for the fat times in the fall. Eric missed the flow of cute coeds who could not decide if the older man at the bar was intriguing or creepy. He was an even six feet tall, short hair graying at the temples, moderately athletic build but with a bit of softness developing around his middle. No ring on his finger, his just-out-of-college marriage lasting less than five years before his wife, tired of his emotional distance and lousy hours, ran off with a criminal defense attorney.

As Eric slowly rotated the beer glass on the coaster, he thought about the dead Border Patrol agent. Pretty girl, 30, engaged to be married. Good reviews, no sign of any problems or whispered connections with the smugglers that sometimes tainted law enforcement on the border. He twisted on his stool and looked around the room. In a corner was a woman about the same age, drinking a martini with a man wearing a red and blue University of Arizona T-shirt. Eric made eye contact with the woman and then looked away. How would this guy feel if his girlfriend were shot in the face? He shook his head and turned back to his beer.

Ballistics on the gun had been un-extraordinary. Nine millimeter hollow points recovered from the victim, and the ejected shells on the scrubby lawn in front of the house, which showed extraction marks, suggested the weapon used in the crime was a Glock. Only a few million of those out there. And what had been so important that the smuggler had been willing to kill a federal agent? It was noteworthy that only two shells had been recovered of the four fired. That suggested that the shooter was careful to pick up his brass in case he had left fingerprints or DNA on them when he had loaded his magazine, but in his rush to leave the scene he had only found two casings, perhaps because they were on pavement. As it was, neither had much in the way of useable DNA or prints.

Eric finished his beer in a long pull, set the glass back on the coaster, pulled a few of the bills from the stack in front of him, and put them in his pocket. He nodded to the bartender and slid off the stool. He pushed the door open and walked into post-monsoon dampness, the street and sidewalks puddled and the sky in the west streaked with lightning. Open the car door, key in the ignition, and Eric was rolling home to a few hours of sleep and a shower.

THE NEXT MORNING WAS BRIGHT, clear, and hot. Eric called a friend at the Drug Enforcement Agency from his cell phone as soon as he climbed into his car to drive to work. When no one answered, he left a message. Just as he was pulling into a parking spot at his office, his phone rang and showed a restricted caller ID he took as a government caller. He put the car into park, left the engine running for the air conditioning, and answered, "West."

He was greeted by his drug-enforcement friend. "Eric, it's Don at DEA."

"Hey, Don, thanks for calling back. You hear about that Border Patrol agent in Nogales?"

"Yeah, we know all about it. The guy you guys IDed works freelance for various traffickers. What're you thinking?"

Eric paused before answering. "Trafficking's your specialty, not mine. But do individual drug smugglers generally use deadly force? Not the big narcos, you know what I mean."

Don chuckled. "Yeah, trafficking is my specialty. We don't usually see armed coverage for small loads of dope. Too much prison risk for the return. A lot more when the loads are bigger, like in Mexico, where a whole load could be ripped off. We don't see that on this side of the border."

"What about people smuggling? I know this is BP's or ICE's area, but could they have been protecting someone important?" Eric asked.

"You mean are there valuable illegals? That's not my area of expertise, but I'd say probably not from Mexico. Any of the big narco guys won't cross the border and risk getting picked up by us and entering the US criminal justice system. They just use their people over here and stay in their *hacienda grandes*, out of reach."

"What about from outside of Mexico?"

Don apparently had known the question was coming because his answer came immediately. "Again, not my area. We hear rumors of Iranians, or Arabs, or Chinese, but I don't think ICE thinks it's as much of a threat as the media presents."

Eric thought about that. "So what drugs would be worth killing a federal agent for?" he asked.

"Like I said, no experienced trafficker would do that. Maybe there was a young hotshot there to make the pickup who got spooked. You don't know your guy was the shooter, right? Just that he was probably in the house,"

Eric thought about that, too. "Yeah, that's true. You saw the BOLO on Rodriguez, right? Any chance your people on the other side have a lead on him?"

"We have feelers out," Don said. "Our office in Hermosillo is asking around, and there are one or two honest guys left in the police over there who haven't been shot and hung by their ankles from a bridge. We might get lucky."

"Thanks, Don, let me know."

"Will do."

When Don hung up, Eric put the phone in his pocket, killed the engine, and walked into the building.

4

_____

When Malcolm McLean invented the intermodal shipping container, he had been trying to solve a problem common to all break-bulk shipping: how to keep cargo intact, dry and un-stolen, as it made its way from a factory or warehouse onto a truck, maybe onto a train, then onto a ship, off the ship, and back onto a truck or train to the recipient. With the intermodal system, most times a container could carry its cargo unmolested—latched, locked, and sealed—throughout this entire sequence without having to be loaded, unloaded, and reloaded multiple times. It was also outside the reach of expensive, moody, sticky-fingered longshoremen. As a result a shipper could have high confidence that what he or she put into the container at one end of a journey would be received at the other. Today, some 17 million intermodal containers ride, float, or rest in nearly every corner around the world.

Twenty of those containers were inside the building in South Phoenix that smelled slightly like pickles. They had been purchased from a company that dealt in surplus containers. The sizable trade imbalance between the US and China made containers much less valuable in the US, from where they might be sent back empty to China or, perhaps, filled with bails of alfalfa grown on farms west of Phoenix or in California's Imperial Valley to feed Chinese dairy cows. These particular 20 containers had the names of Chinese, Korean, and Danish shipping companies on their scuffed sides and were completely unremarkable compared to the thousands of similar containers within a 50-mile radius.

They sat on the floor of the building in various stages of loading, their open doors revealing a row of blue, green, and red steel caves. Inside were rows of plastic barrels, 18 to a row, 4 rows to a container. Near the top of each container, midway down each long side, a small metal box had been attached to the inside of the corrugated wall with self-tapping screws, and a small probe protruded outside the container through a hole drilled in the steel. A little dab of paint ensured that in the hustle of loading the container unto a truck or train, no casual observer would notice the modification.

On the other side of the city, across a desert plain and miles from any airport, a man was experimenting with a large, unmanned aerial vehicle. This particular UAV model was mainly sold to professional photographers and videographers and featured a radio downlink that permitted the operator to see where the camera was pointed. Its six rotors could lift more than 15 pounds of payload, but the man currently operating it was cursing violently, since he was trying to lift more than the rated capacity and was finding that the performance of the UAV, particularly in the hot, less-dense air of the desert, was not what he expected. He shut down the craft and punched in a number on his phone. The voice at the other end of the connection made a few suggestions and hung up after less than a minute. The man returned to his research.

WHILE THE MAN in the desert east of Phoenix was experimenting with his UAV, 5,600 miles away another man was in an apartment in an upscale suburb of St. Petersburg, Russia. He was staring at one of three monitors facing him, streams of computer code reflecting in blue and green flecks from his reading glasses. Every few seconds his hands would crawl across his keyboard and enter a few lines of text, which simultaneously appeared on the screen. Then he would wait for new lines of code to appear from the other side of the world. Vasily was a successful hacker, averaging more than 20,000 euros a month through the theft and sale of stolen credit cards numbers—including those pesky three-digit codes from the back of US cards, which made them much more valuable. He harvested the cards using an army of "bots" that probed internet addresses for poorly secured point-of-sale terminals and captured the numbers while they were in transit. When he entertained his friends with bottles of Dom Perignon champagne in the noisy, flashy bar where he spent his evenings, he bragged about the stupidity of the consumers who trusted their hard-earned dollars, euros, and pounds sterling to such fools who made and serviced the cash registers where they bought their bread and shirts.

This time he was doing something different. While he normally trolled the internet for random vulnerabilities among specific devices, like gas pumps or cash registers, now he was working on a project for someone who called himself Kha and which involved a completely different type of hack. Kha had contacted Vasily, using Vasily's hacker name, Dropper, on a dark-web site called Rescator, where hackers routinely sold stolen financial data. Kha had asked Dropper to look for a specific group of victims, and after Kha had sent him five Bitcoin— worth about $35,000 on the day he sent them—along with the promise of five more per victim compromised, Vasily had happily complied. He had spent the past two weeks seeking his lucrative prey and had been successful enough to earn the promise of another 90 Bitcoin when all was completed.

Vasily turned to look out the window of his apartment. It was well past midnight but the "white-night" sky glowed a pale blue with crimson highlights along the horizon, and he could hear revelers on the street below. He missed his regular evening crowd, but he could not pass up the promise of his richest payday yet. He turned back to his displays and continued his work.

5

Eric and Montez spent the morning at a branch bank in a strip mall northwest of Tucson where, around 10:10 A.M., a short man dressed in black nylon athletic pants, a grey cotton hoodie, and dark Ray-Ban knockoffs had walked into the nearly empty bank and presented the lone teller with a note. The teller had seen the man enter and suspected something amiss since, while many customers violated the posted policy of "No Sunglasses, No Hats," few would choose to wear a cotton hoodie drawn tight over their heads in the already sweltering, summer morning. Written in what looked like crayon were the words, "I have bomb. All money now."

The teller blanched when she read the note, looked back at the hooded man, and turned to her cash drawer. She immediately began withdrawing wrapped bundles of $10 and $20 bills and passing them to the robber, who slipped them into the pockets of his pants and hoodie after quickly checking the money for dye packs. Finding a stack of 20s with a dye pack, he glared at the teller and tossed it back to her. As she dipped into the drawer once more, she carefully brushed a button above the drawer on the underside of the counter, which triggered an alarm that was silent in the bank but not at the alarm company's monitoring station a few miles away. Since that branch of the alarm company received on average of three false alarms from banks per week, the attendant who monitored the alarm first speed-dialed 911 to reach the Oro Valley Police Department, advising them of the alarm and location and telling them she would call the bank to determine if this was another false alarm.

Two patrol cars were dispatched "Code 3"—lights and sirens—to the bank location while the alarm attendant dialed the bank. On the third ring an assistant manager picked up and, looking around, confirmed that there appeared to be a robbery in progress, no weapon displayed. That information was passed to the police, but the robber walked out of the bank as the nearest police car was still about 90 seconds away. He crossed the parking lot and slipped into a dented, gray pickup truck parked out of sight of the bank entrance, where he pulled off his pants and hoodie, the money still inside, and stuffed them under the driver's seat, along with the sunglasses. Within 30 seconds, just as the first police car screeched to a stop in front of the bank, he had jumped out of the truck and was swiftly striding in shorts and T-shirt toward the home improvement store looming beyond his truck. Inside the store he bought a claw hammer and paid for it with a credit card.

By the time the two FBI agents arrived, the Oro Valley police had secured the scene and started interviews with the bank employees, as well as people in the parking lot. No one outside could remember seeing a man dressed for cooler weather. Within a few minutes of the robbery, enough officers had arrived to seal off the six exits to the parking lot, but by then the dented pickup no witness had noticed was gone, along with $8,600.

Eric was watching a crime tech dust the door handle of the bank for fingerprints when his phone rang, displaying a restricted caller ID. "West," he answered.

"Eric, it's Don over at DEA. I have some info on your friend Rodriguez-Marquez."

"Thanks, Don. What've you got?" Eric asked.

"What I've got is your guy with his throat cut behind a bar in Nogales, Sonora. Our guys in Hermosillo passed the BOLO to the

Nogales municipal police, who passed back the bad news a day or two later."

"When did it happen?" Eric asked.

"That's the interesting part. The same night the BP agent was killed."

Eric digested that fact for a minute. "She made her radio call around three A.M. They have any idea when Rodriguez was killed?"

"Sometime between midnight and one," Don replied.

"So he's not our suspect." He paused. "Good thing. He'd be hard to extradite from the great beyond," Eric added sarcastically but also with a trace of puzzlement in his voice. "Nogales have any suspects?"

Don chuckled then said, "No witnesses, but that's not surprising. If they know who he'd been working with, they're not saying. Our guys have little on Rodriguez, mainly that he's a low-level freelancer. I can get them to sniff around and see if they can find out who his last customer was."

"Thanks, I'd appreciate it." Eric hung up and turned to Montez, who had been following Eric's side of the conversation, and quickly brought him up to speed, after which he scratched the back of his neck and looked at the sidewalk. Coincidences bothered him. They usually meant there was more in play than it seemed. "I'm thinking about taking a ride down to Nogales to talk to the Municipal Police."

"Are you crazy? We don't have jurisdiction in Mexico," Montez objected.

"I know. I'm just going as a private citizen."

Montez looked at him a long time, shook his head, and returned to watching the tech dusting fine black powder on the door handle.

6

The next day was a Friday. Eric called the office to say he was taking a few hours of personal time. He left his weapon—no need for an incident with the Mexicans, who do not appreciate the transportation of firearms into their country, regardless of the bearer—but he slipped his badge into a pocket as he closed the door to his apartment and walked to his car. He had already removed the tactical bag containing his ballistic vest, shotgun, and other goodies from the trunk and put them in a closet in the apartment. He opened the car door, climbed in, started the car, and pulled out of his space. He stopped when he saw Montez standing in the parking lot. He unlocked the passenger-side door and Montez climbed in.

"Thought you might need a translator," Montez said as he clipped his seatbelt. Eric nodded and they started south.

The Comandancia Nogales is a modern, reddish-pink municipal building on Boulevar El Greco, not far from the intersection with Boulevar Luis Donaldo Colosio, a street named for an assassinated Mexican presidential candidate. At the intersection is a large supermarket, and a block down Colosio are a Home Depot and a Sam's Club, all the attributes of a modern North American lifestyle. But while Nogales in the past had generally been quieter than border cities like Laredo and Tijuana, the city named for the walnut trees that once flourished on either side of what was now a border fence had seen its share of challenges. These days, paroxysms of violence punctuated days of quiet, the evidence left in pools of clotted blood on the city's streets. Fortunately for the cross-border tourist trade, the violence was usually expressed, not amidst the craft shops, pharmacies, and tequila mills that emanated from the main crossing joining Nogales, Sonora, with its northern namesake at N. Grand Avenue, but in the sprawling neighborhoods that surrounded the day-trippers and climbed the city's low hills.

Eric and Montez had crossed the border 10 minutes before pulling into the parking lot of the Comandancia. They walked up the steps in the middle of the complex, and Montez scanned the signs for a likely place to start their inquiries. Their challenge was that, while the Sonoran State Judicial Police had jurisdiction over murders, the municipal police had found the body and were more likely to know what was going on in the city. Montez found the sign he was looking for, and the two walked through a glass door into a room divided into cluttered cubicles.

When a police officer asked what they wanted, Montez replied in his unaccented Spanish that they wanted to talk to someone about a man who has been murdered. The officer asked who they were, and they both showed their FBI credentials, but Montez said it was an informal visit.

The officer made a quizzical expression with his mouth and walked into an office at the side of the room. He reemerged a moment later followed by a heavy-set man in a slightly too-tight uniform, one hand resting absently on his pistol.

"I am Capitán Garcia," the man introduced himself.

"Eric West."

"Raul Montez."

"To what do we owe a visit from the esteemed FBI?" Capitan Garcia asked, carefully enunciating each letter, "Even if it is ... informal?"

Montez began, Eric following the Spanish as closely as he could. "We are investigating the murder of a US Border Patrol agent in Nogales, Arizona. The agent was killed at one end of a cross-border tunnel, and at the crime scene we found fingerprints belonging to a man who was killed here in Nogales around the same time, José Rodriguez-Marquez."

Captain Garcia motioned them into his office and pointed to two chairs in front of his desk. He sat heavily into his own chair and started rooting through stacks of files that circled a small, open area containing a cup of coffee and a half-eaten burrito. He found what he was looking for and cautiously extracted it from one of the piles, taking care not to let the pile collapse onto his lunch. "You know that this case in not in our jurisdiction. You should be talking to the state police."

He opened the file and looked through its contents as Montez replied, "We know. We're just trying to get some idea of what he might have been smuggling before he died."

Captain Garcia looked intently across the folder at the two men, first at one, then the other. He closed the folder and dropped it on one of the stacks. "What makes you think he was a smuggler?" he asked.

Montez translated, and he and Eric looked at each other before Montez replied, "He had been arrested in the US for trafficking before being deported, or should I say, repatriated, back to Mexico. DEA seems to know about him." Montez continued, "Do you know what he was doing before he died?"

"I believe he was drinking beer in a bar," Garcia replied.

Montez did not let his frustration show, since he was not surprised by the evasion. "Do you think he was waiting for someone?" he asked.

"I have no idea."

"Capitán, if you can just give us something, we can leave you alone," Montez implored.

Captain Garcia sighed. "You have no jurisdiction here. You can leave me alone even if I don't give you anything." He leaned back in his chair, the back scraping against a well-chewed spot on the wall, and sighed. "OK, I will give you something. Your man was not moving the usual products that cross the border. A little bird told me it was something from far away." He smirked cryptically. The two men across his desk looked at him in silence, waiting for elaboration. Garcia rewarded their patience. "It was some things that go boom!"

7

---

onday, the day of the funeral for Border Patrol Agent Margaret "Molly" Walsh, opened dry and hot. The sky was a brilliant blue, the absence of even a wisp of white over the mountains suggesting that the monsoons had taken a *siesta* and the day would be a scorcher. Law enforcement personnel from throughout the southwest had lined up along Stone Avenue to honor the flag-draped casket as it was carried into St. Augustine Cathedral. The men and women stood at attention in beige, green, and blue-black uniforms, solemn under the wilting sun. A small group of family members followed the casket, trailed by dignitaries from DC and Phoenix. Eric and Montez, dressed in dark suits, followed the uniforms into the church and took a seat along one side. Over the next 90 minutes, the choir sang, the organ played, the bishop talked of salvation, the dignitaries talked of sacrifice, and Eric's mind wandered over the disparate pieces of this crime.

The allegation by Captain Garcia that explosives were being smuggled around the time of the murder brought additional visibility to the case in DC and the involvement of new agencies like the Bureau of Alcohol, Tobacco and Firearms and whispers of a role for the CIA. In a place and a culture that values discretion, particularly among members of law enforcement who wished to survive, Montez and Eric had been unable to draw out any more details from Captain Garcia. Perhaps he was simply blowing smoke, telling a good story or sending them on a wild-goose chase, but that type of revelation had to be run to ground and definitively established, whether fact or fiction. The general consensus among the DEA, ATF, FBI, and all the other "alphabet agencies" was that the smuggled item or items were unlikely to be nuclear, given the haphazard way they appeared to have been brought into the country.

Unknown to the FBI in Tucson, the CIA was now sniffing around Latin America, the Middle East, and Southwest Asia for any rumors about explosives sent to North America, but getting a concrete answer among all the noise of intelligence sources was a long shot. Given the legal ability to purchase smokeless powder in any gun store, or to steal more energetic explosives domestically, it was not clear to Eric and his colleagues what would be worth smuggling into the country, unless it was a large amount of Semtex or a similar plastic explosive. Or maybe it was just Garcia playing with them.

In any event, Eric and Montez were not in the SSA's good graces for having "unofficially" interviewed Captain Garcia and then spinning up the intelligence community with his allegation. After the funeral they were scheduled to meet with the SSA to discuss the direction in this investigation, as well as the other items on their plate, such as the previous week's bank robbery.

The organ swelled and the procession started back down the aisle. Eric watched the clergy, then the casket, then the family. Within the latter group was a tall, red-haired woman who raised an irreverent interest in him. *That must be her sister*, he thought. "I'm going to the burial," he told Montez. "Do you want to go or should I drop you off at the office?"

"Drop me off," Montez answered. As the crowd thinned, they walked to their car and drove in the direction of the office on the other side of Interstate 10. At the office Montez hopped out and Eric headed northeast toward the cemetery. He easily caught the procession and turned on the car's emergency lights hidden in the grill to join it.

It was a long walk from his car, parked on one of the main roads in the cemetery, to the burial site, and he took the time to straighten his tie and brush his hair back in place. He neared the grave and joined the large crowd already gathering behind the four chairs that held all of the family who could join Molly Walsh for her last moments above ground. There was an elderly man and woman, dignified and erect, and two younger women, including the red-headed woman who had grabbed Eric's attention in the cathedral. As he studied her now Eric could see she was tall and trim, her hair pulled back from her face, large, dark sunglasses covering her eyes. Her skin was pale and, from this distance, blemish-less. He watched as she faced the casket steadily with an expression that melded emotion and composure.

As the priest completed his prayers, a voice to the side of the grave called out and a Border Patrol honor guard fired a rifle salute, followed by a bugler blowing taps. Eric watched as the dignified woman held her gaze on the casket, not flinching from the rifle report, not looking toward the bugler. Two Border Patrol agents crisply folded the flag that had draped the casket and handed her the blue triangle. She mouthed a "thank you" but never shifted her sight from the casket.

A stream of dignitaries broke her trance. A line of dark suits, dresses, and uniforms lined up to offer their condolences. Much of the crowd lined up behind them, the rest slowly walking toward their cars. He understood there was a gathering at the Border Patrol, Tucson Sector, headquarters on Golf Links Road, but he had to get back to the office. As he walked toward his car, he turned to look back for the woman, but she had vanished into a sea of sympathy. For the first time he realized how hot it was. He turned back and briskly walked to his car, pulling off his jacket as he went.

8
_____

L ater that afternoon, Eric and Montez were in a conference
room with representatives from Homeland Security, ATF,
DEA and a would-be chain smoker who carried US State
Department credentials but everyone knew was CIA. Eric was at the
whiteboard at the front of the room, diagramming the characters in
this drama, with Agent Walsh in the center, José Rodriguez-Marquez
off to one side, and a series of circles with question marks representing the unknown players. Who was the shooter? Who paid to
have whatever it was smuggled? Same person? Where were the smuggled items going? Who was going to use them? The group had too
little solid information to be extremely concerned about the situation.
But since 9/11, no incident where there was a potential nexus
between explosives and unknown, possibly hostile persons could be
encountered without a little extra heartburn. Even almost a dozen and
a half years later, everyone in this group still felt responsible for
preventing another attack.

The covert CIA officer stepped out for a smoke and returned a half
hour later with a red-and white-striped folder, which he conspicuously
placed on the desk in front of him. If local law enforcement sometimes
resented the imperiousness of the FBI, the FBI always resented the

CIA for the way they seemed to make up the rules for intelligence sharing as they went along. As it happened, no one else in the room had the security clearance to know what was in the folder, which the CIA agent had brought from a small Sensitive Compartmented Information Facility—known in the intelligence community by its acronym SCIF—downstairs from the conference room. The SCIF featured solid concrete walls, isolated and filtered electrical service, and double locked doors, the inner door looking like that on a bank vault. The room allowed the dissemination and discussion of high-level classified information, such as counter-intelligence information, to the small number of federal agents with the clearances and the need to know. So the other participants in the room just viewed the appearance of the folder as an assertion of superiority by the CIA man, whose name on his credentials was "John Smith."

They were surprised when John joined the conversation. "I have some information that might be of relevance," he said. The room turned to face him. "We have some moderate-confidence intel that Iranian shaped charges have been working their way from southern Iraq. You will recall that a number were provided by Iran to insurgents supported by Muqtada al-Sadr in the mid-two thousands, but as far as we can tell, only a small number were actually used in IEDs. Since Sadr has been shifting toward more political involvement, these have been 'sitting on the shelf' somewhere in Sadr City. Now it looks like they've gone missing."

There was a pause after John stopped speaking. Finally, a woman from ATF asked, "Moderate confidence?"

"Sources and methods," John responded, "That's all I'm going to say."

"Any idea on the specs?" the ATF agent asked.

"I'll check with the DIA and see if they have anything," he said. More silence followed his comment. Everyone knew how close-mouthed the Defense Intelligence Agency tended to be.

Montez spoke up next. "So where would these be used and by whom?"

No one answered. There was some fragmentary conversation but

John's revelation had put everyone in a pensive mood and the meeting soon ended. Eric and Montez walked over to the SSA's office to brief him on this new development, which guaranteed a higher interest from Washington and maybe even a task force that would take the investigation from the small field office in Tucson and elevate it to a national effort.

THE NEXT MORNING John made a call over a secure phone to a contact at the DIA. After brief pleasantries, he got right to the point.

"Explosively formed projectiles," his contact corrected, "EFPs. A subset of shaped charges. Nasty little bastards. They'll shoot a jet of molten copper about twenty feet. The ones the Iranians sent weren't very big, not much of a threat to an Abrams, but they were deadly to a Bradley or a Humvee. Overkill for a Humvee. I think the idea was to give the insurgents something smaller and more effective than one-five-five artillery shells. Easier to bury, but the bad guys just wired lots of one-five-fives together for a big boom and dug a big hole or put them in the back of a truck."

"How big are these EFPs?" John asked.

"A lot were about ten to twenty centimeters in diameter, like an antitank missile warhead. Weighed about ten pounds. They can get a lot bigger, but I think most of the EFPs the Iranians sent were small."

John was silently amused by the mixture of metric and English units. "Anything else you can tell me that might be useful?" he asked.

"Useful in what sense?"

"Well, there's some reason to believe that a few of these might have made it into the country."

"Shit," his DIA contact said.

9

W hile John was on his call, Eric was at his desk reading reports, waiting to be told he and Montez were no longer on the case because it had been kicked up to headquarters or a larger field office. His phone rang.

"Agent West, this is the guard at the main entrance. You have a visitor," the voice on the line said.

"Who is it?" Eric asked.

"A Ms. Walsh."

"I'll be right down," Eric said, a little too enthusiastically.

ERIC TURNED LEFT from the elevator and strode to the visitor's desk, where Molly's sister was waiting. She looked up from the visitor log she was signing, holding the pen in one hand and her sunglasses in the other. She was dressed in a sleeveless black dress, pale shoulders supporting a long neck and a solemn face framed by hair the color of redwood.

Eric took a half step as he saw her eyes, which were a brilliant, peridot green, perfectly contrasting the red of her hair and lips. He closed the distance and held out his hand. "Special Agent Eric West, Ms. Walsh. What can I do for you?"

"Please, call me Caitlin. I'm Molly's, I mean, Border Patrol Agent Margaret Walsh's sister. I was wondering if we could talk about her case."

Eric had suspected that was why she was here, but it put him in a difficult position. The FBI did not talk about matters under investigation. On the other hand, he did not want to send her away without the courtesy of talking with her. And those eyes. "Not too much I can tell you," he said, "But why don't you come upstairs and we can talk." He signed the visitor log to acknowledge his responsibility of her while she was in the building, and the guard issued Caitlin a numbered visitor badge.

Eric held his left hand in front of him, palm up, as a sign for Caitlin to walk to the elevator, and she placed her sunglasses in her bag and walked that way. He pushed the up button and stood awkwardly as they waited for the car, both of them looking up at the numbers counting slowly down to one. The elevator arrived empty, and Eric again held his hand in front to guide Caitlin into the car. He joined her and pushed the button for his floor, conscious of the seconds until the door closed and the car started to rise. "I'm sorry for your loss," he finally said and immediately regretted it.

Caitlin turned her head slightly in his direction, away from the advancing numbers, and said, "Thank you." Her voice was firm and she was clearly in control of her emotions.

When they arrived on his floor, he led her to the conference room, which, thankfully, was empty. He asked her if she wanted coffee or water and she accepted the water. Eric walked to a small refrigerator at the far end of the room and brought back two water bottles. After they both took appreciative swallows and almost simultaneously replaced the caps and set the bottles on the conference table, Eric asked, "How are you handling the heat?"

Caitlin turned to him and asked, "Are you asking because you know I'm from Alaska?"

"No, I didn't know. It's just hot and we all complain about it," he replied. "How long have you lived in Alaska?" he asked, not anxious to start talking about the case.

"Our dad was in the Air Force and his last transfer was to Elmendorf in Anchorage. Our parents liked it, so they stayed after he retired. After college I stayed, but Molly wanted to see more of the country, so she headed south and ended up in the Border Patrol and ..." Her voice trailed off.

"Were those your parents at the burial?" he asked, uncertain if the term "burial" was too emotional.

"No, my aunt and uncle. My mother's brother. Our ..." She paused. "My parents are dead. The other woman is my cousin." She turned to face him directly. "What can you tell me about Molly's murder?"

Eric was startled by the directness of her question and was not really sure how to proceed. She was looking right into his face, her eyes unblinking. "Well, there's not much we're allowed to say since the investigation is ongoing."

"Was it a coyote?" she asked, pronouncing the slang for a smuggler of humans like the surname of the cartoon character rather than "coy-yo-tay," the Spanish way most in the Southwest said the word.

"We don't think so. She reported suspicious activity near a house, which turned out to have a tunnel into Mexico, so we do think it had something to do with smuggling," he said. Even that was probably saying too much, but he was careful not to expand into dead suspects, etc.

"Do you think you'll catch the killer?" she asked, her eyes starting to moisten.

"We'll certainly try," Eric replied and immediately regretted the non-committal tone. "We have multiple agencies working on it, and we've done some investigation south of the border. We won't rest until the killer is brought to justice," he concluded. He quickly regretted the certainty of the statement, so he reached for his bottle and took a drink, looking away to hide his discomfiture.

When he looked back, she was still staring at him. After a moment she turned away. "I'll be staying for a few days to take care of Molly's estate. Maybe we can talk again," she said, looking at her water bottle.

"I would be happy to." Eric hoped he sounded civil—neither too business-like nor too anxious.

"Maybe I'll give you a call," she said and asked him for his cell number. He gave her his official FBI card and told her to call whenever she wanted. Caitlin held it between her thumb and forefinger, rubbing her thumb idly over the FBI seal at the corner, then she placed it in a pocket of her purse and stood. Eric walked her to the door and escorted her down the hall, into the elevator, and to the guard desk, where she turned in her badge, signed out of the visitor log, and strode across the lobby and out the door into the hot morning.

10

The next day Eric and Montez were in the SSA's office, discussing the turnover of the Walsh murder case. The Phoenix field office and FBI headquarters had decided that the new information regarding explosives elevated the importance beyond what the Tucson resident agency could handle. The Bureau would run an interagency task force initially out of Phoenix, kicking it up to DC if more information developed.

"I know you would like to stay involved, Eric, but there's enough horsepower in Phoenix to handle it going forward," the SSA said. "Let's get these bank robberies solved."

Eric knew there was no winning the argument. Back at his desk, he conferred with Montez regarding the results of the fingerprint dusting at the bank. There were, as expected, a chaotic mish-mash of prints on the door handle, each new finger smudging the older prints. Fortunately, they had obtained a partial print from the dye-pack the robber had touched and rejected.

While the technicians using the fingerprint database could match full prints with very high accuracy, partial prints were a different matter. The process produced a series of partial matches. Possible matches were then checked against the last known addresses of the fingerprint owners, since it was unlikely that a convicted felon from Milwaukee would travel to Tucson to rob a bank. Cross referencing the fingerprint data with the physical description of the robber gave Eric and Montez a short list of possible suspects to interview. There was also a small amount of DNA recovered on the note, but that might never result in a match.

The two drew their weapons from their desk drawers, holstered them, and started for the car.

The first subject was not home, the second was in a wheelchair and clearly not capable of having committed the robbery, but the third was more interesting. Wallace Stoneman answered the door of his trailer, wearing a Harley-Davidson T-shirt and denim shorts. He looked from one agent to the other, dressed in their FBI jackets in the heat.

According to his file, Stoneman had served six years in the '80s for armed robbery, and by all indications had been minimally employed since, but something in his affect as he leaned against the doorjamb struck Eric as not quite right. Eric briefly made eye contact with Montez, who asked if they could come inside and talk.

"Why? Do you guys have a warrant or something?" Stoneman asked.

"If we had a warrant, we wouldn't be asking," Montez replied.

"No need to be defensive. We just want to ask you a few questions," Eric said, trying to dial down the emotion.

"I'm not being defensive. I just don't know what you guys want." Stoneman shifted his stance so he was now blocking the doorway. Montez, who was on the opposite side of the doorway, moved slightly to his right to get a better view inside the house, even as Stoneman tried to block his view.

Eric was getting impatient. He took a step back and placed his hand on the butt of his weapon under his jacket. "Sir, for our safety, you either need to step outside to talk with us, or we can all step inside."

Stoneman relented and stepped aside. The door opened into a filthy living room, and it was clear when they stepped inside that he had been trying to prevent them from seeing the glass meth pipe on the chipped coffee table in front of a dingy green-stripped couch.

"Do you mind if we look around?" Montez asked, pretending not to notice the drug paraphernalia.

"I thought you wanted to ask me some questions?" Stoneman protested, sounding a little less assertive than before.

"Oh, yes, we do," Eric called out as he walked down the hall. Around the kitchen sink were dirty dishes and a half-consumed white paper container of what might once have been chicken lo mein. He stopped at the sink. At the bottom was a pair of nylon athletic pants with red stains around one pocket. There had, apparently, been one more dye packet. Eric smiled. "Sir, you have the right to remain silent. Anything you say can and will be used against you in a court of law," he began as he walked back into the living room.

As soon as Eric started his Miranda warning, Montez grabbed Stoneman's arms and pulled them behind his back. Stoneman half-heatedly tried to squirm free, then his shoulders sagged and he let Montez place handcuffs on him.

After Eric and Montez turned Stoneman over to local police, the FBI crime-scene techs took over. They placed the stained pants in an evidence bag, along with $8,200 in currency found in the freezer.

All in all, Eric and Montez were feeling pretty good. Montez agreed to join Eric at Maloney's, violating his standard practice of leaving Eric to his own drinking. He called his wife, who reminded him they had parent-teacher conferences for their 13-year old daughter that night and he had better not miss them. When he met Eric, he explained why he couldn't stay long then ordered a beer. "If only every case was that easy to close," he said, taking an appreciative swallow of the ice-cold brew.

Eric smiled. "That was just outstanding investigative work." Both men knew that about 60% of bank robberies were solved, so percentages were on their side; nevertheless, they still enjoyed clearing it from their caseload. Eric's phone started to vibrate on the bar and he read the number with an unfamiliar 907 area code. Thinking it was a scam call, he reached to push the 'reject call' button but then changed his mind and brought the phone to his ear. "West," he answered.

"Agent West, this is Caitlin Walsh. I was wondering if we could talk."

"Sure, Ms. Walsh, where would you like to meet?" he replied, looking at Montez, who gave him a look, finished his beer, left a ten on the bar and was gone.

"I am at the Hotel Congress. Can we meet downstairs?" she asked.

"I'll be over in ten minutes," he replied.

On the walk from Maloney's to the hotel, Eric puzzled at Caitlin's choice of lodging. A restored 1919 building with a trendy bar and restaurant, part of its local claim to fame was that John Dillinger and his gang had been staying in the hotel when a fire broke out and they had to evacuate. Two firemen helped them carry their luggage, which was weighted down by stolen cash, and later realized who they were, leading to their arrest at a house a few blocks away. Eric wondered if Caitlin knew the story or if she would even be interested.

He turned the corner to enter the hotel lobby and saw Caitlin standing at a collection of tourist brochures, idly fingering one for the artist colony in Tubac. "Good evening," Eric said as he closed the distance. Caitlin held out her hand and Eric grasped it loosely and gently shook it.

"I just need to talk to someone. Any place nearby for a good beer?" she asked.

"A few just down the street. Might be noisy, though," Eric replied.

"That's OK, lead the way." They walked out onto Congress Street and walked west, the night barely cooling but the lack of sun a relief. They crossed the street and Eric led them into a microbrewery and to a table upstairs and toward the back. It was warm there but quieter, and he thought that better than leaning in to Caitlin and shouting above the din downstairs. They sat and briefly scanned a menu then Eric left and quickly returned with two pints, an IPA for her and an amber ale for himself. They both took sips and Eric watched Caitlin as she stared past the top of the glass at the exposed brick wall beyond. He waited, wondering whether she would choose the topic and start the conversation or whether he should.

After another moment he made his decision. "So how are you handling the heat?" he asked benignly.

She turned to look directly at him and Eric suddenly felt like a buffoon, but then her lips formed a slight smile and she answered, "It is hot here. It never gets this hot in Anchorage, although, believe it or not, the interior can get over a hundred." She sat back a little in her chair and kept looking at him. "Have you lived here long?"

"I've been in Tucson about four years. I like it. It gets hot in May and June then cools down a little with the monsoons. I trained in Quantico, Virginia, which was much more humid, and was assigned to Virginia Beach for a few years. I'll take summer here over summer back there…" After a swallow of beer, he finished, "Any time."

"Where did you grow up?"

"Ohio. My dad was a small-town sheriff. After high school I went into the Marines then realized I was a knucklehead for not trying for ROTC to pay for college. So after I finished my commitment, I went to college on the government's dime and then applied to the FBI," he said, realizing that he had answered a lot more than "where he grew up."

"So you've been in the FBI for about ten years?" she asked, taking a longer sip of her IPA.

"Yes," and he too took a sip of his beer.

"I had an internship in DC a few years ago. I agree the summers are pretty tough."

"What field are you in?" he asked.

"I studied anthropology in college and became interested in the culture of the native peoples in Alaska and across the arctic. I got a chance to study at the Smithsonian, had a few jobs at the museum in Anchorage, and now I am an assistant curator there." She smiled in spite of herself. Curator jobs, even assistant ones, were few and far between, and she was proud to have one. "Do you have any siblings?" she asked, changing the subject. When she thought about what she had just said, her mood darkened slightly.

Eric sensed the change and proceeded cautiously. "A younger brother. He's a fireman in Dayton. Married, with two kids."

A thought occurred to Caitlin and she blushed as she asked, "What about you?"

"Divorced. No kids," he answered, and he watched as a slight expression of relief passed over her face. For a few moments they just stared past each other, drinking their beers and trying not to look at each other. Eric thought about how uncomfortable people are when they are caught staring, how one reflexively looks away if the object of curiosity turns in their direction. He looked at Caitlin, who, sensing his gaze, looked back at him. He did not look away.

11

K halid stood in the sun, a red ballcap barely shielding his face from the glare. His arms and legs were covered in lightweight, sun-blocking synthetic fabric. The man next to him was demonstrating the operation of a UAV with a 16-pound payload, and Khalid was happy. Failure after failure had worn on him and his associate, and while he had been frugal with information to their boss, Khalid could tell his boss was not pleased. A small increase in the diameter of the propellers and a light reduction in the empty weight had provided the capacity, with a small margin, to carry their payload the requisite distance. Khalid could not wait to inform their boss. He clasped the shoulder of the man controlling the UAV and gave him instructions for the next few days' work. Then he walked the 30 yards or so to his SUV and drove west through the desert toward Phoenix.

When Khalid arrived at the building that contained the 20, barrel-filled containers, he was now faced with a more daunting problem than increasing the payload of a UAV by a pound or two. In an inexplicable lack of planning, his men had not realized that the now-filled containers were too heavy to lift with the equipment they had rented to move the empty containers into the building after they were delivered in the parking lot. Indeed, they had ruptured a hydraulic hose trying to lift one end of a container which now weighed almost 50,000 pounds. Not only were they too long and heavy to lift with a forklift, now he was being told that the ceiling of the building was too low to lift the containers with a crane.

Khalid stared at the man he had left in charge of this part of the project and felt his anger rising from his chest, across his face to the top of his head, which burned as if he were still outside in the sun. The object of his ire felt it and visibly shrank as he struggled to explain his carelessness. Khalid looked around him at the other five men standing around him, their lips tight, tension evident in their eyes. He turned to make sure the roll-up doors were closed and, reassured, reached behind his back, returned with his pistol, and shot the man in front of him an inch above the tip of his nose. The man made a gargling exhale of breath, nearly inaudible to the other men due to their temporary deafness from the gunfire, and fell to the floor. "Put him in one of the trailers and reseal it," Khalid ordered. He instructed another man to clean up the blood around the body then he gathered them back together to figure out how they would get the trailers outside without creating too much curiosity.

FAR AWAY FROM the murder in Phoenix, Vasily was uploading a batch of stolen credit card numbers to Rescator when he received an email from Kha. "Success?" it asked.

Vasily thought about how to respond. By now he believed he had 19 of the 27 he had been tasked with compromising under his control. He was careful not to spend too much time inside the compromised systems lest a security scan spot his activities. He typed, "Yes. Nineteen," and sent the reply. He sat back in his chair and waited, for what he was not sure.

"Good. Will send flash drive with payload and instructions," Kha replied.

Vasily knew the conversation was complete. He sat back from the screen and smiled as he thought about the incoming Bitcoin. Then he paused. *How does Kha know my address?*

12

L ater that evening, Khalid reached his rented house in Mesa. The neighborhood on the southeast corner of Phoenix was quiet in July. Most of the year it was flooded with some of Arizona State University's 72,000 students, hailing from all 50 states and from countries around the world. His street had its share of Haram activities—Islamic law forbade drunken parties and indecently clad women—but the chaos was extremely useful to someone who did not want to be noticed. He had even found a Halal butcher for the lamb he liked and an acceptable mosque within walking distance from his home. It was quiet this time of year, with just graduate students and the small number of college students in summer session, but he still felt safe in the relative obscurity that goes with a transient neighborhood. He parked his SUV, walked to the front door and stopped, looking down at the strand of brown grass he had stuck near the bottom of the door. Intact. He took out his key, opened the lock, and walked in.

It was hot inside, maybe hotter than outside, if that were possible. Khalid had turned off the air conditioner when he left and now regretted it, since it would take hours for the creaky unit to cool the small house to a temperature suitable for sleep. He turned on the air conditioner, looked at his watch, and walked to the corner where his prayer rug was neatly rolled up and leaning against the wall. He unrolled it facing east, went into the kitchen to wash, and returned to begin praying the Salah al-Maghrib.

When his prayer was completed, he re-rolled the rug and replaced it in the corner. He walked to the refrigerator and withdrew a glass bowl of lamb and rice, placing it in the microwave for two minutes. He carefully removed the hot bowl and sat at small table to eat. Even after he had finished, washed the bowl, and placed it in the drying rack, it was still very hot in the house, and his clothes clung to him. He took off his shirt and hung it on the back of a chair, but he was still hot. Even though no one could see him, he would not take off his trousers until he climbed into bed.

He walked into the room where he slept and where his laptop sat on a small folding table. He sat down and pressed the button to awaken the machine, which greeted him with a cheery logo and happy sounds. He grimaced, as he always did, at such foolishness. He was very serious about what happened within this machine. Once the computer was completely awake, he opened ProtonMail, which used high-level encryption and servers based in Switzerland to render emails sent with it nearly impenetrable. He opened it in a Tor browser, which added additional security by ping-ponging his internet traffic through a confusing multitude of servers around the world. Khalid opened the email from Hamid, the only one in his inbox. The message had no subject line and only one word. It read, "Initiate."

AT THE SAME MOMENT, back in Tucson, Eric and Caitlin sat in a dimly lit Mexican restaurant on Broadway Boulevard, her with a margarita, him with a Pacifico and lime. Eric was picking at a bowl of *chicharrones*—spicy, fried pork rinds—while they waited for their entrees. Caitlin was telling him about her sister's former fiancé. "Martin is an ICE agent in El Paso. Seems like a nice guy. Not sure where he and Molly met. I can't really read him. I don't know if he's distant because he's so broken up about her, or if he didn't really love her."

"Well, different people deal with tragedy in different ways," Eric volunteered.

"Sure, but I can't help but feel Molly was trying to fix him. That's the way she was, always trying to fix relationships, save abandoned pets, you know. Martin had gone through a hard divorce and then the death of a child, and I think he was a project for Molly."

"I wish I had known her," Eric replied.

"Yeah, you and me both," Caitlin said and stared into the distance. Eric was not sure what she meant and thought about asking, but he waited and Caitlin continued, "I was always the homebody. She was the adventurer, traveling, having wild experiences with her friends. She loved the outdoors. I think if she hadn't joined the Border Patrol, she would have been a park ranger." Her voice trailed off. "I wish she had."

VASILY RECEIVED a Russian Post express package at his apartment on Arkangliskiy Prospekt. He held the envelope with the fingertips of both hands and felt the outline of a flash drive inside. Tearing away one end, he removed the drive and the single sheet of paper that surrounded it. He first inserted the drive into the USB port of a sterile, "air-gapped" computer, one that had no personally identifiable information on it and was not connected to the internet. He used a series of software tools to examine the drive for viruses or other files that might track his movements, either on the dark web, where he frequently operated, or on the normal "surface" web. It was imperative that no one eavesdrop on his email or voice conversations, crash his hard drive, etc.

Satisfied the computer was still secure, he viewed the contents of the flash drive. He found nothing but a small piece of executable code. Next he opened the paper that had come with the drive and read the instructions, then read them again. Vasily ejected the drive, inserted it into his main computer, and began to work.

A FEW WEEKS LATER, in mid-August, a man drove a tractor-trailer north on the Pacific Coast Highway at exactly the speed limit. The traffic had thinned greatly since leaving the San Francisco Bay area, and he tried to enjoy the landscape, the golden hills to the east, the dramatic cliffs and the sea to the west, but the image of his bleeding friend falling to the ground constantly intruded. "Why did Khalid do that?" he asked himself. "Aren't we all soldiers in the struggle?" He shook his head silently and continued his drive.

After a few more miles, he saw the sign for the state park and camping area. He signaled and turned onto the road, westbound toward the beach. He passed a few tourists walking along the road on this Sunday afternoon, the morning fog having burned off to reveal a brilliant blue sky. *Such a beautiful place*, he thought. He saw a building in the distance and could see where he had been instructed to park. He made the turn and used the parking lot beyond the building to enter the opposite lane of traffic and slide the tractor-trailer as far off the road as it would fit, close against a chain link fence. He stepped down and walked back to the fifth wheel, where he released the latch on the kingpin that held the trailer in place on the back of the tractor. He walked farther back and released the crank for the landing gear and began cranking it down, making contact with the ground and slowly lifting the weight of the semi-trailer off the fifth wheel. Then he walked back to the cab, pausing to disconnect the air hoses and electrical cable between the tractor and trailer, and climbed back inside. He released the parking brake and slowly drove forward, feeling the slight motion as the trailer came uncoupled. He continued ahead, making the turn back onto the access road. In his mirror he watched his former cargo disappear as he turned back east toward the Coast Highway.

IT WAS a slow Sunday at the security company that monitored the intrusion alarms and the video cameras for the building. One of the personnel who watched the various screens and displays noticed the truck parking next to the building. That by itself was not particularly noteworthy since long-haul truckers were always looking for an out-of-the-way place to take a nap. What was strange was that the driver uncoupled the semi-trailer from the tractor and drove off. Maybe he wanted to get a bite to eat without dragging the trailer around. Maybe he had a girlfriend nearby and could not make his rendezvous on a back road with the trailer behind him. In any event, the trailer was in a no-parking area. The security company dispatched one of their security cars from Richmond to take a look.

WITH SUNDAY-AFTERNOON TRAFFIC the drive from the Richmond to the trespassing trailer took about three hours, and the security guard was none too pleased by the trip. He got out of his car, walked around the trailer, took down the license plate of the trailer and the identifying numbers on the container bolted to it, and climbed back into his car for the drive home. The guys coming in on Monday could deal with having it towed if the driver did not return that night.

13

When the railroads were laid out across the country during the 19th century, surveyors fanned out across the continent, seeking the most direct routes across the prairies, around lakes, along rivers, and over mountains. After decades of construction, the network of rails looked like the veins, arteries, and capillaries of a reclining body, connecting towns and cities across the continent. One hundred and fifty years later, when the demand for communications bandwidth outstripped the capacity of the Bell System's copper telephone circuits, and later, geosynchronous satellites, the companies running fiber optic cables studied these routes and realized the railroad pioneers had largely done their work for them. So fiber optics were laid along railroad rights of way, joining the same places in data and electronic commerce that the railroads had joined in physical commerce.

While the rails and the trains that run on them are obvious to the casual viewer, the presence of fiber-optic lines along the rails is less obvious. If you walk along the lines, you may see a narrow sign warning of buried telecommunications cables. Or you might notice that every 50 miles or so a cluster of brown, prefabricated buildings sits beside the rail lines, surrounded by a chain link fence. At 9:16

A.M. Pacific Daylight time, Burlington Northern-Santa Fe Locomotive 7828 was near Stockton, California, leading a "stack train," 131 cars carrying intermodal containers, one or two containers high. As the 44th car in the train reached one of these small clusters of buildings, the bottom container exploded with the equivalent of 20 tons of TNT, throwing the mangled container above it several hundred feet into the air and tossing cars ahead and behind it in all directions. The buildings and their contents were completely obliterated, their foundations now part of a crater 60 feet deep and 130 feet wide.

The explosion that pulverized the container and shattered the car and the rails below also cut the brake pipe, and as air spilled, the brakes on both ends of the now-severed train set hard, but they could not prevent 40 of the cars behind the 44th from zig-zagging off the opened rails and scattering across the crater and surrounding countryside like so many dominoes. The locomotives and many of the cars ahead of the explosion came to a stop less than a mile from the damage, the engineer and conductor in the lead engine dazed by the motion the explosion imparted to their cab through the remaining tons of train and by the realization that something very violent had occurred behind them.

The engineer keyed the microphone of his radio and told the dispatcher that they had an emergency. "There's been a derailment behind us, and what we think was an explosion," he explained.

The dispatcher queried, "Aren't you a stack train?" Then he quickly asked, "You aren't pulling any tank cars, are you?"

The engineer confirmed the first question and assured the man there were no tank cars but said that he and the conductor could see an enormous plume of smoke and dust a mile behind them. The dispatcher contacted local first responders, fire and police.

A different set of first responders was already aware of the event. A major national telecommunications company experienced a massive outage of one of their main bundles of transcontinental fiber, 400 fibers in total, of which about 200 were currently in use. With the bundle completely dead, they had no way of knowing that is was not a simple fiber cut but the destruction of one of their regeneration stations. These stations were normally unattended, so loss of life was generally not an issue.

The same could not be said for the building along the California coast where the semi-trailer had parked illegally. Two technicians were inside, performing diagnostics on some of the fiber optic lines that had crossed the Pacific from Asia and landed in the US inside the unmarked building. One of the technicians, an older woman with four children and a new grandchild, was in an aisle among the racks of equipment and facing the side of the building opposite where the trailer was parked. When the container exploded, she saw without comprehending the tons of concrete block, electrical conduit, and racks of electronics suddenly flying in her direction at a few hundred miles per hour. Her colleague two aisles over had just milliseconds more to live. One of the major internet connections between the US and Asia died with them.

Fifteen minutes later, another BNSF train exploded. An hour later it was a Union Pacific one, then another BNSF, and so on for the next few hours until nine trains had exploded, all near enough to fiber optic regeneration sites to destroy the fibers and the fabulously expensive equipment that massaged the signals within them. Finally, a container exploded on a train at the crowded Port of Oakland. And just an hour later, a container exploded on board a giant container ship being loaded at the Port of Long Beach.

The Department of Homeland Security received an alert from BNSF as soon as the first container vaporized. The railroad also notified the Federal Railroad Administration and the National Transportation Safety Board. DHS staff at first had difficulty understanding why a train derailment was a DHS concern. When they saw the first video of the smoking crater on CNN, courtesy of a local news helicopter, they suddenly realized this was not an ordinary derailment. Two minutes after the second container exploded, the Secretary of Homeland Security, Barbara Nelson, was on the phone with the president's national security advisor, whose staff organized a meeting in the White House Situation Room for later that afternoon. That schedule was "blown up" by the seemingly unrelenting explosions of containers across California. The national security advisor, John Keelers, briefed the president, who was on a golf holiday in New Jersey escaping the humidity of an August in Washington, and rescheduled the meeting in the Situation Room for an hour hence, with the president patched in via secure video link.

WHILE OFFICIAL WASHINGTON was scrambling to manage a crisis they did not yet understand, a piece of software code disseminated by a hacker in St. Petersburg began its mischief. Vasily had infected the Supervisory Control and Data Acquisition (SCADA) systems at 19 major electrical transmission substations in the San Francisco Bay Area with a routine that increased the overcurrent values of a series of protection relays and then switched the entire customer load onto a single transformer, causing it to overheat and fail explosively within about 20 seconds. The routine then repeated the process for the remaining transformers at the substation. In less than five minutes, the electricity failed across broad swaths of the Bay Area, punctuated by plumes of black smoke as thousands of gallons of oil burned in the stricken transformers.

Since Vasily had only been able to compromise some of the substations, due to different vendors' SCADA software and their vulnerability to hacking, Khalid and his men had prepared a backup solution for the remaining eight substations. Now the work of the man in the desert proved its worth. Khalid and seven of his men had driven to the area with similar UAVs programmed to fly to specific GPS coordinates. As the traffic lights and the air conditioning and the rest of modern life flickered off around them, they launched their UAVs on their missions. Each man launched three, one after the other, with a one-minute delay between them, and the craft began their short flights.

This part of the plan proved less successful, as there was more error in the locations of the substation transformers than Khalid had thought. The first UAV to arrive at its location established a hover 100 feet above what it thought was a transformer and began a slow descent, stopping at what it believed was 40 feet above the ground. The program running on the UAV then triggered the detonator on the EFP suspended below and the charge exploded, obliterating the UAV and propelling the jet of molten copper into the dirt and gravel below, spattering the side of the transformer 16 feet away with stones but otherwise leaving it unscathed. But most of the UAVs squirted their jets of destruction through the steel upper shell of their targets, and the residual stream of copper and molten steel shorted the windings. At a minimum, the damage took the transformer out of service; at best, it turned it into another useless, burning tank of oil.

Once the UAVs had done their work, Khalid drove to the rooftop of a parking garage in Santa Clara. There was no place to park but he did not plan to stay. He just wanted to look north and east across the Bay to see what he had accomplished. Khalid had not planned to be there to watch the execution of the plan, but events in Phoenix had left him short one man. Standing in the sun, watching plumes of smoke rise on both sides of the Bay, he smiled at what he had accomplished. Hamid would be pleased.

14

By the time official Washington had gathered to assess the situation, the chaos generated by the onslaught of rail and internet disruptions, and then the electrical outages, had created panic not just in California but on Wall Street as well. The NYSE plunged 800 points and the NASDAQ 400 points in one hour, leading both exchanges to suspend trading for the rest of the day. Traders joined their fellow citizens glued to CNN, Fox News, Bloomberg, and CNBC, trying to make sense of what was happening in the Bay Area. More than a few stared beaded in sweat or fighting tears as they relived a similar day of chaos and destruction on their own coast less than two decades before.

With the president patched in via secure video link, the vice president, Mark Parker opened the meeting in the White House Situation Room at 3 P.M. eastern daylight time, less than three hours after the first explosion. Even as the meeting began, reports were still coming in describing additional disasters on the West Coast. Parker turned to Barbara Nelson, and asked, "OK, what do we know?"

Nelson cleared her throat and began, "At approximately nine fifteen Pacific Daylight Time, a freight car on a westbound Burlington Northern-Santa Fe train exploded east of Stockton, California, derailing the train and destroying a fiber optic regeneration site alongside the tracks." She paused to take a drink of water. "There have been multiple, similar explosions on other trains along the West Coast between Los Angeles and San Francisco. We also have a series of explosions or failures at electrical substations in and around the San Francisco Bay Area, with widespread loss of electrical power. We're still trying to establish a timeline, damage estimates, and repair estimates."

"There are still explosions taking place, uh, happening?" the president asked.

"Yes sir," Nelson replied.

"Do we have deaths?" he asked.

"At this time, we don't know for certain, Mr. President. Aside from the explosions at electrical substations in the Bay Area, most of the explosions have been occurring in fairly rural areas." As she finished speaking an aid was sliding a piece of paper in front of her. The room watched as she blanched and turned back to the video screen. "We just received a report of a container exploding at the Port of Oakland. It appears there are fatalities."

"Jesus," the president muttered.

John Keeler, chimed in, "Mr. President, I believe we should order a halt of all railroad traffic and perhaps an evacuation of all container ports until we know what's causing all this."

"Just like nine-eleven, except trains instead of planes," the president said. "Do it. I'll be back in Washington in a few hours," he added and turned over the rest of the meeting to the VP.

Once the president was off the call, the conversation around the situation room settled into details. "Do we have statutory authority to do this?" the Parker asked, looking at the attorney general, John Seavers.

"I'm not sure," Seavers replied. "But in a situation like this, I suggest we act now and let the others figure that out. I'm sure we can find a way. We could just call the railroads and the ports and ask them to suspend operations."

The VP looked back to Secretary Nelson. "Can you handle that?" he asked.

"I'll take care of it," she replied and turned to speak to an aid seated behind her.

On two walls of the Situation Room, monitors displayed CNN, without volume but with closed captioning enabled. Suddenly, one of the aids who had been monitoring the news program called out, "Look!"

There was a sudden rush to find the volume control, and then the TV's speaker blared, "... claims responsibility. The previously unknown group claims this is the first phase in their war against the west. CNN has translated the Arabic text transmitted to various news organizations. The message reads..." The screen switched from the news anchor to Arabic text with an English voice overlay:

"On this day, the anniversary of our victory for Allah at Yarmouk,

We, the Global Warriors of Jihad and Righteousness, the Sons of Khalid ibn al-Walid

Celebrate a new victory over the infidels, the apostates, the Romans and the Jews.

The Umah will crush them all until all know Allah and his prophet, Mohammed,

Blessed be His name. Allahu Akbar, Allahu Akbar, Allahu Akbar."

Parker asked over the TV voice, "Was there a battle against ISIS that I missed? And where's Yarmouk?"

An aid muted the monitor.

"Yarmouk's near the Golan Heights in Syria, but that battle was in six thirty-six AD," the Secretary of Defense, John Martin, volunteered. "Thirteen hundred," he paused and calculated in his head, "and eighty-two years ago. Ibn al-Walid was the leader of the Muslim forces that defeated the Byzantine troops. So this is apparently a new group with a long memory."

The Director of National Intelligence, Dave Colby, chimed in, "We don't know if this is a new group or any group at all. We need to verify the claim." He leaned back to speak with an aid, who silently shook his head. "We don't have anything on this group right now," the director said, turning his attention back to the VP.

Parker did not comment, but the unsaid command was, *Then figure out just who the hell they are and fast*. He turned to the Martin. "Do we need to raise the DEFCON level?"

"I would recommend raising it one level pro forma, but I think intelligence and law enforcement will be carrying the weight here. SOCOM is always on alert these days if we need them. We'll increase air-defense readiness and maybe increase surveillance against unidentified shipping." He looked across at Nelson, who was nervously twirling a pencil in her fingers. "I'm sure the Coast Guard and CBP can help with that." The comment brought a nod.

Parker brought the meeting to a close and the participants rushed to their respective offices, knowing it would be a very long night.

15

It turned out that Colby had misspoken when he said the intelligence community was unaware of the group. The intelligence community, and the wider press-fed populace, were painfully aware of the "Islamic State of Iraq and al-Sham" or ISIS. The group had recently added its own color to the claim of a radicalized "lone wolf" in Arkansas, who had spent too much time in online chatrooms populated by other sexually frustrated, disaffected young men. He had legally purchased a used 9 mm Beretta 92f pistol and walked into a local bar with murder in mind. The man had stepped inside from June twilight into a bar's brown-wall dusk and stood in the doorway long enough to get his bearings and let his eyes adjust. But it was also long enough to be sized up by an off-duty Arkansas state trooper seated at a rear table opposite the bar. The would-be jihadist ostentatiously shouted *"Allahu Akbar"* several times, raised his weapon, and fired three rounds into the patrons leaning over their beers at the bar before the trooper drew his off-duty service weapon and dropped the shooter where he stood. The trooper was hailed as a hero and feted on the cable news channels. The terrorist went to the hospital in restraints, to recover from two gunshot wounds to the abdomen.

Investigators from the Arkansas Department of Investigations and the FBI had interviewed the terrorist's neighbors and coworkers but had been unable to identify a "friend" per se. All reported the man, who had recently moved to the area from another southern state, to be quiet, remote, and unremarkable. One FBI agent quipped, "'He kept to himself' must be the motto of guys who suddenly decide to slaughter their neighbors."

Law enforcement scoured the terrorist's cell phone, laptop, online accounts, and bank records, looking for clues as to motive and potential offshore support. Between web-browser caches and various fragments left behind in other locations of his hard drive, they were able to ascertain that he had searched for stories on jihadi killers and tried to contact ISIS but had, apparently, received no response. The FBI liaison to the CIA checked whether the CIA counter-terrorism unit had connected the terrorist to ISIS, either through electronic surveillance or through human sources. The answer was no: the shooter was the perfect definition of a lone-wolf terrorist. FBI computer forensics did discover, however, that he had been emailed by an entity calling itself the Global Warriors of Jihad and Righteousness, the Sons of Khalid ibn al-Walid. That was news because no one in the intelligence community had ever heard of the group. Now, two months later, they were hearing about it again—and in a big way.

The intelligence community convened its Interagency Terrorism Working Group (ITWG) at the offices of the director of national intelligence the morning after the White House meeting. Present were experts from the CIA, DIA, FBI, Homeland Security, and other organizations whose job it was to catalogue radical groups, monitor them, and prevent their hostile activities against the US or friendly countries. The chair, a trim, gray, CIA assistant director nearing retirement, opened the meeting by requesting to his deputy, "Wardlaw, bring us up to speed on these events."

"Yes, sir. Yesterday, at zero-nine-sixteen Pacific Daylight Time, a Burlington Northern-Santa Fe freight train consisting of three locomotives pulling one hundred thirty-one cars, themselves carrying two hundred thirty-four intermodal containers, suffered an explosion and derailment. It appears that the explosion occurred in one of the containers, and it was somehow timed to occur as the train, or the explosive container, was passing a fiber-optic regeneration station along the tracks. So the one explosion derailed the train, destroyed the tracks, and destroyed one of the main trunk paths for internet communication to California."

"A triple play," someone chimed in, without getting many responses.

"We've had three explosions that also took out pipelines running along the tracks as well. Gasoline and natural gas," Wardlaw continued as the mood in the room darkened. "After the first explosion, BNSF seventy-nine forty had a container explode around car number eighty-four at zero-nine-forty PDT just south of Fresno. Union Pacific ninety forty had a container explode around car number twelve at ten thirty-eight PDT about ten miles south of Merced. UP eighty-eight twenty-four had a container explode near car one-oh-four just east of Colton at twelve fifty-five PDT. Another BNSF train, number eighty-five twenty-five, had a container explode around car fifty just outside the Port of Oakland at fifteen eleven. A container exploded on another UP train, sixty-nine ninety-six, at the Port of Long Beach at sixteen thirty. I don't know the car number on that one. The times are all PDT." He paused to take a drink of water. "Finally, there was an explosion on UP ninety-three ninety-seven in Oakland at seventeen thirteen and on UP seventy-four eighty at seventeen forty. The last explosions are a real mess since they occurred in urban or dense areas. We know there are casualties among rail and port workers and civilians. No idea on how many."

"Jesus, how many exploding containers are still out there?" a woman from Homeland Security asked.

"We don't know. The president has ordered all rail traffic west of the Mississippi halted until further notice and the West Coast container ports evacuated—that's Long Beach, Los Angeles, Portland, Oakland, and Seattle."

"Didn't I see something about an explosion on a truck north of San Fran?" someone in the back of the room asked.

Wardlaw shuffled through his notes. "Yes, that was a container on a truck parked outside a landing point for a major trans-Pacific fiber optic cable."

The CIA assistant director chairing the meeting leaned forward and directed, "Please bring us up to speed on the attacks against the grid."

"Of course, sir," Wardlaw began and pulled up another set of notes. "Around the same time as the first train detonations, about ten hundred PDT, a series of casualties occurred among the major electrical substations in the Bay Area. At this time we don't know what caused them, but it appears that explosives were used in at least some of the attacks. The major damage seems to be to large distribution transformers. You will recall that these transformers are designated as critical infrastructure. Because of their size and cost, utilities companies don't generally keep spares. Or at least not many spares."

Homeland Security chimed in, "Right now about eighty percent of the San Francisco Bay area is without electricity, that includes San Francisco, Palo Alto, San Jose, Santa Clara, Fremont, Oakland, and Berkley." There was a light "whew" in the back of the room.

"When you say explosives, are we talking car bombs? Someone cutting the fence and entering the substation? What are we talking about?" a man from the CIA asked.

An FBI agent spoke up. "We think it could be mortars, since what we've seen so far shows the fences are still largely intact."

"Those are some pretty accurate mortars," a representative from the DIA said skeptically. "Have you found the launch locations? Unless they fired multiple rounds, they either got very lucky or they used some kind of guided projectile."

The FBI agent responded, "Too soon to tell. Some of the damage looks minimal, aside from fire damage."

That piqued the interest of a CIA analyst. "Any sign of a cyberattack? Like someone penetrated the SCADA system and deliberately overloaded the transformers?"

"From what I've seen, there are definitely signs of explosives. We'll know more when we've investigated all the sites."

"What about attribution?" the chair asked.

Wardlaw began, "Well, we have the claim from the Global Warriors of Jihad and Righteousness. This group, if it exists, has not been on our radar except for what we thought was a lone-wolf attack in Arkansas in early June. We don't have independent confirmation of the claim. CNN received a message from an encrypted email service and ran with it."

"Hard to believe these guys go from one lone wolf to this level of sophistication in two months," one of the analysts asserted to broad agreement. "There must be something more going on."

The room devolved into multiple conversations, but after a few minutes the chair brought the meeting back to order. "OK, CIA will take the lead on evaluating the claim and IDing this group. FBI, needless to say, keep us up to speed on what you find domestically." He turned to the woman from Homeland Security. "How long do you expect the president to maintain the halt at the rails and ports?"

"I assume until things stop blowing up," she replied.

The president would have to wait, because containers continued to explode at random intervals all night until the twentieth explosion destroyed the tracks near Barstow, California.

16

E ric woke up, Caitlin lightly snoring by his side. He smiled at the sound, pausing to look at her red hair painting the pillow. He pulled on a pair of shorts and walked to the kitchen, softly pulling the door shut as he went. His phone was on the kitchen counter, silenced, and he saw a string of missed calls without caller ID—he assumed those were from the office—and two missed calls from Montez's cell phone. He assumed that meant an all-hands effort related to the terrorist attacks. A call to Montez, who was already in the office, even though it was only 6:30, confirmed it.

"Where've you been, man? The SSA has everyone going up to Phoenix. Looks like one of those exploding containers came out of there or at least passed through."

Eric whistled lightly through his teeth. "OK, let me shower, and I'll see you in half an hour or so."

Caitlin was still asleep when he returned to the bedroom. He quietly opened his dresser and gathered underwear, socks, and a polo shirt, then slacks from the closet as he stepped into the bathroom. He softly closed the door behind him and ran the water hot to shave. When he was done, he started the shower, felt the water was warm, and climbed in. A little while later he felt rather than heard the door open and, behind him, the shower curtain slide across the rod. Caitlin stepped into the shower and hugged him, soft here, firm there, as she pressed across his back.

WHEN ERIC and Montez arrived at the industrial building off I-17, they pulled to the rear of the parking lot, as the front was filled with Phoenix PD cruisers, black FBI and ATF Tahoes, evidence vans, and unmarked cars. News media, local and national, were assembling at a building across the street, and the food trucks that normally served the blue-collar workers in the neighborhood were doing record business in burritos, coffee, and cold, bottled water.

The two walked under the police tape and moved toward an opened roll-up door where a pair of uniformed Phoenix police officers were standing in the shade, controlling access to the inside. Eric and Montez showed their badges and one of the cops handed them white Tyvek booties, which they slipped over their shoes.

The interior of the building was alive with investigators and techs —distinctive in their white Tyvek suits and masks—in clusters around specific locations. One group wearing respirators was standing around a pallet piled with bags of some sort of powder. Another was studying a collection of perhaps three dozen dirty, empty steel barrels. Still another stood near three plastic folding tables covered with electronic circuit boards and soldering irons in a distant corner of the room. The image bothered Eric. *Why does a criminal leave so much evidence? Do they want to tell us something? Do they not care? Or was there just not enough time to clean it up?* He did not ask the questions aloud, knowing there were as yet no answers.

An FBI Agent Eric knew from the Phoenix Field Office saw Eric and Montez walk in and joined them in the center of the room. She shook their hands and pointed around the room at the different groups. "Over there are bags of ammonium nitrate. ATF already figured they used ANFO—that's ammonium nitrate and fuel oil. Our guys are running down the sourcing, but we suspect they purchased it from the distributors that supply the farmers in the west valley, maybe all the way to California." She turned to her right. "Looks like the barrels over there contained some kind of oil, smells like diesel. Fuel oil only makes up a small percentage of ANFO, so they didn't need more than a few barrels." She paused, "That's assuming there are no unexploded containers out there." The three exchanged glances. "And over there's the most interesting," she continued, pointing to another area of the large room. "There's a lot of examining yet to be done, but it looks like they built some kind of timing or trigger boards here. We don't know how they got so close to the fiber repeater stations."

"What's going on there in the middle?" Montez asked, pointing to three men on their knees facing each other.

"Not sure if they've tested it yet, but it looks like blood," she replied. "We have teams on the fertilizer, the fuel, and the containers. We could use your help running the container transportation to ground."

"What do you have?" Eric asked.

"We found this place because a security guard got the plate off the trailer that carried the container that exploded by the beach in Northern California. Local rental company rented the trailer and the tractor to two men. We haven't been there to interview them yet."

"We're on it," Eric replied, maybe too enthusiastically. They walked to a table set up near the entrance covered with laptops, printers, and stacks of paper. They picked up the address of the equipment rental company and stepped back into the sunshine.

A FOREST OF BLUE MACHINES—SCISSOR lifts, high-lifts, and reach-forks—in the distance beckoned as they neared the equipment rental facility. As they drew closer they saw a few white tractors and a flatbed semi-trailer. They parked in front of the office and walked past smaller equipment—stump grinders and cement mixers outside, air compressors and saws inside—until they reached the counter. They showed their credentials and asked for the manager.

The man behind the counter next to the one they had approached spoke up. "Martin Cruz. I'm the manager. What can I do for you?"

"Is there a place we can talk in private?" Montez asked.

Both men behind the counter looked uncomfortable. "What's this about?" Martin asked.

"Let's talk in private," Eric responded.

The three walked into an office at the back of the building and sat around a desk. Montez started the conversation. "Did you rent a tractor and flatbed trailer last week?"

"Yeah, several. Do you have the name of the renter, the company?" Martin answered.

"No, just the license plate of the trailer. DMV traced it to you folks." Eric handed over a slip of paper on which he'd written the license plate number.

Martin searched in the computer and came up with the rental information. "Warren Smith. Connecticut Class A driver's license. Paid with a credit card."

"We're gonna need all of that information. Copies of the rental agreement, too," Eric said. "Do you have video cameras?"

"Not inside, but outside in the yard. What's this about?" Martin asked again, squinting.

"You're gonna need to make an insurance claim for that trailer. It's in a million pieces up in California," Montez responded.

ERIC AND MONTEZ sipped from complimentary water bottles as they waited for Martin to find the date and time the rental had taken place on the digitized video recording. When he found what he thought was the spot, the two agents crowded in closer to the monitor. One image gave them a view across the front of the office, including the front door. Two other views showed the equipment in the yard, with one showing the location of the rented tractor and trailer. They waited until they saw a black SUV, maybe a Ford Explorer, park in front and two men exit it and walk into the office.

Martin fast-forwarded about six minutes to show the two men now exiting the building, accompanied by one of the rental company's employees. Another camera picked up the trio as they walked to a tractor. One of the men, the driver of the SUV, turned and walked back to the front of the office, where he could be seen entering the vehicle and driving off. The other man climbed into the truck and skillfully backed it around to mate with the flatbed. He connected the hoses and cables, raised the landing gear, and drove out of the frame.

"We'll need to take this with us," Montez said, reaching into his pocket and placing an evidence sticker over the front of the recorder.

Martin nodded and then said, "I almost forgot. I think these guys rented two forklifts from us as well. Big ones."

"Did they pick them up?" Eric asked.

"Oh, no, they were big, sixteen-ton Cats. Never had someone rent two at the same time before." He walked to the filing cabinet and pulled the rental paper for them as well. Same credit card.

Martin went back to searching the video recorder. After fifteen minutes they saw an image of the same black SUV and the same driver. This time the man looked around and up in the direction of the camera before putting on a ballcap.

"Stop!" Eric yelled.

Martin paused the recording and slowly stepped it back to the moment the man looked up. The quality was surprisingly good. They saw a dark-skinned man with sharp features and a closely trimmed beard. Black hair, freshly cut and neatly combed. Eric and Montez looked at each other. "Yeah, we're definitely going to take this with us," Montez said softly.

17

"So, you're not looking for Molly's killer anymore?" Eric and Caitlin were sitting at his dining room table, and he had just had the unhappy task of telling her that all available agents were working the terrorism case.

"We're still working the case," he replied cautiously. "It's just that these events in California have taken priority for now. We don't know if there are more bombs or more attacks coming." He reached over to put his hand on hers and she pulled away as if his touch had stung. He looked at her pleadingly, but her eyes were filled with tears and she looked away. "We *will* get the killer, I promise you that," he said, less certain than he sounded, "It just might take a little time."

She looked back at him. "I feel like my life is in limbo until I know why my sister died. Can you understand that?"

"Certainly, I understand. Just give us a little time," he pleaded, but her eyes were still cold to him. Eric's head spun a bit as his thoughts raced. *What was their relationship? Did she care about him for himself or was she so obsessed with someone finding Molly's killer that she felt she needed to stay close to him?* He leaned back in his chair and took a drink from his water glass. Those were not questions he wanted to ask her. He was content to coast for now. Was she?

18

The rental company provided a fertile start for identifying at least two of the unknown terrorists. While "Warren Smith's" license was certainly a fake, the Xeroxed picture in the rental paperwork gave investigators a start toward identifying him, and the surveillance video provided a possibility for the second man. Even before they were identified, the FBI issued a BOLO for the two unknown men. The "Be On the Lookout For" request went to police agencies around the country, as well as Immigration and Customs Enforcement and the CIA.

In the meantime Eric and Montez were interviewing employees of the logistics service that had delivered containers to the rail terminals and the crane service that had lifted the containers onto trailers. A "Melvin French" had used a credit card to hire the logistics service and a "Frank Suppa" had used a different card to hire the crane. The crane operator described a group of four men on the site over the course of two days who had helped to chain each container to the crane and then watched as he set each container onto the semi-trailers. It had struck him as odd that they had to be told how to run the chains through the castings at the corners of the containers. Normally, labor on site had a supervisor who directed the work, but these four seemed somewhat adrift. In any event, no one had been hurt and the crane service had been paid, so he moved on to the next job without dwelling on it.

Eric and Montez took down descriptions of the men, vague as they were, and copies of the paperwork, including the credit card and ID info. Driving back, the air conditioner blasting away the August heat, they puzzled over what they knew. "It doesn't sound like the driver of the SUV is one of the four who were on site when the containers were loaded," Montez said.

"Well, that's hard to say, since the descriptions of the four aren't that clear. What about Warren Smith?" Eric asked.

"I don't know. We have the containers loading for transportation to the railyard on Thursday and Friday. We have the one on the flatbed loading on Friday. So maybe our Warren Smith is one of the four, maybe not. We don't even know if he drove the one on the flatbed all the way to Northern California," Montez replied.

"I heard California Highway Patrol found the tractor in Oakland. Lots of prints, who knows how many drivers before Warren Smith or whoever drove it," Eric said as they pulled into the parking lot of the Phoenix Field Office.

THE DAILY COORDINATION meeting was just starting when they walked in, nodding to their colleagues in the room and looking up to see the field offices in San Francisco and Sacramento on the video screen, along with headquarters. The Bureau had divided the investigation into one focused on the containers, and one focused on the substation attacks. Phoenix—augmented by Tucson—was part of the former, despite the fact that Eric and Montez had identified the possible source of the explosively formed projectiles used against some of the substations.

As they took seats near the back of the room, an assistant director in DC was making some housekeeping comments and then asked one of her deputies to summarize the status of the investigation.

"ATF has verified that the explosive was ANFO. Physical evidence at the sites suggests between twenty and fifty polyethylene barrels were used in each container. The ammonium nitrate was sourced from a fertilizer distributor in Arizona and three in the Imperial Valley in California. All were purchased using stolen credit cards and picked up using rental trucks. We don't have a license on the truck or trucks and don't have a rental location yet. We also don't have sourcing on the fuel oil or the barrels yet. Analysis of the fuel oil shows it to be standard, low-sulfur diesel fuel. It wasn't dyed red, so it was street diesel. We don't yet have a source for that, either."

Slight chuckling rippled around the room, since everyone knew street-grade diesel could be purchased at any of a thousand service stations in the area.

The deputy continued, "ATF has identified the detonators as ones commonly used in mining and construction. No sourcing on that yet. No information yet on the timing circuits or whatever was used to command detonation at a particular time or place, but we have found some debris that resembles GPS antennas, so they may have used GPS for location and timing. We have the containers themselves coming from a seller of used containers in Phoenix. Purchased with a stolen credit card. Director?" On the screen he turned slightly toward his boss.

"Phoenix, update us on your crime scene."

The Phoenix SAC cleared his throat and began, "We have the rental agreement for the truck that was used to transport the container to Northern California. The guy used a fake Connecticut driver's license in the name of Warren Smith and a matching stolen credit card. The same individual also arranged the rental of two fork-lifts from the same company with the same credit card. We have surveillance video of two males, dark complected, possibly Hispanic or Middle-Eastern. Multi-agency BOLOs have already gone out." He turned to look at Eric and Montez. "You guys have anything to add?"

Eric and Montez briefly looked at each other and Eric began, "Yes sir. We have the logistics company that transported the containers from the site to the respective freight terminals. The company was hired by a Melvin French, using a credit card in that name. And we have the crane service that loaded the containers. They were hired by a Frank Suppa, also using a matching credit card. We don't know yet if the cards are stolen, but it sounds like a good bet."

Eric received a slight scowl from the SAC for opining. "Anything else?" the SAC asked.

"No sir," Eric replied but made a mental note to mention the smuggled explosives when they were offline.

The assistant director asked, "Are we sure all of the containers are accounted for?"

The room went very still, and the SAC and Eric looked at each other. Eric began, "The crane company said they loaded twenty containers over the course of two days. I believe at this point," he looked at the SAC for confirmation, "we've had twenty explosions."

There was a pause, then the assistant director said, "Then in so far as there is only one cell active in this attack, there should be no more explosive containers."

There was some back-and-forth about details of the investigation. An agent in Sacramento pointed out that there should be a significant evidence trail associated with transporting the tons of fertilizer. The assistant director pronounced herself generally satisfied with the investigation but said, "I'm concerned we don't have IDs on any of these guys. Phoenix, concentrate on that. Headquarters will track down those credit cards. And for God's sake, keep your eyes open for any other atrocities these guys might try to commit!"

The conference room slowly cleared out, but a few agents stopped to talk with the SAC. Eric waited his turn, deliberately positioning himself to be last. Smiling, the SAC shook the hand of the last agent ahead of Eric and Eric stepped forward. "Sir, is anyone working the smuggling connection with the explosively formed projectiles?"

The SAC eyed him skeptically. "That investigation was kicked up to headquarters. There's no evidence the EFPs were smuggled through Arizona, and we have enough on our plate. Do you have any new information?"

Eric shifted uneasily. "No, sir, it just seems like a loose end, and it might be related to the murder of that Border Patrol agent in Nogales."

The SAC smiled slightly, paused for a moment, and then replied, "Ah, that unsolved murder of a federal agent." He paused again and the smile slipped away. "Rumor has it that you're keeping company with the deceased's sister. That wouldn't be the reason you're interested, would it?"

Eric felt the heat rising from his neck, past the collar of his shirt, across his face, and all the way to the part in his hair, but he spoke evenly. "You said it, sir. It's the unsolved murder of a federal officer. And the timing is too coincidental."

"Too coincidental *if*,"—he emphasized the "if"—"that's what was being smuggled." He paused, looked slowly around the empty room, and then sighed slightly. "OK, take a day to try to run it to ground. But no more. I want these perps in Phoenix IDed."

Eric's hairline cooled slightly. "Yes, sir."

19

W here did these guys get all those stolen credit cards, the headquarters investigators asked themselves? When they looked at the credit-card-processing information for the various rentals and purchases, it was clear that the cards had valid data on their magnetic strips, as well as valid security codes on the backs. An interagency team from the FBI, Department of Justice, Secret Service, and the CIA looked back at their surveillance of stolen credit cards and personal information from dark-web sites like Rescator and found an interesting pattern. The cards in question appeared to be part of batches of stolen cards that had been posted for sale over the last few weeks, but these cards had never been posted. Someone had saved these cards for a particular client.

The now-daily meeting of the ITWG convened with the credit cards high on the agenda. Wardlaw opened for the absent chairperson and began, "What can we learn about this group and its network from the credit cards they used?" He looked around the table.

An FBI agent lightly cleared his throat. "All the cards appear to have been stolen from compromised point-of-sale terminals in the New York-Connecticut-New Jersey area. What's unusual is that the data was likely stolen more than four months ago, because four months ago the POS terminals had a firmware update that included encryption that has, since then, made the data in those terminals inaccessible. Combine that with the encryption across the Point-of-Sale network, and we don't think these were stolen recently."

A CIA agent asked, "Why is this relevant?"

The FBI agent replied, "Because if these cards are part of a larger batch, more than five thousand that just came up for sale after the attack ...." He let that sink in for a minute. "*After* the attack, and I emphasize 'after,' suggests coordination. It suggests the individual or group that stole them held all of the cards back so these cards would not be compromised and unusable."

"You mean compromised as in cancelled, right?" the CIA man clarified.

"Yes. The hackers held onto a lucrative batch of cards for months instead of selling them right away. They just don't do that. Too much risk that the data breach will be discovered and the cards become worthless. These were valuable, since they had the CSCs along with complete stripe information. Pretty soon cards like that will no longer be in circulation, since all the issuers are going to chipped cards. So these five thousand were very perishable."

The room soaked that in for a moment. "Where were the physical cards made?" someone asked.

"Hard to say," the FBI agent replied. "Could have been printed overseas or made here. We see a lot made here. Both Europe and the US see cards made in Belarus, Ukraine, and Russia, too, though."

"How do we find out?"

"We'd have to have the physical cards, which have probably been destroyed by now." Wardlaw brought the conversation back to the hacker. "How do we find the hacker or hackers who stole the cards and then held them? That seems like the key."

The conversation meandered for the next 15 minutes until the meeting was adjourned with action items focused on finding the hacker.

∾

TWO HOURS LATER, Bert Loggins was in his home office when the
doorbell rang. Loggins was well-known in cyber-security circles for
intrepidly investigating criminals and criminal organizations associated with identity theft, denial-of-service attacks, credit card and ATM
skimming, and other nefarious profit-making activities of the internet
age. His published work had generated such anger among cyber criminals that he had been "SWATed" multiple times. Those "SWAT" calls,
which had maliciously reported to the local police a hostage situation
or other violent act taking place at his home, had led to heavily armed
and apprehensive law enforcement personnel showing up at his door.
So when the doorbell rang today, he first viewed his doorbell-mounted
camera on one of the three monitors facing him before walking downstairs and answering the door. He was greeted by a short, stocky man
in a blue suit who displayed CIA credentials and asked if he could
come in.

Once they were seated in the living room and Bert had poured
them both cups of coffee, the CIA man began, "Mr. Loggins ..."

"Please, call be Bert."

"OK, Bert, I'm Leonard. My colleagues and I have followed your
work closely for years, ever since you were at the paper."

"I suspected you would." Loggins smiled.

"We know you follow carders, among others, and we'd like your
help," the man continued.

Loggins stopped him. "You know I cooperate with law enforcement, but I'm not comfortable getting involved in an intelligence
operation."

"I wouldn't call this an intelligence operation." The CIA man
looked around the room and said, "More like a law-enforcement
operation."

"May I see your credentials again?" Loggins asked, uncomfortable
with the cartoonish way the conversation was proceeding.

Leonard showed his credentials again and said, "Let's go one
better. Would you mind coming with me to the Agency?"

They drove in Leonard's Subaru the few miles through Northern
Virginia to Langley, talking baseball. They were waved through the

main gate and parked on the side of the main building. They walked to the entrance, picked up a visitor badge (escorted) for Loggins, and left his cell phone with visitor control. Then it was through the electronic gates and up to the third floor. Leonard swiped his badge at a door marked with a cryptic acronym, and they entered a room of cubicles radiating from a central conference table. They settled at the table and were joined by several young analysts. After introductions they got down to business.

Leonard began, "You cannot use anything we're going to discuss in your blog, and you cannot disclose anything about this to anyone outside this room. Is that understood?"

"Yes," Loggins replied, amused by the seriousness. This was not his first rodeo.

"Ok, we're trying to identify the source for credit cards associated with Monday's terrorist attacks." Leonard turned to his colleagues and let that sink in.

Loggins was not really surprised, but hearing it still had an impact, which he tried not to show. "What do you know so far?" he asked.

"We believe the cards were stolen from POS terminals in the New York area sometime in the last few months."

"Last few months?" Loggins asked, a slight look of incredulity showing. "Why weren't they cancelled?

"Since none of them showed up before this, they weren't reported as stolen. We think they were held specifically for this purpose," Leonard replied.

"Pretty risky," Loggins said.

Leonard smiled at him and said, "Yeah, but it worked."

20

Eric saw Caitlin that night at Molly's former apartment, which Caitlin had moved into after checking out of the Hotel Congress. What had started as a few days to attend the funeral and deal with Molly's financial affairs following the mind-numbing reality of her sister's death had, depending on her mood, blossomed into a romance or mushroomed into a giant pain in the neck. Caitlin paid off Molly's bills, cancelled her cell phone, and donated her clothes and most of her furniture to the Salvation Army.

She had become attached to Molly's dog, a scruffy Schnauzer stray Molly had found near the border, half-starved and covered in burrs and bunches of cholla spines. He had not been wearing a collar—and, Molly found out later, was not chipped—and immediately flattened himself into a submissive pose as soon as Molly got close to him, suggesting he had been abused. She fed him some water and part of a protein bar and sat with him for quite a while on the passenger-side floor of her Border Patrol SUV. After a trip to the Humane Society and multiple trips to the vet, he became her dedicated companion, now confused and sad that he had not seen her for seven weeks. *Seven weeks*, Caitlin thought as she stroked the dog's back. *Seems like a lifetime.*

When Eric arrived early that evening, he had flowers and pizza, hoping to get back on Caitlin's good side. She opened the door and smiled softly but did not kiss him as she stood aside to let him enter the apartment. The living room was bare and all that remained in the apartment, other than a bed in the bedroom and some boxes, was a small table with four chairs next to the kitchen. He looked under the sink and in the cupboards for a container for the flowers but found nothing but a few plates and water glasses. He turned and looked plaintively at Caitlin, who shrugged and pointed to an empty soda bottle waiting to be recycled.

Eric scrunched his lips and silently took the bottle, washed it, and cut the narrow top off with his pocket knife. He filled the bottle with water and inserted the flowers, placing them ceremoniously on the table. They sat down to eat, still not having said a word. After a bite or two, Eric faced Caitlin and said, "I wanted you to know that I'll be working on Molly's case again." He did not tell her it was peripheral to the terrorism case.

But that was enough. Caitlin reached over and touched his hand, finished chewing, and said, "Thank you." They went back to their meal, occasionally making eye contact but again not speaking.

Eric left not long after they had finished eating, giving her a gentle, almost brotherly kiss on the cheek as he walked out the door. He drove to the office and spent a few hours looking over the images he and Montez had gathered from the video recordings. He stared at the men, their grainy features enhanced somewhat by the techs at Quantico. Nothing had popped up yet domestically, and certainly not yet internationally, even though Interpol and friendly intelligence services had copies of the pictures. There had been some dark amusement among the investigators when it became apparent that the man driving the SUV had put on a "Make America Great Again" hat, whether to shield his face or protect himself from the sun. A terrorist with a sense of humor? More likely a sense of irony.

21

Bert Loggins called Leonard from a phone whose Caller ID said "Eastern Rent-A-Car" but actually rang at his desk. When Leonard answered, Bert told him, "I think I've got something." Leonard invited him over to the Agency immediately.

They gathered around the table, and Bert passed around screen grabs from his investigations. "I visited the main carding sites, at least those I'm aware of, and on Rescator I found a guy I've seen before who goes by the handle 'Dropper.' Now, as you know, these sites are all well isolated through Tor or other anonymizers, but we're pretty sure Rescator is in Ukraine, so Dropper is probably either in Ukraine or Russia." The analysts nodded approvingly and Loggins continued, "Since DoJ helped take down much of the 'Infrafraud' group, Dropper has been bragging about not having been caught, both in blogs on carding sites and in social media. It seems like these guys can't help themselves. Everyone wants to be the King of the Thieves. Don't know if it's ego or testosterone or both. Now, I don't have access to Dropper's Facebook page, and I can't find it, but I know from comments on another carder's page that he's there." He pointed to screen grabs, first from carder blogs and then from a Facebook page.

Three analysts got up from the table, carrying the screen grabs, and led Loggins to a computer in a nearby cubicle. After covering some classified documents on the desk, a woman sat down and started typing, first a username and password and then some additional phrases. "You're not seeing this, right?" she asked with a grin, and he shook his head no. In a few seconds the screen displayed the original Facebook page shown in the screen grab. The analyst typed additional commands, and two or three dozen more Facebook pages opened. The quartet of analysts, now joined by Leonard, looked carefully at each page, minimizing them as they went. After about a dozen and a half, they paused. Before them was a thin, 20-something with a wispy mustache and pale skin, each arm around an attractive young blonde in a tight dress. In front of them was a table littered with glasses, empty champagne bottles, and an ice bucket with an unopened bottle directly in front. One of the analysts read the Cyrillic out loud. "Vasily Dobrovsky."

"Dropper," said another analyst, not seeing the words written on the page—since they weren't—but saying out loud what everyone was thinking. "Where is he?" he asked.

"Looks like a club in a big city. Could be Moscow, or St. Petersburg, or Kiev," another one said.

"We can't find him from his IP address?

"Facebook allows Tor connections," the woman at the keyboard pointed out. "Those virtual connections make pinpointing a user's actual internet protocol address nearly impossible. But we can try, using his email address or login information."

Leonard turned to Loggins, smiling and holding out his hand. "Thank you, Bert, we'll take it from here."

22

A cross the river the president was being briefed by law enforcement and national security officials at what would have been a regular cabinet meeting, but four days after the attacks there was only one subject to discuss. "Ok, where are we?" he asked.

Secretary Nelson began, "Mr. President, we still have a total stoppage of rail and container traffic on the West Coast. We've had twenty container explosions, and we believe that's the entire number of containers the terrorists filled with explosives. Between the rail explosions and the explosion adjacent to the Pacific fiber optic landing, the San Francisco Bay Area, which includes the Silicon Valley, now has less than twenty percent of its normal internet connectivity. More problematic is that as of today, about eighty percent of the Bay Area's communities don't have electricity and ..."

The president interrupted. "Can't they lay some temporary cables or something to restore the Ethernet and the power?"

"Unfortunately, sir, the solution isn't that simple. The damage to the internet connections isn't just severed fiber optic cables. It's also the electronic equipment that's used to transfer the signals in the fiber optics. Not only will thousands of individual fibers need to be repaired, all of those electronics will need to be replaced."

"How long do they think it will take?" the president asked.

The secretary paused before answering. "It could take as much as a year or more to restore all of the connections, at least temporarily."

The president sat back in his chair and rocked a few times, then leaned forward again. "What about the power?" he asked.

"That could take just as long. The transformers the terrorists damaged are custom units that are made to order. They're so large and expensive that the utilities don't keep spares, and there are just a few companies in the US that make them."

"Do we have to buy them from China?" he asked.

The secretary turned and whispered with an aide, then continued, "Not China. Maybe Germany, maybe India, but hopefully the US will be able to handle the orders."

"Well good, at least we don't have to ask China for help," he said and waited for a laugh that did not come. He continued, "FEMA, what are you doing?"

The Administrator of FEMA began, "Mr. President, we have multiple IMATs, I mean, Incident Management Assistance Teams, deployed to the area, one to San Francisco, one to Oakland, one to Berkley, one to Fremont, one to San Jose and one to Santa Clara. These teams are liaising with local governments to establish their requirements for assistance. We've already moved more than two hundred temporary generators to the areas and we're transporting more. We're working with the local governments to make sure their fresh water supplies are uninterrupted and that sewage continues to be treated. These are the priorities, along with making sure that hospitals have power, as well as fire stations and police stations. Oh, and I should say we're trying to get power to supermarkets, as well." As the grim implications of that last statement sank in, there were concerned looks around the room.

"Two hundred doesn't sound like nearly enough," the President's Chief of Staff stated emphatically. "There must be thousands of police and fire stations and hospitals. And how are we going to keep people from starving?"

The FEMA administrator continued, "Most of those facilities already have backup generators. The problem is that they're generally not designed to run twenty-four seven for very long. And the supermarkets, of course, generally don't even *have* backup generators. Right now some have rented generators, and more are coming in from across the country from commercial rental companies for supermarkets and other food stores. Our IMAT teams are working those issues, as well as trying to keep up the flow of diesel fuel to fuel the generators."

"So those places could run out of generators after a while?" the president asked.

"That's the danger," the administrator replied.

"Are there problems with stalled traffic? Looting?" the chief of staff asked.

The administrator looked at the Barbara Nelson, who answered, "Most traffic lights are out, but fortunately or unfortunately, there isn't that much traffic, because people aren't commuting to work. If they go out it's for food or medical care. The local governments have instituted dusk-to-dawn curfews, and by and large they're using their earthquake preparedness plans for providing essentials—food and water and public safety. There have been some isolated examples of looting, more extensive in Oakland than elsewhere, but so far the police and National Guard have it under control."

"Well, do everything you can to help these people," the president ordered, looking around the table. "I've already declared a state of emergency in the whole area. That should help. What about the railroads?"

"I think the picture is a little better there, Mr. President. We should have the rails mostly cleared up and repaired within a month or so," the secretary of transportation said. "It's mostly just removing damaged cars, re-railing some of them, filling in holes, and replacing ties and rails. There's some signal damage, but the railroads have the capacity to make these repairs pretty quickly. And they're getting crews from CSX and Norfolk Southern to help out."

"Well, at least there's *some* good news," the president said. "Where are we with the investigation?" He looked past the attorney general to the director of the FBI. The director stood from his chair along the wall and began, "Sir, we've found the location in Phoenix, Arizona, where the twenty containers were filled with explosives."

Here he was interrupted by the president. "Twenty! I just can't believe so many. Only three planes on nine eleven and we have *twenty* containers."

The director did not correct the president by reminding him of the fourth plane, United Flight ninety-three, that crashed in Shanksville, Pennsylvania, on its way toward Washington. He simply continued with, "Yes, sir. We believe the twenty containers are the extent of the explosives, based on the witness accounts from the crane service that loaded them onto trucks for transportation to the railroads' inter-modal terminals. We have descriptions of five men and we have multiple agencies searching for them."

"Do you think they're still in the country?" the president asked.

"We have no way of knowing, except that none of them have shown up at airports or border crossings. So they may still be here." What the director did not say was that could mean there would be more attacks. He continued, "We know they purchased the fertilizer, containers, and various services using stolen credit cards, so we're working on that area as a source for funding."

"How did they get things to explode where they did to take out the fiber optic equipment?" the president asked.

"We were able to recover some of the trigger boards at the Phoenix site that they didn't use. ATF believes they built trigger boards that used GPS to determine if the containers were at one of a series of pre-determined locations within a certain window of time. We think that if the triggers never reached that location, they were set to explode at some other time. The fact that all of the containers detonated within twenty-four hours suggests they knew we would figure out where the containers came from pretty quickly and isolate any that were unex-

ploded. That is, we would had isolated any that hadn't detonated," the
director finished.

The president turned to CIA Director Haller. "What do we know
about the group that claimed the attacks?" he asked.

"Unfortunately, very little, Mr. President. The group was unknown
prior to a few months ago, when they claimed the shooter in
Arkansas. We're working on tracing the source of their credit cards, as
well as what communications we're aware of. We're working closely
with our international partners in Europe and the Middle East."

"OK, good. Treasury, what's this doing to the economy? The stock
market is killing us," the president said, noting that the Dow Jones,
S&P and NASDAQ had all fallen more than fifteen percent since the
attacks.

"Mr. President, the rail and port shutdown has severely limited our
Asian imports and exports."

"That should help our trade deficit," the president interrupted,
getting a little chuckle from the room this time.

"Yes, sir," the treasury secretary responded. He continued, "That's
true, but the Bay Area also accounts for about four percent of our
GDP, and productivity in the area has plummeted. Businesses are
closed because they don't have power and workers can't get to and
from work. Many of the big tech companies like Google or Facebook
have server farms in other locations, but management is largely
handled in the Silicon Valley. Also, manufacturing business across the
rest of the country, like automobile plants, are starting to suffer from a
lack of parts coming in from Asia, with the railroads and West Coast
ports shut down, so we could see a broader slowdown across the
entire manufacturing sector develop very quickly." He paused for a
moment then added, "I think there's a good chance we'll slide into
recession very shortly."

The president winced but did not say anything.

The secretary of defense asked, "Since we don't think any of the
explosives reached the Pacific Northwest, Mr. President, should we
consider reopening the ports in Seattle and Portland and the associated rail lines?"

The president looked around the room and asked, "Any objections to that?" The assembled cabinet and staff largely shook their heads no to the question.

The secretary of homeland security turned to look at the FBI director, who mouthed. "Caution," and then said, "Mr. President, I think that's a good idea, but we should maintain high security and institute one hundred percent screening of containers until further notice." Unspoken was how much the screening would slow shipments on the reopened lines and the broader question of what they would be screening for.

"OK, then," the president responded. "Let's do that." Then, forcefully leaning forward in his chair, he added, "FBI and CIA, I want these guys found and the people that paid for this found and punished. Severely."

"Yes, Mr. President," they responded and the meeting was over.

23

First thing Monday Eric and Montez were conferring on how to proceed on the smuggling investigation and, ultimately, on the murder investigation, when Eric received a call from a special agent at a DHS Homeland Security Investigations unit that was part of ICE. After introductions the special agent said, "Eric, we think we have your guy in the ballcap entering Mexico at Nogales on the twenty-first. A day after the explosions."

Shit, Eric thought. *We lost him before we even knew to find him.* "Did he drive in?" he asked aloud.

"No. Walked in with the tourist crowd around dinnertime," the ICE agent responded.

Eric thought about that. Maybe his car was still near the port of entry. "Can you guys look around on the American side? See if his car is parked nearby? Black, late model Ford Explorer. We don't have a plate. I'm on my way down."

They hung up and Eric briefed Montez. They discussed how to identify the suspect's car. "The guy at the rental place thought the car had Arizona plates. No plate in front, so it wouldn't be California. Arizona DMV lists about four hundred cars matching the description. About thirty have changed ownership in the last six months, about as long as the warehouse in Phoenix was rented, so that gives us some plates to look for," Montez said.

"That's assuming he didn't steal a plate."

ON THE WAY TO NOGALES, they discussed how to track the vehicle and what they could do to rejuvenate the smuggling investigation. Eric's phone rang, interrupting their discussion. It was ICE again.

"I think we might have the car. It's got a few tickets on it dating back to the twenty-second. It's parked about a quarter mile from the port." The ICE agent gave Eric the address.

"We're about ten minutes out," Eric said and hung up.

When they got to the address the ICE agent had given them, they saw the black SUV with tinted windows surrounded by Nogales police cars and a few ICE Tahoes. Yellow police tape kept out curious bystanders. Eric and Montez slipped under the tape and showed their credentials, shaking hands with the ICE agent who had made the phone call. They circled the vehicle and stopped at the back by the tailgate, squinting to see what was in the back behind the rear seat.

Out of the corner of his eye, Montez saw a Nogales police officer with a Slim Jim approaching the driver's side door. As the officer started to slip the thin metal between the glass and the rubber weather stripping, Montez yelled, "Don't do that. Wait for EOD. The car might be booby trapped." The officer froze then sheepishly stepped away and put the Slim Jim back in his cruiser.

Eric looked at Montez. He had thought about that, given the volume of explosives these guys had handled, but since they had not booby trapped the crime scene in Phoenix, he had pushed the thought lower in his consciousness. *Stupid*, he thought. *That's how cops and FBI agents get killed.* As he said that, the wind changed direction and he caught a whiff of something. Kerosene, maybe diesel fuel. He lowered his head to touch the window and was able to make out a gray blanket covering something large and regular. "Everyone back," he yelled, "I think there's a bomb in there."

The crowd stepped back and the uniformed officers pushed them back another thirty yards.

SANTA CRUZ COUNTY EOD spent the next three hours carefully inspecting the vehicle, finding four 5-gallon pails that had once contained paint but now held 120 pounds of ANFO. The four detonators were wired into the dome-light circuit, so that if a door had been opened, the resulting explosion would have leveled half the city block. Most importantly, ATF was able to recover the booster charges that magnified the detonators' explosion into a blast sufficient to ignite the ANFO. This could be an important piece of evidence, since every other booster charge had been consumed in the container blasts.

Eric and Montez did not wait around for EOD to do their magic. After the evacuation of the area around the vehicle, they headed to the port of entry with the ICE agent to see the video of the ball-capped terrorist. What they saw was a clear video of a tall, well-built man, dark complected, with sharp features and a closely cropped beard. It was the same man they had seen on the rental company video. "Did you pick up any of the others in the BOLO?" Eric asked.

"Those descriptions were pretty vague. This one popped up as an automated match, but since we only had pictures of the one other guy, and that one wasn't too good, I'm not surprised we didn't get another match," the ICE agent replied.

"Do you have him coming into the country?" Montez asked.

"We searched the video archives going back a year for a match. Nothing. Nothing in the passport or visa database, either. So he didn't come in by air or ship, at least not legally."

They thought about that a moment. "What about other points of entry from Mexico or Canada?" Eric asked.

"Nothing," the ICE agent replied, looking for confirmation from a Customs and Border Protection officer who had joined them.

"Is it possible the automated system missed him? Is there any way to look manually?"

"In theory it's possible to look at all of the video for all of the cameras at all of the ports of entry around the country," the CBP officer began. "For a year, that's millions of hours of video. No one has the manpower to look at all of that video. If we can narrow it down in time or location, maybe."

"I can tell you the automated system is pretty damn good since it's positioned so the individual is looking right toward the camera," the ICE agent said. "We might get false alerts on an image, which are then reviewed manually, but unless the guy's wearing a disguise, a decent picture like you guys sent us will give us a match."

Eric was skeptical that the computer system could be that good. The FBI's system did not seem to be. But he let it pass for now. He mused, "So if we don't have a record of him coming in legally, maybe he was smuggled across. Do your intelligence people have any resources on the other side we might use to run this to ground?"

"We get better cooperation on people smuggling than drug smuggling. There's less money involved, but it's still hit or miss," the CBP agent said. "We'll see what we can come up with."

Eric and Montez took prints of the best images, as well as copies of the video, and thanked their colleagues at ICE and the CBP. They walked north from the border to the lot where they had parked. Eric looked up at the sky, a brilliant blue with a few cotton-ball clouds forming over the mountains in the distance. He stopped. Montez stopped too and looked at him. "Let's go see Capitan Garcia," Eric said.

Montez tilted his head, a habit he had when he was thinking. "I don't think that's a good idea. This case has too much visibility now and we need to stay inside the lines."

Eric was not dissuaded. "We're not gonna to catch this guy waiting around. Garcia seemed to know about the smuggled EFPs. That sounds like a connection to me."

"What the hell. I'll be very surprised if he's still in the neighborhood." Montez was not convinced, but he shrugged and they walked to their car, where they locked their service weapons in the trunk.

They drove through the port of entry into Mexico, trusting the Mexicans would not search their trunk.

IT WAS early afternoon by the time they reached the Comandancia, and the building was nearly empty of police. The absent included Captain Garcia. Eric and Montez stepped back outside. They felt sticky and uncomfortable, thunderheads building gray and black over the mountains confirming the humidity. They walked a few blocks to the Costco, ate Sonoran hot dogs and wandered the aisles, marveling at what was different and that was the same compared to the same chain store over the border, just a few miles north. After an hour they walked back to the Comandancia and found Captain Garcia returned from his patrol, or his *siesta*, whichever it had been. Montez greeted the policeman in Spanish, "*Buenos tardes*, Capitán Garcia. It is nice to see you again."

Garcia leaned back in his chair, scraping that same spot on the wall behind. "I remember you two. Looking for a dead *traficante*." He fished out a cigarette from a pack on his desk, poked it between his lips, and lit it from a disposable lighter.

Eric smirked slightly. The cigarette gesture looked like something the Captain had seen in a movie. As Eric handed over pictures of the man in the ballcap, he said, with Montez translating, "We're looking for this man. He entered Mexico last Tuesday."

Captain Garcia leaned forward and lifted one of the pictures between his thumb and index fingertips, his remaining fingers extended as if he were daintily holding a tea cup. He studied it, tossed it onto his desk, and looked briefly at the other photos. "Many people enter Mexico, including last Tuesday. Why is this one so interesting?"

"Well, for one, there's a reward for finding this one," Eric responded and sat back in his chair.

"How much?"

"One million dollars," Eric replied.

Captain Garcia leaned back again and rocked slightly a few times.

He took a long drag on his cigarette and blew the smoke above him as he looked at the ceiling. "I will make some inquiries." Eric leaned forward and dropped a business card on top of the pictures. Captain Garcia stood and said, "You left me your card last time. I know how to find you."

As they walked out Montez turned to Eric and asked, "Are you sure that was a good idea? For all we know, Garcia is tight with the traffickers and will tip off our man."

Eric smiled and replied, "I thought he wasn't in the neighborhood? It was worth a shot. Maybe we can generate some action around our trafficker." He froze. *Jesus*, he thought. *Why didn't we think of that before?*

Montez looked at him as if he were reading his mind, "Think maybe it's the same guy?" he asked.

"That's what I was thinking, but I don't know. Too neat. Too circumstantial," Eric replied.

The afternoon rush hour was kicking in so they stopped at a small bar that mercifully was air conditioned and had a beer. Montez took a long pull of his Modelo Negra, looked around for eavesdroppers, saw that the bartender was at the other end of the bar, and asked, "So if our guy's still here, why? And where are the others? Back in wherever?"

Eric finished a pull of his Pacifico and answered, "Why still here, if he is here? Maybe he can't get out. Problems with his escape plans. Or maybe he's planning something else. We're making an assumption that this guy's the boss, when we really don't know the structure of the cell. If he *is* the boss, it bothers me that he would have put himself at risk with smuggling the EFPs. Maybe he doesn't trust his people." He paused and took another pull on his beer. "Maybe he's playing with a pickup team that isn't really trained."

"If he's not the boss, who's pulling his strings?" Montez asked.

24

A few hours prior to Montez and Eric's conversation, a man in black had been standing in the dark entryway of an apartment building. The entryway was dark because he had broken the bulb in the light overhead. He stood quietly for a few moments but saw little movement on the street or inside the building, so he turned to the electronic lock panel next to the door and quietly set to opening it. In a minute he had tricked the micro-controller into granting him access. The electric door lock buzzed and he stepped into the vestibule and climbed the marble stairs to the third floor.

When he reached the apartment he was looking for, he looked carefully for a "tell" at the door jam, a thread or piece of paper that, if dislodged, would tell the owner the door had been opened in his absence. About two feet from the floor he found one, a tiny white speck protruding from the door jamb. He reached into an inside pocket of his jacket and withdrew a fiber optic camera, which he plugged into his phone and used to view the inside of the apartment for occupants—human or animal—and then the back of the door for any unusual locks or alarms. He saw none.

He replaced the camera in his pocket and now used his phone, which looked externally like an iPhone 10 but had some additional, non-Apple features built in, to scan for strong radio frequency signals that might be used for remote audio or video surveillance. He found none. He replaced the phone in a back pocket of his trousers and withdrew from an inside jacket pocket a shiny cylinder that looked like a small flashlight but, instead of a lens, had a metal pin protruding from the end. He inserted the speed pick first into the deadbolt lock, opening it in less than 30 seconds, then into the knob, which he unlocked in less than ten. He gripped the knob and slowly swung the door open, remembering to pick up the "tell" and hoping to remember exactly where to replace it when he left.

The first room he entered was neat and spare, furnished with just a couch, chair, and table. To the right was a kitchen, a large cuckoo clock ostentatiously ticking on the wall next to the refrigerator. His target was the room to the left, a combination bedroom and office. He walked along the edge of the room until he reached a window then slowly drew the curtains. He wouldn't turn on the lights, but he didn't want to be seen illuminated in the glow of the computer displays either.

The man felt around the back of the three computers in the room and found unused USB ports into which he plugged what looked like USB memory sticks. One of the computers woke up, while the other two stayed in hibernation, but inside all three their hard drives were slowly being read and archived like a parasite sucking the life out of its host.

He looked at his phone, which gave him a status on all three devices. This was going to take a while, which was no surprise but, nonetheless, was not welcome. He opened the messenger app and texted, "in process." Twenty seconds later he received one word: "stable." He texted back, "advise if unstable." *For God's sake*, he thought. *Don't let him walk in on me.*

While he was waiting, he used his phone to take pictures of the room, the computers, and the few sheets of paper lying around. Then he found the apartment's cable modem and Wi-Fi router. He reached into his pocket and found a small, cylindrical object with threads on each end that would screw in between the cable and the modem. It was marked "Surge Suppressor," but it had some additional capabilities. He replaced the modem as precisely as he could and continued studying the apartment. He took pictures of the books on the bookcase, the magazines in the bathroom, the pharmaceuticals in the medicine cabinet, the food in the fridge. When he walked back into the bedroom, he saw that one of the devices was finished, one close, but the one on the computer with three monitors still had a long time to complete. He looked at his watch, a Rolex Submariner, and sighed, then smirked just a bit. The watch was an extravagance and, even more so, an anachronism in the age of GPS-accurate cell phone time, but he always felt that time was "better" on the Rolex than on the phone.

Just at that moment the phone buzzed in his pocket, and he looked at the text: "unstable." Given the distance, that gave him perhaps ten more minutes. He looked at the archive display. Not enough time. He texted, "need 20 more." A few seconds later the reply came: "K."

AT A BAR A KILOMETER AWAY, a woman approached a couple rising from a table and putting on their jackets. "Oleg, it has been so long," she said exuberantly and kissed the man.

The man stepped back, looked at his attractive assailant, and sat back down, puzzled but interested. The woman who had been with him stopped putting on her jacket and also sat down, eyeing the interloper warily, the jacket hanging off one arm.

The woman who had kissed the man had the advantage of being sober, which the man and his companion were not, and she enthralled them with tales of her most recent travels to Minsk, to Berlin, and to London, how she was liking her new job, what she thought of the mayor of St. Petersburg, etc. The man listened, smiled, and nodded, while his companion just slumped in her seat and frowned, idly picking light-colored lint from her black skirt. After 15 minutes the phone buzzed in the sober woman's purse. She reached in to look at it and said, "Well, have to go," and she disappeared into the crowd.

The man watched her go, confused by her abrupt departure, and called after her dolefully, "But my name is Vasily!"

25

E arly Saturday morning Eric walked into the office and found Montez on the phone. He walked around behind him and saw on his computer display a picture of their suspect in the ballcap in a file naming him as Khalid al-Hassan. Montez held the receiver against his chest and quietly told Eric, "Forensics got a print from the SUV and a friendly intelligence service IDed him." Montez went back to his call and finished a moment later. He hung up the phone and turned to Eric, who had pulled up a chair from an empty cubicle. "Turns out the SUV was pretty well wiped down, but we got a really clean thumb print from the glove box door. Our 'State Department' friend helped get the print overseas a lot faster than normal channels."

"Well, that's helpful," Eric said. "What's his story?"

Montez leaned forward and read from the text on the screen, "Given name: Khalid al-Hassan, born in Homs, Syria, thirteen July nineteen seventy-nine. Immigrated to Lebanon in nineteen eighty-two. Looks like he joined Hamas as a young man and was arrested by the Israelis in March, two thousand three. That must be how we have him." He took a drink of his coffee and a bite of a bagel that sat in wax paper on his desk. "Released by the Israelis in two thousand four, then disappeared for a while until he gets stopped entering Jordan from Iraq on a Syrian passport in two thousand fifteen. Lots of moving parts there," he added parenthetically. "Disappears again until he pops up here."

"So we have ourselves a real Islamic terrorist," Eric said. "Is there any reference to the group that claimed responsibility, the 'Sons of what's his name'?"

"No."

"Anything that would help us nab him?"

"No."

IN LANGLEY a larger meeting was just starting among a half dozen CIA agents, four from the NSA, four FBI agents, and cybercrime experts from both DoJ and Treasury. The group sat at a large table populated with computers and already littered with water bottles, coffee cups, and the odd breakfast burrito.

Wardlaw opened the meeting, "On this server we have mirrors of hard drives sourced involuntarily from a Russian who we think provided the credit card used in the August twenty attacks. I want you to try to decrypt them and figure out if there's any lead to his customer."

Lisa, a woman from the NSA, asked, "How many machines are represented here?"

One of the CIA analysts answered, "Three. Two were connected to the internet, and one looked like it was air gapped."

"Which one was air gapped?" she asked.

"Drive marked 'C'"

"OK, that's the one I'm working on," she replied and opened the image of the drive from her computer. She saw the familiar file structure of Linux. She opened a diagnostic program and ran it against the image, then ran another one to give herself some confidence that the files would not self-destruct if she tried to access them. In the long run it would not matter, since there were multiple backups of the image, but it would waste time.

Lisa next used a tool to evaluate the encryption used on the hard drive. She smiled. Maybe, because this machine had never been connected to the outside world, the hacker had used dm-crypt, which came with the Linux distribution, to encrypt the drive. Lisa knew at least three ways to crack that encryption. She saw, as expected, the boot sector was unencrypted. Why bother, she thought, as she methodically worked to break through the encryption.

The other analysts were less sanguine. Vasily had used a much more sophisticated encryption on his two computers that were connected to the outside world. The team made a request to the NSA to reserve supercomputer time to try to break the encryption keys. That could take days or weeks, they worried. After a few hours of work, it appeared from the file structure that one of the remaining computers had been used for email, while the other had not; they decided to focus their attention on the former.

It was late afternoon when one of the analysts called out, "It looks like he was using Hushmail for his email. Do we have his IP address?"

The senior member of the group from the NSA said, "Yes. Let me make a call."

Lisa looked up from her display. "I don't have any email or anything like that, but I do have fragments with the name 'Siemens' and a copyright date. Looks like some executable code." A few of her colleagues got up from their computers and gathered around her, pointing to text on her display.

One said, "Siemens, like the electronics company?"

A CIA analyst volunteered gravely, "They make electrical equipment, like electrical substation controls."

LATE IN THE day Wardlaw briefed his boss. "Here's what we have so far," he began. "We have partial decryption on the air-gapped computer."

"That's the one not connected to his network?" the assistant director clarified.

"Yes, sir. That drive has some suggestions that this individual was somehow connected to the attack against the electrical substations. There are fragments of code that look like parts of the Supervisory Control and Data Acquisition, or SCADA system, at some of the substations. We're running that to ground. Then we're trying to access email that was sent using an ostensibly secure email system but for which we think we might have an entree. Should have an answer on that in a day."

"The director has to brief the president on Monday. I need some progress for her to give him," the assistant director said, leaning back in his chair and placing his feet on a file folder on the corner of his desk. He was wearing Saturday clothes, and in place of his normal, highly polished Oxfords, he sported a pair of scuffed Docksiders, as befitted a man who would rather be sailing his boat on the Chesapeake Bay than sitting in his office.

"We'll keep working it. The problem is going to be the encryption of the other two drives. The NSA is working on the keys, but it's impossible to tell how long that will take," Wardlaw responded.

"Well, buy the kids pizza and keep them on it," the assistant director said. He thanked Wardlaw and sent him back downstairs.

26

On Sunday Eric and Caitlin escaped the heat by driving up to the top of Mount Lemon and hiking the Aspen trail, which rises to 6,500 feet above the desert floor. Eric was not much of a hiker, but he had lived in Tucson long enough to know that, besides hunkering down in air conditioning, altitude was the only way to beat the heat.

This time of year, a sudden thunderstorm could drench them on the trail, so wearing just a pair of jeans and a cotton T-shirt could be a problem. And while Caitlin had a closet in Anchorage full of name-brand outdoor wear in all the right synthetic fibers, she had not packed any to come to her sister's funeral, so Eric had taken her to a local outdoor shop and bought her enough to acquit herself properly in the wild.

When they reached the trailhead, they found a place to park, climbed out, and started assembling themselves for the hike. Caitlin slipped on Eric's Camelback and Eric dropped three, quart-sized bottles of water into his own backpack that also carried Mylar blankets, a compass, trail mix and jerky, a flashlight and a whistle. Eric was not one to take chances in the wild. Though off duty, he still carried his backup service weapon in an ankle holster.

They started on the trail, both panting slightly, surprised by the difference the elevation made. "How's your investigation going? The whole thing, that is," Caitlin asked in between breaths.

"We're making progress," Eric said, silently cursing himself for not keeping in better shape. "Have you climbed Denali?" he asked, changing the subject.

"I haven't *climbed* Denali," she answered, emphasizing the word "climbed." "I *have* hiked around it quite a bit. It's a really big mountain, not just tall but wide. On a clear day you can see it from Anchorage."

"How far is that?" Eric asked, tripping slightly over a root.

"About two hundred and sixty miles," she answered.

"Wow, that *is* a big mountain."

THEY WERE on their way back, about six miles into the eight-and-a-half-mile loop, when the thunderstorm hit. Through the treetops they had seen the sky darken, then a half mile later heard the thunder, then a half mile later still the skies opened and they were being drenched. Eric pulled the backpack off his back and dug through it for the Mylar blankets. He wished he had thought to bring rain jackets.

He pulled Caitlin toward a slight slope where the water would not pool under them, and they sat on the forest floor and covered themselves with the waterproof blankets. The thunderhead felt close enough for them to touch, and the sound and flash of the lightning striking all around was at once terrifying and mesmerizing. Eric silently prayed lightning would not strike the tree they were under or one nearby. When Caitlin pressed herself into him and started to cry, he whispered into her ear, "We're fine, the lightning won't hit us."

Caitlin pushed herself away and looked at him with damp, narrowed eyes. "This has nothing to do with lightning," she stated emphatically and wiped her eyes with the back of her hand. She looked at him for a few moments. She had pushed herself far enough away that the rain was now running down her back. She sighed and eased back toward him, looking down and to the side, watching the drops splash on the dirt, turning it to mud.

After ten minutes the rain started to ease. Eric looked at her and when she nodded, they both stood up, Eric holding the sheet above them as they rejoined the trail and continued their hike. When they reached the car, they brushed the mud from their legs and behinds as best they could, dropped their gear in the trunk, and climbed into the car. They sat, silent, watching the last few drops run down the windshield before heading back to Tucson.

27

The Monday ITWG meeting opened with good news and bad news. "The NSA was able to crack one of the computers and found evidence that the hacker we're investigating was associated with the destruction of the twenty substations," Wardlaw began.

"Nineteen," someone corrected.

Wardlaw smiled and continued, "The *nineteen* substations that were damaged by corrupted control software rather than EFPs. So this fellow might have been a one-stop shop. The bad news is that we still don't have the other machines cracked, so we still don't know who his contact was."

That was a serious issue since the intelligence community still could not figure out who the Global Warriors of Jihad and Righteousness—their new acronym was GWJR—were. Neither US intelligence nor friendly foreign intelligence services could find a whisper of this group before August twentieth or, rather, before the Arkansas shooting in June.

"How long does the NSA think it will take to break the encryption on the other two machines?" an FBI agent asked.

"Well, he used a two-fifty-six-bit encryption key, so we won't be

able to crack it using brute force. We're attempting to harvest his pass
phrases, and we'll try them as they come in," a representative of the
NSA answered.

"So, back to the identity of this group. Roger, bring us up to
speed," Wardlaw prompted.

One of the CIA analysts opened the file in front of him and began,
"Israelis were able to ID one of the terrorists, the one we think might
have been the leader. His name is Khalid al-Hassan, DOB thirteen July
nineteen seventy-nine, Homs, Syria. Nom de guerre: Khalid al-Fajr.
'Fajr' literally means 'dawn' or 'daybreak' and is used to identify
morning prayer, that is, before daylight. It's also the title of the eighty-
ninth Sura of the Quran, which describes the destruction of unbelievers and those who value wealth. His father was active in the
Muslim Brotherhood, and he, his mother, and brother fled to Lebanon
during the Homs massacre in February nineteen eighty-two. We
believe his father was killed in the Homs massacre, but we don't know
if he was killed in combat or captured and executed.

"At some point Khalid became acquainted with the Muslim
Brothers in the Palestinian refugee camps, because he shows up in
Gaza during the Second Intifada and gets arrested by the Israelis in
two thousand three. They worked him over for a while and kept him
in prison but really didn't have anything major on him, so he was
released as part of the big two thousand four prisoner release. He's off
the radar again until the Jordanians prevented him from entering
Jordan from Iraq in two thousand fifteen. He was carrying a Syrian
passport giving his home as, you guessed it, Homs. Now, that's interesting because by two thousand thirteen Homs was completely in
Syrian government control. So what was he doing? We don't know."

"Any connection with Daesh?" someone asked, using the Arabic
acronym for ISIS.

"We don't know. We have no evidence he was in ISIS-controlled
territory, but how does a guy with his background survive in areas
Assad controls?" Roger asked rhetorically.

"What do we have working backward from the contact with the
Arkansas shooter? If this al-Hassan guy has no contact with ISIS, then

how did GWJR contact him?" Wardlaw chimed in, referring to the email purportedly from the Global Warriors of Jihad and Right-eousness.

One of the FBI agents said, "Between the shooter's computer and metadata provided by the ISP, we were able to trace the internet address through a few hops, but we lost it in Europe when it went hard into TOR."

The room was quiet for a moment. Then someone asked, "How was he paid?"

"How was who paid?" Wardlaw asked, his face betraying his confusion.

"The hacker in Russia that we're exploiting. Was it crypto-curren-cy?" The analyst asked, using the generic term for digital or virtual currencies like Bitcoin.

Someone volunteered, "I don't think we know."

The man who had asked the question said, addressing the Treasury contingent, "Well, you guys are routinely tracking Bitcoin payments, right?"

"We think we get most of them, yes," one responded.

"Well, why don't we see if a payment went to our guy and try to figure out who sent it," the questioner suggested. As he was speaking, the faces around the room brightened as they saw where his thoughts were going.

"Let's get on that," Wardlaw commanded.

28

E ric and Montez were in the daily coordination meeting when
Eric's phone rang silently. He looked down at the number
and jumped up when he saw it was from Mexico. He showed
it to Montez, who followed him outside the room.

"Agent West?" Captain Garcia asked in English.

"Speaking."

"Come down and talk to me. I think I can get you your man," said
Captain Garcia and hung up.

Eric turned to Montez, "He says he can get our man."

Montez smiled. "Let's go."

CAPTAIN GARCIA WAS WAITING for them when they arrived at the
Comandancia. He closed the door after they sat down and asked in
English, "How soon can you get the money?"

Eric and Montez looked at each other. "How soon can you get our
guy?" Eric asked.

Captain Garcia switched to Spanish and Montez translated for
Eric. "It is an interesting situation. Your man crossed over and had

arrangements to leave the country, but those who made those arrangements found out about the reward and, how do you say, 'stalled' him."

That made sense, since the president had announced the one million dollar reward on national television on the night of the attacks. That type of information travels fast.

Eric and Montez exchanged glances again, and Eric leaned in to Montez and whispered, "I have an idea. Stay with me." He turned back toward Captain Garcia and said, "It might take a few days to get the money. Maybe the people who have him can do us a favor? Use some of their techniques of persuasion to ask him some questions. Nothing permanent, of course ..."

Montez stopped translating, turned to Eric and protested, "No man, that's wrong!"

"Raul, if we bring him in now and he clams up, it will be days, maybe weeks before he starts to talk. Maybe they send him to Guantanamo. Then we have nothing on the attacks, and nothing to help us solve the Walsh murder."

Montez was unconvinced. "You can't cut corners that way. It's wrong and it'll cost you your career. And maybe your freedom."

Eric pushed back, whispering, "If Khalid doesn't know we know he's here, if he thinks he's just a 'guest' of some cut-throat traffickers, maybe he'll be willing to talk to save his skin. Literally."

"That's a mucho big 'if'," Montez said, not taking his eyes off Eric.

Captain Garcia was getting impatient with the colloquy. "Gentlemen, what is going on?" he asked in Spanish.

"Nothing, Capitán, just a discussion about tactics," Montez replied similarly, then turned back to Eric. "What would be the logic for the traffickers to question him?" he asked.

Eric thought for a moment. "OK, how's this? The murder of the Border Patrol agent brought heat on the traffickers. There's their motivation. Then they ease into other topics. I know none of it's admissible. I just want a head start before he's in the system and we lose him."

Montez looked at him. "You're on your own on this one. I'll translate for you, but that's it. I don't want anything to do with it." He turned to face Captain Garcia, stone-faced.

Eric also faced the Captain, with Montez translating. "Capitán, I would like you to ask the men holding our man to interrogate him about the murder of the Border Patrol agent. Then I would like them to ask about the terrorist attacks. Why he did it, who paid him. Make it sound like they're interested for their own reasons, not ours."

Captain Garcia leaned back in his chair. "Why would I do this?" he asked.

"Professional courtesy," Eric answered.

"These men, they don't have 'professional courtesy'," Captain Garcia replied.

"They're getting a big payday, and I'm sure you are too. Just make sure they don't mention the gringos when they're questioning him." Eric stood up to leave and Montez silently followed.

THEY DID NOT SPEAK until they were halfway back to Tucson. "You're taking a very, very big risk, and I don't like you including me in it," Montez said heavily. Montez was a stickler. If he couldn't put it in his "302," the standard form the Bureau used to document witness interviews, it was not part of the investigation.

Eric glanced at his friend. He thought about what he had done and the fact that Montez was right. What he had done was professionally risky, probably morally wrong, and might not even provide any action-able intelligence. Despite the frigid air-conditioned air blowing right on his face, he felt sweat break out on his forehead and upper lip. He was conflicted right down to his bones. But he needed answers for Caitlin, even more than he needed them for the official investigation. "I'm sorry, man, I'll keep you out of it," he said sincerely.

"What are we going to tell the SSA?" Montez asked.

"We're pursuing a lead on Khalid down in Mexico," Eric answered. "We should have more in a few days."

"What if he brings in other agencies to help us?" Montez asked, "What then?"

"He won't. If he does, we throw them on the guys whose names we still don't know," Eric said.

Montez shook his head slowly but said nothing.

29

In Washington the investigators from Treasury and the FBI were slowly paging through thousands of Bitcoin transactions they had tracked over the last year. Every one of them was like deciphering its own code, since the sender and receiver frequently used some means of shielding their electronic and, thereby, their physical identities. After two days of sorting through transactions, they had found eight that had gotten close enough to Vasily to warrant further scrutiny. They wondered whether the computer team had been able to crack either of the two hard drives that might contain transaction information.

One of the investigators called over to Langley via secure telephone to find out the status. "How are you guys coming with the decryption?" she asked.

"We got one passphrase on Saturday, but he hasn't been on his machine since."

That seemed odd to the caller, since Vasily made his money sitting in front of a screen for hours at a time. "Any idea why? Is he out of town?" she asked.

"No idea," was the reply and the conversation ended, the caller startled by her interlocutor's lack of interest.

Elsewhere in the CIA, Vasily's sudden absence was causing more concern. The device that had been left on the back of Vasily's cable modem had provided a continuous, covert stream of data from his apartment, including a reasonable re-creation of his computer keystrokes, as well as the encrypted data flowing to and from his modem and continuous audio monitoring of the room. The last recognizable sounds the monitors had heard were late Saturday, or rather, Sunday morning. They heard Vasily putting his computer to sleep, then filling a glass of water from a faucet, probably in the kitchen, and finally a series of rustling sounds that were interpreted as getting ready for bed. Aside from street sounds and the occasional creak, there had been no discernible movement in the apartment for the last two days.

MUCH AS THE Agency hated to do another "black bag" operation, breaking into Vasily's apartment again was very much on the agenda if they did not literally "hear" from Vasily in the very near future. First, agents in St. Petersburg used a disposable, "burner" cell phone to call Vasily's phone. No answer, and no sound inside the apartment. That by itself was not of concern, since the ringer on the phone could be silenced, although on Saturday they had listened to one side of a social conversation, and that time the incoming call had been signaled by a ringtone that sounded like a well-known rap song. So what was going on now? Had he left the apartment, quietly and unobserved? The decision was made to go back in.

The first step was a fake delivery. A covert agent dressed as a delivery man stood at the door to Vasily's apartment building with a package from Ozon, the Russian equivalent of Amazon, and rang Vasily's apartment. No answer the first time, and no answer two hours later. By now there was continuous surveillance on the entrance to the apartment, Vasily's living room window on the front of the building, and, from the adjacent alley, Vasily's bedroom. There was no movement visible in either room.

That night the same man who had broken in three days before repeated the process, except for breaking the overhead light, which was still broken from his last visit. As he approached Vasily's door, he noticed the tell on the ground, which meant either that Vasily had forgotten to pick it up, that he had chosen not to pick it up, or that someone had been in the apartment and did not care about being detected. The man's heartbeat accelerated slightly. He repeated his observation with the fiber optic camera, and radio-frequency sniffer before deciding it was safe to pick the lock.

A moment later, he slowly opened the door and quietly walked into the apartment, standing first by the closed door. He listened for sounds, any sound—snoring, breathing, screwing—and heard nothing. Streetlights lit the living room a dull amber. Everything looked as it had before. He compared the scene with the pictures on his phone. The same. He peeked into the kitchen and saw nothing noteworthy. When he turned to the bedroom, the light was dimmer, so he walked through the doorway and caught the familiar smell of decay and feces. The bed was empty but stained red. As he slowly walked to the opposite side, he saw Vasily, face down on the floor, a pool of clear vomit and coagulated blood framing his head like a scarlet halo. *Saint Vasily, the Hacker*, the man thought morbidly. He did not have a sample bag for the secretions, but it looked like a poisoning.

Careful not to step in anything puddled around the deceased, the man approached the computers. He glanced out the window and, as before, slowly pulled the shades. He chuckled at the thought that the surveillance team would conclude from this action that the apartment was unoccupied. Well, it was in a sense. With that thought he stopped abruptly; someone had opened all three computers and removed the hard drives. He looked behind the cable modem. The tap was still connected, but it was covered by a small blanket that appeared to have been carelessly tossed against the wall. He removed the tap, placed it in his pocket, and reconnected the cable. He slowly looked around the room for anything he had not seen before, anything that might have intelligence value. He saw nothing. He took a few pictures of Vasily, the room, and the computers and carefully made his way through the apartment, into the hall, down the stairs, and back into the night.

30

Vasily's demise alarmed and confused the intelligence community. Wardlaw opened the ITWG meeting with the question, "Who killed him?"

There was a pause before the first response, and when the response came, it didn't really answer the question. "It was very professional. We didn't hear them. Last we heard conclusively was we think him drawing a glass of water and then going to bed. After that it was just random noises, no sound of a scuffle."

"Could they have entered previously and applied a poison to the glasses?" Wardlaw asked.

"Possible," a CIA agent with experience in the field replied. "The mike in the tap isn't great at picking up low frequencies like footsteps, particularly far away, so we could have missed someone entering."

"Or maybe the assassin had entered the apartment before we first got in," another added.

"OK, let's decide who it *wasn't*. A rival hacker?" Wardlaw asked.

"That's not their style. Online character assassination, yes, but not physical violence," an FBI agent volunteered.

"Russian organized crime?" Wardlaw asked.

"Their hits tend to be much more visible—bombs, shootings in the street, things that send a message," a CIA analyst replied. His answer was accompanied by several nodding heads around the room.

"The GWJR?" Wardlaw asked. Another pause.

"That one's a real puzzle," a senior CIA analyst began. "We've never heard of these guys before a few months ago and never seen them operational before a few weeks ago. And they have the sophistication to carry out a very elaborate terrorist attack which, by the way, caused relatively few casualties, at least initially. We don't know what the long-term effects of the Bay Area power outage will be. But they come out of nowhere, prosecute a highly complex, coordinated, multi-prong attack, and then stealthily kill a potential witness? We must be looking at a group that includes highly trained, maybe former intelligence agents or Spetsnatz types," he finished, using the name of the highly regarded Russian Special Forces.

There followed a series of side conversations around the room until Wardlaw brought the discussion back to the initial topic. "So what are we saying? That the GWJR is populated with Special Forces types?"

"We can't make that statement. There's not nearly enough data," an analyst stated emphatically.

"There is another possibility for the killer. A national intelligence service," another analyst volunteered.

"It wasn't us," a woman from another directorate at the CIA called out to muted laughter.

"Interesting point," Wardlaw said. "What's their motive? Did they know we were interested in him? Maybe he's done some work for the SVR?" The acronym referred to the Russian foreign intelligence service. "Or GU?"—the Russian military intelligence service—"and they wanted to keep it quiet? Maybe it's unrelated to our interest."

"It's true they didn't look for the tap. At least they didn't find it," an NSA analyst said. "Thanks to Snowden they would have known it was there if they knew we'd been in the apartment."

"That suggests it's just coincidental," said an analyst who had been trained not to believe in coincidences.

Wardlaw leaned back in his chair and looked up at the ceiling for a few minutes, then back around the room. "I want you to be sensitive to any Russian government "involvement," but do not go open loop on this. I don't want this getting across the river and becoming a political issue. For that matter I don't want it getting upstairs right now, either," he said, referring to CIA upper management. "Just be open to data pointing in that direction."

31

C aptain Garcia called the next morning. "You can come and pick up your man," he told Eric.

"On our way," Eric replied.

"Do you have the reward money?" Garcia asked.

"No, we have to show the boss we have Khalid first."

"I think I will trust you. I think I know enough that you will not fuck me." Before Eric could reply, Captain Garcia hung up.

When they arrived at the Comandancia, Eric and Montez found the courtyard filled with Mexican television cameras and police from multiple jurisdictions—the Sonoran State Judicial Police, the Federal Police, even a few Mexican Marines—in a variety of uniforms and a few with their faces covered. Everyone apparently wanted some credit for the capture of the wanted terrorist. It was also apparent that the Mexican Government was happy not to waste time with extradition procedures; they just wanted Khalid out of their country. Eric and Montez pushed their way through the crowd, which was focused on the various law-enforcement sideshows: interviews, poses for pictures, etc.

Inside it was just as crowded. Eric's head was spinning. He and Montez had expected a low-key affair, and now he was worried about blowback, not just because of the "extra care" he had requested for Khalid before he was turned over, but because the Phoenix office or FBI headquarters might resent two lowly special agents parading in front of the cameras, perp-walking their alleged terrorist mastermind. They pushed their way to Captain Garcia's office, where they found Khalid, wearing a black nylon tracksuit, handcuffed to a metal chair. Captain Garcia was sitting behind his desk, giving an interview to an attractive, dark-haired news anchor from the largest television station in Hermosillo, the state capital.

He introduced the two FBI men to the newswoman, who asked them a question first in Spanish, then in perfect English, which both Eric and Montez refused to answer, although Montez did tell her, "*Sin commentaries,*" his standard "no comment" reply.

Captain Garcia was wise enough to know he needed to end the interview and the rest of the circus, so he politely ushered the news anchor out of his office then called one of his police officers to move Khalid into an empty conference room and handcuff him to something solid. When that was done, Captain Garcia closed the door to his office and sat back down. "So, my friends, what brings you to Nogales," he asked in an excessively jovial mood. As before, Montez did the translating.

"We were hoping to pick up a prisoner," Eric replied and then more quietly added, "And I was wondering if he said anything interesting."

Captain Garcia chuckled. "Ah, our little version of 'rendition.'"

Eric was not so cheerful. His face hot, he just stared at the captain, saying nothing.

"OK, our friend Khalid says he did shoot the lady border patrol agent, and here is his gun," Garcia finally admitted, motioning to a semi-automatic pistol inside an unmarked, clear plastic bag on his desk. The pistol's slide was back and the chamber empty, rendering it safe, and there was what appeared to be a full magazine accompanying it. "It has his fingerprints, I am sure."

Eric was stunned upon hearing the words spoken out loud but not surprised by what they meant.

"No chain of custody. It will be inadmissible," Montez half whispered, half spoke to Eric.

"Do you have chain of custody paperwork showing you or another law enforcement person removed this pistol from Khalid's person and that it has not been tampered with since?" Eric asked, switching his gaze from the captain to the pistol and back to the captain, whose levity was rapidly evaporating.

"I am sure we can produce the required paperwork," Garcia said.

"Can you testify under oath in a US court that the chain of custody was unbroken from the time the pistol was retrieved by law enforcement from this person to the time you turned it over to us?" Montez asked.

"Yes," Captain Garcia answered in English, clearly getting impatient.

"*Bueno*," Eric answered, which drew a small smile from Captain Garcia and seemed to release some of the tension in the room. "So what else did Khalid say?"

"He said he is part of, where did I write it, 'Global Warriors of Righteousness and Justice, Sons of Khalid Walid,'" Garcia put down the paper he had read from and looked up.

"What else did he say?" Eric asked, trying not to sound impatient. He could not tell if Captain Garcia and the interrogators were ineffective or just incurious.

"He said he is from Syria and he is a warrior for jihad."

"Did he say anything about his organization?" Eric asked, less successfully hiding his impatience this time.

Captain Garcia was himself now getting impatient. In Spanish he asked, "What did you want, you want us to waterboard him? Knock his teeth out? Pull out his fingernails? The people who held him would have happily done that, and more, but then you would not have a suspect and they would not have their money from the gringo government."

Eric suddenly thought he understood: the traffickers had not tortured Khalid; they had a witness who knew that Khalid had shot

Molly. "Will you be able to provide a witness that Khalid killed the border patrol agent?"

Captain Garcia looked at Eric as if he had just asked if the traffickers would confess their sins and become social workers. His jaw dropped, his mouth opening without a sound. He slammed it shut and quickly, shallowly, shook his head back and forth—the universal "no."

Montez caught Eric's eye and shot him a "that's enough" look. "Capitán Garcia," he said in Spanish. "Thank you for capturing this suspect. Is there some paperwork we need to complete?"

The captain stood up and said, "Yes, thank you for asking." He handed them the extradition warrant and other documents that would make it legal for them to take Khalid out of Mexico against his will. When the signing was complete, they stood and followed the captain out of the room, Eric carrying the pistol in the plastic bag.

When they entered the room where Khalid was handcuffed, Eric was able to study the man for the first time. Khalid looked squarely at him, jaw clenched, eyes attentive but not afraid. The first adjective that occurred to Eric when he looked at Khalid's face was "sharp." His nose was straight and well defined, ending in an almost sharp point like the tip of a pickaxe. His chin was thin but prominent, and his face was narrow so his gaze seemed to cut, both with his eyes and with his bone structure. His beard had grown a bit from the well-tended stubble they had seen on the video and photos, and his hair was unkempt, but there was no doubt this was the man in the picture.

Montez asked, "Do you speak English?"

Khalid said nothing, his expression not changing.

Montez read him his Miranda rights and then started to read a translation of the warning in a sort of phonetic Arabic. After the first two sentences, Khalid winced and said, "OK, I understand," in clear, slightly accented English.

They removed his handcuffs and returned them to Captain Garcia, who was quietly standing next to them, and re-cuffed him with Eric's cuffs. While they were pretty sure the Mexican authorities had searched Khalid, Eric was not willing to bet his life on another peace officer's unknown competence, so he thoroughly patted him down head to toe, even looking in his ears and taking off his sandals to look under his feet and between his toes. Eric was not sufficiently motivated to make a more extensive cavity search before he pronounced him "clean."

Eric took one of Khalid's arms and pulled him through the door and into the larger room. Once there, Montez took up his station on the other side, securely holding their prisoner, and they started walking through the army of police, reporters, ice cream sellers, and civilians outside, alert for any signs of trouble. They had not counted on publicity, and each was now thinking about the possibility of a "Jack Ruby" in the crowd killing their suspect and maybe themselves in the bargain. Maybe they should have "tacted up"—put on their Kevlar tactical vests with the big yellow "FBI" on the front and back, but they ended up making it to their car unmolested.

Sonoran State Judicial Police Ford F-150 pickups with police in the beds were positioned in front of and behind Eric's FBI-issued Malibu, and the convoy started for the border a few miles away. They made the border crossing without further drama and were waved through the Mexican checkpoint, where their police escort turned around. At the US checkpoint, they stopped and showed the CBP officer their paperwork and credentials. He took a quick scan through the car and waved them through as well, even as a crowd of CBP officers gathered to take a look at the man in the back seat.

The ride north on I-19 was uneventful, Montez calling the Tucson SSA to tell him they had Khalid al-Hassan in custody and were bringing him in. The plan was for Khalid to be processed in Tucson and then be immediately transferred to Phoenix. From there it was unclear where he would be sent, but both Eric and Montez knew this could be the last time they would have access to Khalid.

He had been legally Mirandized, so there was no harm in questioning him. He was seat-belted the middle of the back seat and was looking out the left window. Eric watched him in the rearview mirror, stealing glances forward to keep in his lane. "Why did you kill the border patrol agent?" No visible reaction. "Was it because she was a woman doing's men's work?"

That brought Khalid's head around. He gave a slight scowl then returned to looking out the window.

"Where are the men who helped you in Phoenix?" No reaction. "Why did you come to America and commit these crimes?" No reaction. Eric was not the least surprised by Khalid's stoicism. He would have been surprised if he had been at all forthcoming. An ideological terrorist was every bit as hard to interrogate as a hardened criminal. They had no incentive to provide information to their captives unless offered something in return: a lighter sentence, privileges inside the prison, even a better prison location. Eric had nothing to offer that compared with 72 virgins in paradise. But maybe he could get Khalid talking on a subject he *was* interested in. "Tell me about the Global Warriors of Jihad and Righteousness. Who was Khalid ibn al-Walid?"

Khalid turned to meet Eric's eyes in the mirror. "Do you not have Google? Did you not search this man?" he asked, his neutral expression changing to a slight smirk.

"I've been pretty busy. I left it up to the intelligence folks to figure it out. I'm just curious now, and we have some time ..."

Khalid knew Eric was playing with him, but after his two-week captivity in Mexico, he relished the opportunity to proselytize. "Abu Suleiman Khalid ibn al-Walid ibn al-Mughirah al-Makhzumi, the Sword of Swords, the Drawn Sword of God. He was a companion of the Prophet, peace be upon him, and he defeated the Romans and the Jews and the idolaters from Arabia to Mesopotamia. Al-Walid was the greatest general in history, much greater than your Washington or your Patton. In one battle he broke nine swords and was still victorious."

"Hmm, that's a lot of swords." Eric let his sarcasm get the better of him.

Khalid was undeterred. "Allah was with him. We are victorious with Allah."

"Is Allah with you?" Eric asked.

"Of course. We are doing his will."

"I didn't know Allah hated the internet and electricity," Eric said, earning a sideways, questioning glance from Montez.

That comment angered Khalid, who leaned forward and spat, "Allah hates all unbelievers and those who choose wealth over submission to him."

Montez turned to Khalid, ordered, "Settle down," and pushed him by the shoulder back against the seat. They didn't speak again until they reached the Tucson Resident Agency.

32

T hat afternoon the president was briefed in the Oval Office on the capture and extradition of Khalid al-Hassan. "Mr. President," the director of the FBI began, "this morning FBI agents arrested Khalid al-Hassan, who we think is the leader of the terrorists who committed the August twenty attacks. He was captured in Mexico as the result of field work by our agents, the efforts of the Government of Mexico and Mexican law enforcement. And as a result of the one million dollar reward you offered on the day of the attacks, of course."

"Money talks. And I guess I should thank Mexico," the president interjected to light chuckles.

The director was aware of the critical role played by the traffickers in Mexico as well, but he thought better about commenting on it. He continued, "Al-Hassan was read his Miranda rights as soon as he was taken into US custody and transported to the FBI Resident Agency in Tucson for initial questioning. From there he was transported to the FBI Field Office in Phoenix for further questioning. We expect to keep him there for a few days before he's transported to Camp Delta at Guantanamo Bay for more interrogation and for detention pending trial."

"Good, I'm glad I didn't close it," the president said.

"Yes, sir. Al-Hassan is also the primary suspect in the murder of a US Border Patrol agent in Nogales, Arizona, about four weeks before the attacks. The Mexican government provided as evidence a handgun that was taken from Al-Hassan that may be the murder weapon. We're currently performing ballistics tests to establish if it is, in fact, the murder weapon."

The president's chief of staff asked, "Do you think the murder was related?"

"We don't know, but we suspect it may have been," the FBI director admitted. He looked to the director of the CIA, sitting on the opposite couch, who remained expressionless. The director continued, "The CIA believes the shaped-charge explosives used to destroy some of the substations were smuggled in from Mexico, so the tunnel that ended at the house where the agent was killed may have been used for that purpose."

"And those explosives came from Iran," the president said emphatically. "When you people have all of this figured out, I want the people who did this to pay a very, very high price."

That was definitely not going to be the FBI director's responsibility, but since no one else said anything, he responded, "Yes, sir."

The president turned to the CIA director and asked, "Anything new in your area?"

She shifted on the couch to face the president. "We're still trying to decrypt the computer information we recovered from the hacker's apartment. We've made some progress, but he used a very high level of encryption and we've only been able to harvest a few passphrases to decrypt files." She paused for a moment and looked briefly at the FBI director. "That process was complicated by the hacker's murder a day after we compromised his apartment."

A few seconds of quiet were interrupted by the president, who asked, "Who killed him?"

"We don't know, sir."

"Did you have an OPSEC failure?" the chief of staff asked, using the acronym for 'operational security.'

"We don't believe so. We think the murder was coincidental with our compromise of the apartment but possibly still related to the Eight-twenty attacks. Someone wanted to cover their tracks."

"Who?" the president asked.

"That's what we're trying to figure out, sir," the CIA director answered.

BACK IN TUCSON ERIC and Montez were sitting in the SSA's office. "I want you to go to Mexico City to work with the *federales* on the smuggling angle," the SSA said.

Eric looked at Montez then said, "Sir, I would rather participate in questioning our suspect."

The SSA was unmoved. "We have a dozen agents in Phoenix who will be doing that. I want you guys to trace the route the EFPs took into the country." Eric started to say something, but the SSA raised his hand, palm out in a "stop" gesture, and continued, "This is not a punishment. You guys did good work bringing al-Hassan in, although I'm not sure your methods strictly followed FBI procedure." He paused, looking at Eric to let the comment sink in. "But you're getting kudos from Washington. And the EFPs are actually an important part of the investigation."

"I understand that, sir, but we'd like to complete the investigation of the Walsh murder, tie a bow on it," Eric said, looking to Montez for support. Montez was expressionless.

"I'm sure you would. Al-Hassan will be questioned on that murder as part of the terrorism investigation, which you will recall involved quite a few more fatalities. And when ballistics comes in on the weapon, we may have enough to charge him. Where are we on chain of custody?"

They were quiet for a moment then Montez said, "We've been promised paperwork. It wasn't ready when we picked up our prisoner."

The SSA looked at them long and hard. "Well, let's hope you can produce that paperwork or the prospect of Mexican law-enforcement testimony before we meet with the US attorney, and certainly before they convene a grand jury." He shook his head and looked down at the floor. It was nearly impossible to get Mexican cops to come to the US to testify at trial. "Come on, guys, didn't they teach you this at the Academy?"

Eric felt a familiar sensation—heat under his collar rising across his face to the top of his head. He said nothing. When the SSA dismissed them with an admonition to follow procedure this time when working with the Mexican Federal Police, he and Montez walked silently back to their desks.

THAT NIGHT ERIC and Caitlin sat on the terrace of Eric's apartment, sipping wine and looking across the desert to some lights beyond. As the dusk fell, the hulking mountains showed as shadows against the first splotch of stars. It was hot still, but with the sunset and a little breeze, it was tolerable. Eric enjoyed the heat, a relief from the too-cool, air-conditioned office where he spent his days. It did not feel too cool when he was inside, but outside he was reminded of the futile, phony attempt they made to divorce the inside world from the desert all around. "When are you heading back?" he asked Caitlin.

She took a shallow sip of her rosé and said softly, "Soon."

"I don't want you to go," Eric said, almost whispering to himself. He wondered if he sounded too trite.

Caitlin did not answer, but later, as she was moving against him in the dark, she felt drops on his chest that she knew were tears. She welcomed his embrace when he pulled her close.

33

The next day the Treasury/FBI team was reviewing the suspect Bitcoin transactions with a group of CIA analysts. Of the eight transactions that looked most likely, four appeared to originate from a Moscow IP address. One of the analysts cross-referenced the IP address with a database of addresses used by various internet malefactors and noticed something interesting. He sat back in his chair, double-checked his search results, and walked from his cubicle to the boss's office. "Looks like we might have an endpoint for some of the Bitcoin transactions," he announced.

His boss looked up from the file he was reading. "Fill me in, Trent."

"You know we're trying to back-trace Bitcoin transactions that might have terminated at IP addresses we suspect Vasily Dobrovsky, the dead hacker, was using, right? We found eight that looked like they ended up at what we think were his IPs, so we then used our penetration of the Bitcoin network to backtrack to the originator of the transaction. Four of the suspect transactions trace back to an IP address we haven't seen before but which is suspiciously close to a bank of IP addresses the GU used during the DNC hack." Trent paused for effect. DNC, of course, meant Democratic National Committee.

His boss sat back in his chair, rocked a few times, and asked, "How certain are you about the IP address?"

"The WHOIS is, of course, private," Trent replied, referring to the internet search that provides information on the ownership of web domains and IP addresses. "And the IPs would all belong to cutouts," he added, this time referring to fake owners who could not be traced to a government entity. "But we've compromised enough ISPs to have reasonable confidence these addresses were all registered to the same user."

"OK, Trent, let's say the GU paid him. What is there to prove they were paying him for anything related to Eight-twenty? The guy could just have been doing other things for Gizunov." They both knew Gizunov was the man believed to be head of the GU's cyber-intelligence unit. "After all, we know the connection between the FSB and Humpty-Dumpty." The former was the Russian internal intelligence organization, the latter a group of cyber-criminals allegedly connected to it.

"We haven't seen any sign of that," Trent said but then conceded, "It's always possible."

"RG involvement is a very serious development, if true. We can't just throw that out without corroboration. How do we do that?"

"Has the team decrypting the computers made any progress? Can we see his email?" Trent asked.

"Not yet." They both stared past each other for a moment, thinking. "Keep at it," Trent's boss ordered. "And keep this between us for now. I'll see if there's another way."

"Yes, sir," Trent said as he turned and walked back to his desk.

34

L iz Sanders strolled along the Moscow River on a sticky
September afternoon. Visitors to Moscow were often amazed
that a city with a reputation for brutal winters could be so
hot in the summer and early fall. Compared to St. Petersburg, its
cosmopolitan sister to the west, relatively few tourists from outside
the boundaries of the former Soviet Union came to Moscow to suffer
the weather, whether hot or cold. No cruise ships with overstuffed
semi-centenarians in shorts and long socks sailed up the Moscow
River, just the odd dinner excursion and the Russian version of the
booze cruise, the latter both more alcoholic and more expensive than
its western equivalent. Instead of tourists it was government officials
and business people who walked the streets around the onion domes
and brick walls of Red Square or the skyscrapers of the International
Business Center on Leninsky Prospekt.

Liz had lived in Moscow for the last three years, serving as the
major-account sales representative for a luxury-goods distributor
based in Miami. As part of her marketing budget, she organized
monthly parties at the Ritz-Carlton hotel on Tverskaya Street. These
were regularly attended by high Russian and Moscow government officials, foreign ambassadors, oligarchs, and other favored folks whose

black, 7-series BMWs were equipped with flashing blue police lights that let them fly past the traffic on the Moscow Ring Road.

Liz knew who the best gossips were. When the tales were flowing, she made sure the vodka, 18-year-old single malt, and Chateau Margaux flowed freely, because she had a second career—she was a NOC, a CIA agent operating under a non-official cover. The owner of her company, an OSS officer during World War II, had agreed to carry Liz as an employee using a front company in Pennsylvania and even to supplement her budget beyond what the Agency was providing. Thus, not bound to the US Embassy or any US Consulate, Liz had infinite deniability but also no diplomatic cover if the FSB or SVR found out about her activities. As a NOC she risked prison or worse if discovered, not deportation.

Today, Liz was meeting an acquaintance who worked in the Ministry of Foreign Affairs of the Russian Federation, specializing in relations with Ukraine and Belarus. His opinions regarding relations with those countries were interesting, but what was more interesting was his gossip about his alcoholic brother-in-law, who happened to work in the FSB.

Liz turned away from the river at 1905 Year Street and halfway down the block stepped into an excellent Georgian restaurant called Kazbeck. She let her eyes adjust to the dim interior. When she saw her acquaintance facing her at a table in the back corner, she smiled and started walking toward him, discretely glancing around her for any other familiar faces. She saw none, but when she reached the table, she apologized, saying, "I'm sorry, but would you mind if I went to wash my hands before I sit down?" As she walked away from the table and toward the restroom, she had a chance to see another part of the room, and as she returned, she had yet another view. She saw no one she recognized, and the few men in the room had the right level of interest in their eyes as she walked by, not trying to be too discrete as an FSB watcher might. So far so good.

Liz approached the table for the second time and embraced Anatoly, who squeezed her and gave her a slightly sloppy kiss on the cheek. She could smell alcohol on his breath already, even though there was nothing on the table other than a glass of water. "How are you, Anatoly?" she asked in just slightly accented Russian as she pulled away smiling and sat down.

"I am quite good, Liz. How are you? Anatoly asked, smiling broadly and waving down a waiter. "Wine or vodka?" he asked.

"Why do I have to choose?" Liz replied, grinning.

Anatoly laughed heartily and ordered a bottle of expensive Georgian wine and a bottle of Moskovskaya Osobaya vodka. He knew Liz would pay for it. The vodka arrived in less than a minute, accompanied by two glasses buried in ice. Anatoly quickly poured glasses for them and raised his glass in a toast. *"Za vashe zdorovie!"* he said, adding in English, "To your health."

Liz responded in kind and they both emptied their glasses in one gulp. Anatoly refilled them but in deference did not immediately drink his. But when the wine arrived and the waiter opened the bottle and poured two glasses, Anatoly took a drink and pronounced it, "Excellent."

"So, Anatoly, what's new in your life?" Liz asked, wondering how to get him drunk and talking before she was under the table. She had a very high tolerance for alcohol for someone of her body weight, but everyone has their limits, and Anatoly was probably twice her weight and no slouch as a drinker.

"Oh, nothing is new. Same idiots running around kissing Popov's ass," Anatoly quipped, referring to the powerful Russian president. "Same idiots in Ukraine trying to piss him off."

"Have things cooled down in Eastern Ukraine?" Liz asked, waving down the waiter and asking for two orders of *khachapuri*, cheese-filled Georgian bread served hot, and two of *shashlik*, Caucasian shish kebab.

"No, you do not hear very much, because they pushed all the journalists out, but there is still fighting. The idiots who run the separatist groups are fighting among themselves, and we can barely keep them from killing each other instead of Ukrainians."

Liz knew that when Anatoly said 'we' he meant the GU, but she decided to needle him a bit. "Is your brave brother-in-law standing in the middle of them?" she asked with a grin.

Anatoly was taking a drink of vodka and almost spat it out as she asked the question. "No, no, it is the idiots in the GRU," he said, using the older designation—Main Intelligence Directorate—for Russian military intelligence. "The idiot hates the idiots in the GRU. They create nothing but trouble for him." He refilled his glass and took another long drink.

Liz did not want to distract him from this line of conversation, but she also did not want to seem too interested. "How's the wine?" she asked.

"Excellent, as I said." Anatoly took a sizable drink from his wine glass and Liz refilled it. The khachapuri arrived and they both dove in, Liz to protect her sobriety, Anatoly because he was hungry.

After a few bites Liz resumed the conversation. "Delicious. I was very hungry." She licked her fingers in emphasis. "I'm sorry," she continued. "What were you saying?"

Anatoly finished chewing, took a sip of wine. "I don't remember," he said, looking at Liz intently.

Liz had a judgment call to make. If Anatoly was trained and practicing counter-intelligence tradecraft, he was testing to see if Liz was deliberately pumping him for information on a specific topic. But she looked into his dewy eyes and her intuition told her he really had forgotten what he was saying. "You were talking about your brother-in-law and the idiots in the GRU."

Anatoly smiled. "Ah, yes." He took another bite of khachapuri. "The idiots in the GU. They all want to suck up to Popov and make the FSB and SVR look bad. They take a lot of risks, but Popov loves them because they have balls." The shashlik arrived and Anatoly dove in.

Liz thought about how to dig a little more into what he was saying. "The FSB must have balls. Your brother-in-law must have balls."

Anatoly laughed through bites of roasted chicken. "The FSB used to have balls, but they fucked up in Ryazan and now Popov has their balls in a vice. My brother-in-law, his wife has his balls." He laughed some more and took a drink of vodka.

Liz knew the Ryazan reference was to FSB agents caught planting explosives in an apartment building so that the bombing could be blamed on Chechen separatists. She thought the time was right to dig some more. "So what trouble are they causing for your brother-in-law with no balls?" she asked with an impish smile, taking a long, visible drink of her vodka.

Without further thought Anatoly replied, "Those GRU idiots are helping Islamic idiots fuck up other idiots' countries."

Liz masked her reaction and asked, knowingly off base, "I thought the GU hated the Chechens?"

Anatoly took the opportunity to educate Liz. "Not every Islamist is a Chechen, my dear. You would know that if you did something besides sell expensive handbags and perfume to rich idiots." When Liz feigned offense and sat back in her chair. Anatoly apologized. "I am sorry, yes, the GU hates Chechens, everyone hates those Chechen idiots. Popov is killing those ISIS idiots, but the GU likes to keep one or two to make trouble for other idiots." Anatoly felt he had vindicated himself and took another bite of shashlik and a drink of vodka, followed by a drink of wine that emptied his glass.

Liz quickly refilled his wine glass. "How about some *chakhokhbili?*" she asked, referring to a "Georgian Eagle," a roasted, spatchcocked chicken she knew Anatoly loved.

Anatoly drank some wine and, laughing, protested, "No, no, I must go or my wife will have *my* balls." They drank a little more wine and vodka, gossiped about mutual friends, and then Anatoly stood, wobbled a bit, and pulled Liz's chair back from the table for her. He hugged her and gave her a sloppy kiss on the mouth. "It is too bad you only like girls, because I would love to put you in an apartment where we could drink vodka and, well ..." His words trailed off and he nodded to her and ambled across the restaurant and out the door.

Liz did not "like girls," but it was a convenient way to keep her unwitting sources, almost all males, from forcing the relationship in an awkward direction. She remained at the table after Anatoly left, sipping her wine, which was quite good, while waiting for the waiter so she could settle the bill. She removed a compact from her handbag and, pretending to refresh her makeup, used it to look behind her. The restaurant had filled up and there were a number of fresh faces, none that she recognized. The waiter brought the check, and she paid it in cash, adding a 20% tip, for which the waiter thanked her. She got up from the table and walked back to the restroom, knowing she would find it occupied, which gave her an excuse to study the remainder of the restaurant with a casual glance while she waited. Liz saw nothing that concerned her by the time the door to the restroom opened.

A FEW MINUTES LATER, Liz walked straight through the restaurant and onto 1905 Year Street. It had cooled enough that she decided to walk the four kilometers to her apartment. Liz reached into her handbag and retrieved a pair of flats. Holding onto a light pole, she swapped her heels for the flats and slipped the heels into her bag. Then she started toward the river, rejoined the path, and retraced her steps back to New Arbat Avenue as she worked her way east and north. The walk gave her time to think. She replayed the conversation with Anatoly, particularly the last part, and parsed his words carefully. "Islamist idiots to fuck up other idiots' countries." *Did that mean the GU controlled Islamic terrorists?* That would not be tremendously surprising since the Soviet Union had supported the PLO and splinter groups like the Abu Nidal organization and the Popular Front for the Liberation of Palestine. The rise of Islamic militarism inside the former Soviet Union made the subject much more complicated.

Anatoly had specifically said they were not Chechens, although ISIS had attracted Chechens to fight in Syria. *Had he been referring to Arab fighters?* It was not clear if having Chechens fighting in Syria was a plus or a minus for the Russian Government, since their forces and the US-led coalition were killing large numbers of ISIS fighters, including, presumably, Chechens. If they were going to Syria, they were already radicalized, so that was not much of an issue. Perhaps the biggest problem would be the tactics they would learn or the connections they would make. Liz rolled these ideas around in her mind as she thought about how to frame what she had heard in a report to the Agency.

Liz was tired when she opened the door to her apartment building, so she took the elevator up four stories to her apartment. She turned right from the elevator and opened the door with her key, noting that the blonde hair she had left as a tell was still stuck between the lower part of the door and the jamb. She kicked off her flats, sat on the couch, peeled off her hosiery and rubbed her feet. In the kitchen she pulled a bottle of Borjomi mineral water from the refrigerator, opened it, and took a long, deep drink as she walked to her desk. It faced the window, the gauzy curtains letting in the waning twilight but granting her some privacy, particularly with the lights off in the apartment.

Liz booted her laptop, and as the machine's screen flashed its greeting, she looked past it to the building across the street where lights shone in a patchwork of windows. As a little girl she would look at a hotel or an apartment building and spend hours creating stories about the people framed in each window. Even now, when she was lonely, which was often, she would spin a narrative about the man in this apartment or the woman in that one.

Liz snapped out of her daydream and opened her Facebook page. She wrote a quick entry about an interesting ceramics stall she had found at the Izmailovo Market. The way she phrased the post was in fact a covert meeting request, asking to meet her contact on the following Saturday a dozen stalls to the west of the one she mentioned. Once the message was posted, she checked her email. The inbox contained the usual innocuous messages consisting of business correspondence, advertising, notes from friends and acquaintances, and spam. She made sure she received a lot of spam messages so that anyone monitoring her email would become very bored.

Then a long, hot bath and a rub with a thick towel and she was feeling better. Wrapped in a white robe, she walked through the darkened living room back to her laptop. She saw that her Facebook post had received a response from one of her friends, ostensibly in Minnesota. "Looks so cool. Would love to see it in person sometime." Liz smiled. The meet was on.

35

Eric and Montez peeled themselves out of their airline seats at the end of their three-and-a-half-hour flight from Phoenix to Mexico City and joined the crowd walking to passport control. After a surprisingly brief stint in the arrivals hall, they continued through the baggage area, retrieved their bags, and continued through customs screening. "Do we have to declare our weapons?" Eric asked, half in jest.

"We're not going to pay duty on them, so I think we're OK," Montez replied. While firearms in Mexico were strictly regulated—but not that rare—as US federal agents on official business, they had received permission to carry their service weapons. With that permission came an admonition of discretion: only display them if absolutely necessary; that is, don't pull them unless you really need to shoot someone.

As they waded through the crowd leaving the arrivals area, Montez spotted a tall, trim man in a dark suit holding a sign saying "Montez / West." They walked toward the man, who had already spotted them in the crowd, and introduced themselves.

"Raul Montez."

"Eric West."

"Inspector Rafael Ruiz-Arraiza, Mexican Federal Police, Intelligence Division. You can call me Ralph." Hands were shaken and Inspector Ruiz pointed them toward an exit and a black Tahoe that was parked at the curb beyond. As they climbed in, he introduced them to his driver, a young corporal named Sanchez, who pulled the SUV away from the terminal. As they started their journey to police headquarters through Mexico City's legendary traffic ,they made small talk. Inspector Ruiz' English was excellent, and he only reverted to Spanish for an occasional word, which was a relief for Eric, whose Spanish was spotty.

When they arrived in the Intelligence Division offices, Inspector Ruiz led them into his small office, closed the door, and turned to them. "You will notice that I did not speak about our case in front of Corporal Sanchez. That is not because I do not trust him. It is because you must assume that you cannot trust *anyone*. Even if you think you can, you must be very cautious."

"I am assuming we can trust you," Eric replied with a slight smile.

Ruiz had been expecting a comment like that and he smiled. "Do you have a choice?"

Eric grinned. "I can see we'll get along just fine."

AROUND THE SAME TIME, which was late afternoon in Fort Meade, Maryland, Lisa was in her NSA office, working on one of Vasily's encrypted hard drives. Since discovering the fragments containing malicious Siemens SCADA code on the air-gapped computer, she had turned her attention to one of the other two machines, the one that investigators suspected had been used for email. A secure encryption required a long, not-easily-guessed passphrase. Since they had not been able to harvest a working passcode, Lisa was trying various phrases and number sequences that analysts had guessed based on what was known of Vasily's life, lifestyle, etc. She had tried hundreds of passwords, using combinations of his name, his parents' names, his brother's names, their birth dates, addresses, etc. No luck. She and her CIA colleagues had methodically studied the pictures the black-bag man had taken of the items in the rooms, the books on the shelves, and the magazines in the bathroom to try to understand his interests and thereby his mnemonic processes. The agents had even taken a picture of the contents of his refrigerator to figure out his favorite food, which seemed to be *pelmeni*, Russian dumplings. Lisa tried countless variations using items in the photos—with various iterations of a word by itself and in combination with others—but again had no luck, either in Russian or in English.

Frustrated, she leaned back in her chair and looked out the window. It always amazed her that one of the most secure intelligence facilities in the world had windows you could actually see in and out of. But humans had an innate need to see the outside world at least once in a day, and these were long days. She was surprised to notice it was now dark outside. She grabbed a bag of sourdough pretzels and extracted one, then another, and popped them into her mouth, rolling them with her tongue so she could bite each the way she liked, right across the middle so she had two equal pieces to chew. She put the bag down, rolled the top so the contents would not get stale, grabbed her purse and badge, and started for the door.

When she was outside, she noticed the air had cooled, and she looked up at a clear sky with just an occasional cloud glowing amber in the parking lot lights. She walked across the lot to her car, unlocking it as she walked, climbed in, and started it. She reached into the glove compartment and turned on her phone—forbidden inside her building—and placed it next to her on the console.

As she drove toward the gate and the guard standing there, her phone chirped a melody that meant she had a text message, and she stopped abruptly in the middle of the road. She picked up the phone, read the message, and called one of her friends who worked at CIA.

"Hey, Lisa," he answered. "What's up?"

"What was the ring tone on his phone?"

"Whose phone? Oh, *his* phone. I'm not sure, but it sounded like NWA's 'Fight the Power,'" her friend replied. "Why?"

"I'll let you know." She hung up, waved to the guard, and drove back to her parking space. Before she locked up her phone, she opened the YouTube app and searched for "NWA Fight the Power." A second or two later, there was the video. Lisa was not much of a rap fan—Taylor Swift was more her style—so she watched the video to refresh her memory, bobbing her head to the beat. After she had watched it a second time, she threw the phone into the glove box and hurried back to the building.

BACK IN HER office Lisa started typing before she even sat down. "Fight the Power."

No success. "FIGHT THE POWER." No. "fightthepower." No. "FightthePower." No. 'She tried more iterations, without success. She had started to lose hope when she reminded herself just how long the passphrase had to be. A 256-bit encryption would require at least 128 bits of entropy, or about 20 characters. "Fight the Powers that Be." No. She counted the characters and thought about the lyrics she had just listened to. Lisa slowly typed "You've Got to Fight the Powers that Be." The disk started processing the decryption. "Yes!" she shouted and pounded her desk.

36

After a day of introductions and an excellent dinner of Mexican street food, Montez, Eric, and Inspector Ruiz were sitting at an outdoor table, drinking cold Victoria beer and discussing trafficking routes. "The Venezuelan military formed the 'Cartel of the Suns' ten or twelve years ago to move cocaine from Columbia through Venezuela to Mexico and the Caribbean," Inspector Ruiz told them. "The Cartel of the Suns supplies the Mexican Gulf Cartel by ship and by air and the Sinaloa Cartel by air. We try the best we can to stop the boats and airplanes, but there is too much country to patrol and too much money that they have and we don't. Not the good guys, at least." He paused and took a long pull from his bottle.

"I assume it was the Sinaloa Cartel that was helping our guy?" Eric asked.

"Sinaloa or Zetas. The Sinaloa controls Nogales, so it's probably them."

"Have you seen weapons come in from Venezuela?" Montez asked.

"Not in any great quantity, which is surprising. We know the Hezbollah is very active in Venezuela. The Hezbollah has been involved in smuggling tons of cocaine out of Venezuela, and they have certainly supplied weapons to the Venezuelan government, as well as to the Ecuadorean government and Columbian rebels. We don't see as much because, frankly, it is so easy for the cartels to smuggle weapons from the north. Maybe we see more weapons from the Hezbollah in the south, closer to Guatemala. AK forty-seven and AK seventy-four, some SKS, both Russian and Chinese, you know, from Norinco. We are pretty sure those come in from Venezuela and are obtained from Iran."

"What about explosives?" Eric asked.

"Again, explosives are so easy to smuggle from the north that we don't see much come in from Venezuela. Maybe a little plastique from the Czech Republic, you know, Semtex, but it seems the cartel guys prefer shooting people or hacking them to death to blowing them up."

"We Mexicans like to look you in the eye before we kill you," Montez said to laughter all around.

"So where do we go with this? How are we going to run down the route for the EFPs?"

Ruiz twirled his now empty beer bottle between his fingers. "The cartels are very good with operational security, so it is hard to get wire taps or any useful electronic surveillance, at least with the technology we can afford. I would suggest two things: we give your NSA some targets, and maybe they have something we can use. And we shake the tree a little bit."

"Whose tree are we shaking?" Eric asked.

"Most people are afraid to talk about what they know, but it is always a question of what they fear more."

THE NEXT MORNING the trio met at the federal police headquarters before walking a few blocks to a tall, glass-and-steel building with the name of a major Mexican bank over the door. The few-block walk actually took 20 minutes because they first walked through a busy department store in an attempt to lose anyone who might be following them. Feeling reasonably confident they were alone, they entered the bank and took the elevator up four floors to the office of a bank vice president. "Miguel, nice to see you," Inspector Ruiz called as they walked into a small office.

"*Buenos dias, señor*," answered the tall, 40-ish man behind the desk who rose to close the door behind his visitors. His office was decorated with all the accoutrements of middle management: framed photos of wife and family; framed certificates on the walls attesting to his competence and accomplishments. He offered his guests chairs, one of which he must have borrowed from an adjacent office since it did not match the other two, and sat back down uncomfortably behind his desk.

Inspector Ruiz continued in English, "Gentlemen, this is Señor Miguel Guzman-Salazar. Señor Guzman is a very respected executive at this bank, where he has brought in some very important clients. Unfortunately for Señor Guzman, many of those clients have shady connections, and also unfortunately for Señor Guzman, I happen to know that some of his clients' investment losses were actually gains for Señor Guzman, so we are now best friends, right, Miguel?"

"Anything I can do to help, Inspector," Miguel replied unenthusiastically.

"Miguel, as you might have guessed, these men are from El Norte. They are not here to take you back to face American justice, so do not worry." Inspector Ruiz was having fun with him. "Today, we have some questions that maybe you can help us answer."

Miguel did not answer, just nodded slightly and looked at the two FBI men.

"Your clients do a lot of business with the Venezuelans?" Inspector Ruiz began.

Miguel nodded, not sure if it was a statement or a question.

"We are looking for information about a certain transaction with the Venezuelans in, about, June or July. A small shipment that was not the usual product."

Miguel shifted slightly in his chair and answered, "I just see the money, I don't see the product."

"Yes, but you see the amounts and where they come from. We think maybe this one would look different from the others. Maybe a different source or a strange amount. Perhaps you can remember, or you can look for it?" Inspector Ruiz was smiling solicitously, but there was no mistaking the force behind his words.

Miguel sat still for a moment, then turned from them and took a key from his pocket. He unlocked the dark wooden credenza behind his desk and withdrew a small box from which he took a USB drive. He returned the box to the credenza and turned back to face them, shutting down his computer as he did so. He waited for the shutdown sequence to complete, then he inserted the drive into one of the USB ports and rebooted the computer. Inspector Ruiz got up from his chair and went around to the back of the desk to see the screen, and Montez and Eric joined him.

On the display they watched Miguel enter a long string of characters, all showing as asterisks as he typed, and when he finished, a spreadsheet opened on the screen. Miguel opened one of the dozens of workbook tabs displaying at the top and scrolled to a point toward the bottom, where he studied a series of rows. Eric and Montez looked at each other. If there were ever a graphic illustration of the amount of money passing through the cartels other than piles of wrapped bills, this was it. Every cell in the spreadsheet seemed to have six figures in it, adding up to tens of millions at the bottom of each column. And these were dollars, not pesos. "In July there was a transaction of five million dollars from Petroleos de Maracaibo," Miguel told them. "I have not seen that entry before."

"What was the product? Oil?" Eric asked, sarcastically.

"I do not know specifically. The products are coded A, B, C, D. I do not know what those letters correspond to and do not want to know. This is coded as an E. I have only seen that once before," Miguel answered then quickly shut his mouth as if realizing he had already said too much.

"When?" Inspector Ruiz asked pointedly.

Miguel thought for a moment, closed the workbook and opened another. Again he scrolled down until he found what he was looking for. "In August of last year."

Inspector Ruiz turned to Eric and Montez, put his arms around their shoulders, and led them away from Miguel to the corner of the room by the door. He whispered, "In October of two thousand seventeen, Federal Police discovered a drone with an IED attached to it during a traffic stop in Guanajuato. Sinaloa Cartel territory. Maybe your man was working for them?"

Eric and Montez looked at each other, confused. How did that fit? "That's a new development. We just don't know," Montez said.

THE THREE WALKED SLOWLY, conversing quietly on their way back to the federal police headquarters building. "Did your people arrest any of the technical people who were involved with the drones?" Eric asked.

The inspector looked sideways at him and said, "Do you have any idea how well protected, how insulated people like that are? We never see them and top insiders never, uh, flip, so no, we have no way of knowing who they are nor we get a chance to arrest them. We do know that, because of the money they can pay, the cartels can get very good technical talent."

"So they could still be out there. Have you seen any more drone activity?"

"Yes, along the border, where it is the latest technique to transport high-value cargo like fentanyl across the border. Not too heavy but very valuable."

"Good thing cash is heavy. Can't drone it back," Montez volunteered.

"So are guns," Eric said. "They have to smuggle them the old-fashioned way." He had another, more serious thought. "Could you find out what the model number and manufacturer was of the drone you captured? Might be interesting to know if it was the same as the ones in San Fran."

Inspector Ruiz nodded, and the three finished their walk in silence.

37

L iz left her apartment and started the 20-minute walk to the Ploschad' Revolyutsii metro stop. The day was bright and cool, perfect for walking, and the bonus was that Ploschad' Revolyutsii was one of her favorite metro stations. Built by Stalin and restored under Popov, the station featured larger-than-life-sized, crouching bronze figures of idealized socialist men and women: farmers, workers, aviators, scientists, and soldiers. As many times as she had traveled through the station, she still passed the time between trains pacing its length and breadth, trying to view as many of the 76 figures as time allowed. The long walk and the layout of the station also gave her time to assess if she was being followed and, if so, to attempt to lose the tail. As she walked this Saturday morning, pausing to look in shop windows and ducking into a cafe for coffee, she felt comfortable that she was "clean."

Forty minutes or so later, Liz was emerging from the Partizanskaya station, named for the statues of brave partisans that decorated the station's marble columns. Ironically, the station had originally been named for its location near the famous Izmailovo Flea Market, but on the 60th anniversary of victory in the "Great Patriotic War"—what most in the West knew as World War II—the station had been renamed for its denizens.

Another ten minutes of walking and she arrived at the great, eclectic market. She walked through one of the elaborate entrances and passed stalls of all sizes selling baskets, clothes, toys, Russian Orthodox icons, and Soviet militaria. Every time Liz came to Izmailovo, she stopped at a famous stall overflowing with nesting Matryoshka dolls. She loved to see the latest representation of Popov and other politicians and famous Russians displayed alongside the traditional dolls painted as girls in peasant dress. Liz considered the depiction of politicians on the Matryoshka as one more data-point in assessing their relative power and popularity.

Slowly making her way down a long aisle, memorizing faces and doubling back to see who followed, she was again comfortable that she was alone. Even though she still had probably 20 stalls to go to reach her meeting point, out of the corner of her eye she saw her contact performing the same dance of spy tradecraft, walking then doubling back. Without being obvious she watched him for any potential watchers and was again satisfied. She made her way to the stall and started looking at the wares—dish towels and tea cozies in a variety of patterns. Fingering a white towel with red and green embroidery, she covertly slipped a paper inside, patted it, and walked away to look at the ceramics stall she had described on Facebook. She bought a small, hand-painted dish and started walking toward one of the exits.

Her contact arrived at the designated stall a few minutes later, picking up towels and buying the one she had handled but not before carefully extracting and palming the paper Liz had concealed. He took his parcel with him and continued his sojourn, continuing to study the crowd for familiar faces. After a few minutes of seemingly aimless wandering, he turned into a restroom and entered a stall. He took a quick look around for anything out of the ordinary, but seeing only typical public restroom grime, he placed his parcel on the toilet tank, removed the paper from his pocket, and photographed it with his phone. Then he tore the paper into small pieces and tossed them into the bowl, urinating over them for good measure. Finally, he retrieved his parcel, flushed the toilet on his way out of the stall, washed his hands, and started for an exit.

Once he was outside the market and alone on the sidewalk, he pulled his phone from his pocket and entered a code to unlock it. The normal code he entered would have revealed a standard iPhone, with the picture he just took revealing what looked like a typed grocery list. The code he entered instead enabled a few non-standard functions, with the grocery-list photo becoming a summary report of Liz's meeting with Anatoly. He read the report as he walked, looking up frequently to make sure he didn't walk off the sidewalk or into a tree or that another pedestrian wasn't approaching him from ahead or behind. With his peripheral vision he watched for approaching cars.

After he had read the report twice, he rebooted his phone and walked in the direction of a restaurant where Liz was waiting for him. She sat at a table toward the rear, her back to the wall but rose to greet him with a hug. He softly kissed both her cheeks in continental style. "How are you, Liz?" he asked.

"Wonderful, John. Always love a stroll through the market," she replied and took a drink of her tea. John waved down the waiter and ordered the same—hot tea served in a glass cup with a silver handle. They continued with small talk, discussing new items they had seen at the market as they looked around to see if anyone showed interest in their English conversation. After a few minutes the conversation shifted as they lowered their voices and leaned in to each other, hunching over their tea until their faces were no more than two feet apart.

"This is going to generate a lot of heat back home. Do you have another friend to confirm or deny?" John asked.

Liz had known the question was coming but she did not answer right away. She leaned back a little and took a drink of tea before leaning forward again, "I might. Not sure how to ask it, though."

John smiled. "You'll figure out a way. You always do."

38

T he Monday ITWG meeting was preceded by a smaller meeting on a much higher floor. At the moment, the CIA director and her deputies were reviewing the implications of the report out of Moscow. "If this story continues down this path, the secretary and I will need to give the president some options or else he'll come up with some on his own ... and we may not like them," she told them. "So keep this very close and think about proportionate responses if we're tasked."

"Is there a scenario where we can fix the blame on Syria but privately tell the Russians we know what they did?" a deputy asked.

"I don't think so, I think once we make the judgment about RG involvement, we have to tell the president," the director replied and adjourned the meeting.

AT THE SAME TIME, 1,200 miles to the south, Khalid al-Hassan was clothed in an iconic orange jumpsuit, sitting in a steel chair and mana-cled to a steel table. Two men in khakis and polo shirts were asking him the same questions they had asked for a week:

"Who funded your operation?"

"Where are the rest of your men?"

"How did you acquire the drone technology?"

"How did you acquire the explosives technology?"

The latter two questions were almost rhetorical, as other investiga-tors, including the FBI, had high confidence that they understood the purchase of the fuel and oxidizer for the ANFO used in the container bombs and the smuggling route for the EFPs. But there were thou-sands of minuscule details that could illuminate other potential plots or risks or criminal activity, and the interrogators desperately wanted to get Khalid talking. But Khalid evidently had no motivation to talk, and the interrogators had not been able to find a lever to create that motivation. They knew nothing of his family other than his deceased father and his mother and brother, whereabouts unknown. He had not been on intelligence or law-enforcement radar since his release by the Israelis in 2004. What had he been doing?

Khalid looked at his interrogators with disinterest, leaning as far back in his chair as his manacled hands allowed. His hair was trimmed close to his scalp, his beard close as well, and a jagged scar was now visible on the back of his scalp.

"Where did you get that scar?" one of the interrogators asked, touching the back of his head for emphasis.

Khalid decided to play with him, "I fell off my bike."

"Your English is pretty good. Where did you learn it?" the other interrogator asked, noticing the western colloquialism. When Khalid did not answer, the man persisted, "Did you learn it from the Israelis, or did you already speak English before you were arrested?"

"The Zionists did not teach me anything but to hate them." Khalid nearly spat his reply.

"Why hate them? You were trying to blow up their settlements. At least they didn't kill you like you would have killed them," the first interrogator replied.

"Their *settlements* are on Muslim lands," Khalid snarled. "They must leave them or die. And I would not recommend spending time in a Zionist prison if you are a Muslim."

"Not too friendly, were they?" one of the men said and chuckled. *Could we use this to build rapport?* he wondered. *Create some traction with Khalid.*

The interrogators glanced at each other and the other man said, "One of my friends was over there in deep cover. The Israelis picked him up and knocked him around pretty good before they released him." It wasn't a true story, but it did earn a confused look from Khalid. The interrogator explained, "Deep cover means he was a spy, and the Israelis didn't know he was one of ours."

For the first time Khalid smiled. "So the Zionists can be your enemies too."

"Everyone is someone's enemy sometimes. And everyone is someone's friend sometimes too."

Khalid stopped smiling. "You cannot be my friend if you are an enemy of Allah."

"Would you prefer if we asked a Muslim colleague to ask you some questions?"

"Why, are you Jews?" Khalid snapped.

The shorter of the two said, "No, I'm a Catholic, and my friend here, well, I'm not sure what he believes, but I am sure we're both people of the Book."

"It would not matter if you were both Muslims. You both serve the oppressors of Muslims."

"Come on, now, there must have been some things you liked about living in the US," the taller one said and offered him a plastic bottle of cold water. "Water?"

Khalid motioned with his hands that the manacles would limit his ability to drink. The interrogator reached into his pocket, withdrew a single key, and unlocked one of Khalid's hands, placing the bottle in the now-freed palm. Khalid took a long drink and placed the bottle on the table, using his free hand to scratch the back of his head. "If you have lived in places where there is no clean water, you appreciate this," he said, pointing at the water bottle with his hand and a tip of his head.

"Not much clean water in Syria or Lebanon?" the taller man asked

Khalid shook his head. "No."

"What about Gaza?"

"Better but still not so good."

"Clean water in Jordan?"

"I never lived there."

"Chechnya?"

"Not so much in the cities, but the countryside is good." And then Khalid realized what he had said. He slumped a little in his chair and then looked off distractedly, away from the two men.

The interrogators pretended they were not paying much attention to what he had said, but they knew exactly what they had done: get him a little comfortable and let the conversation flow. They were even a little surprised it had been so easy, albeit after a week of monotony.

In order to diminish the importance of his admission, the shorter man asked, "Where was the best food? Besides here, of course." All three chuckled, which was a good sign. Khalid and the other Muslim prisoners were served Halal food, but no one would mistake it for gourmet fare.

Khalid brightened slightly. "My mother's, in Homs."

"Of course, a mother's cooking is always the best," the shorter man said and began to reminisce. "My grandmother was from Naples and was the best cook in the family. Sunday dinners started with antipasto, you know, cheese and salami, then we had soup, maybe escarole soup—what they call Italian wedding soup—with tiny meatballs. Then pasta, you know, macaroni with red sauce, or as she called it, gravy, since there were meatballs or sausage and maybe a bracciole —rolled flank steak—that had been cooked in the sauce but were always served on a separate plate." He paused and involuntarily licked his lips. "Then roast beef or lamb with oven-roasted potatoes. She would spoon on lard to make the potatoes crispy on the outside. Then salad, then a little break before desert—Italian pastries with coffee— and finish it off with nuts and dates and figs. You had the same dates and figs in Syria, I bet."

All three men were hungry from the discussion of food, and Khalid agreed, "Yes, dates and figs were very good."

"What would your mother cook?" the short man asked.

Khalid smiled as he thought. "Lamb with rice. I always liked eggplant. My mother would buy from a man down the street very fine baklava. I was too young for coffee, but I would always eat as much baklava as I could."

The men made a mental note to have some baklava air-freighted in from Detroit. "Could you get good baklava in Gaza?" the taller one asked.

"It was good. Not as good as Homs."

"Lebanon?"

"It was good."

"I don't think they have baklava in Chechnya," the short man said.

"They do, but it is not as good. Not enough honey," Khalid said.

"Was your mother with you in Chechnya?" They knew she wasn't, but the question would keep the thread moving.

"No, it was my brother." And now Khalid really knew he had said too much. Neither of the other men said anything for a moment, both taking a drink from their water bottles. Khalid looked at them and did the same.

"How long were you in Chechnya?" the taller man asked, staring straight at Khalid as if to say, "playtime is over."

The shorter man defended Khalid, "We don't need to ask him that now. We were having a nice chat, weren't we?" He looked at Khalid, who had straightened in his chair, wary now, no longer casual. But the isolation and hopelessness of Guantanamo worked on all of the prisoners, and sooner or later they would start to talk to their inquisitors if only for the companionship. "How *is* your brother?" the shorter man asked.

Khalid slumped a little in his chair. "He is well, as far as I know."

The shorter man fought the urge to smile and shot a quick look at the taller man. "His name is Hamid, right? That means 'praiseworthy', right?" he asked.

"Yes," Khalid responded disconsolately.

"When was the last time you spoke with him?"

Khalid held back for a moment, but the desire to speak, to

converse, was overwhelming and at this point it really did not matter. He had done his duty, and he was proud of what he and his brother had accomplished. He suddenly felt liberated. He straightened in his chair and the words streamed freely. "I have not spoken to him in many years. We communicate via email."

"When did you last communicate with him?"

"Just before we inflicted the damage on the infidels."

"What did you talk about?"

"I told him that the preparations were complete."

"And he responded?"

"He said to proceed."

"Have you spoken to him since the attacks?"

"No"

"Are you sure?"

"Yes, we have not spoken. I destroyed my computer, and I have not communicated with my brother since."

The two interrogators glanced at each other and walked to a corner of the room to talk. They wanted to keep Khalid talking, but they also needed to consider what they wanted to ask him and in what order.

Khalid turned to watch them, then turned back to face the table where one arm was still immobilized. He took his free hand and massaged his wrist where the manacle gripped it, seeing a slight red mark where he had involuntarily pulled against the steel as the men questioned him.

The two men ended their caucus and turned back to Khalid. The taller spoke first this time. "Is Hamid still in Chechnya?"

"As far as I know."

"How long has he been in Chechnya?"

"For about two years."

"Where was he before he went to Chechnya?"

"Syria."

"Where in Syria?"

Khalid paused for a moment. He did not think his words could hurt Hamid. There was no way the Americans could get to Hamid in Chechnya. He spoke one word: "Palmyra."

39

E ric and Caitlin drove to the airport, the first 15 minutes in silence, the air filled with tension and sadness. The weather had cooled, and Eric asked over the open-windowed flutter, "What time do you arrive?"

Caitlin looked straight ahead. "About seven." She turned to look at him and added, "You can come with me."

Eric held her gaze as long as he could without hitting the car in front of him and smiled. "I would like to. But there's work to be done. You could stay here," he said, half teasing her because he had asked her before, many times.

Caitlin smiled back. "What does an anthropologist specializing in Alaskan native peoples do in the desert?"

"I have a few ideas," he said and grinned.

If she were younger she would have playfully punched his arm, but she was more serious now, both from age and the experience of the last months, so she just looked at him.

"Seriously," Eric began again. "You could study the Tohono O'Od-ham, or the Yaqui, or the Yavapai."

She looked at him quizzically, her green eyes sparkling now. "I'm not sure they want to be studied," she replied, emphasizing the word "studied."

"You know what I mean."

"There's no museum here like I have in Anchorage. My job is in Anchorage. My life is in Anchorage." She regretted how that sounded as soon as she said it and, sure enough, Eric's lips tightened as he continued to look at her. "Come up to Anchorage," she said softly.

Eric's expression softened somewhat, and he said, "I will, some day." As he said it, he realized how mawkish it sounded, like they were playing roles in a bad melodrama. Where was the boundary, where was *their* boundary, between infatuation and love? Even after months, he was not sure. Did it take a lifetime? No, but it took more time than they had enjoyed together, and that was why right now she was going back to Anchorage, and he was staying in Tucson.

As if they both realized there was nothing more to be said, they completed the journey in silence.

ERIC PULLED to the front of the terminal and parked. He walked around to open her door, but she was already on the curb, so he continued back to open the trunk, lightly squeezing her upper arm as he walked past her. He opened the trunk and extracted four large suitcases and two smaller ones, which attracted the attention of a sky cap with a cart. Eric and the sky cap loaded the cart and Eric tipped him. Caitlin handed over her ticket and the sky cap, pushing the loaded cart, headed toward his stand, which left Eric and Caitlin alone to say goodbye.

At first they just looked at each other, an arms-length apart. Then Caitlin moved toward him and they hugged tightly. He kissed her once on the cheek, once on the lips, and once more on her cheek before she gently broke the hug. "I love you," she said.

Eric smiled widely. "I love you too."

Caitlin leaned in to him again and moved her head to whisper in his ear, Eric grasping her arms as she drew closer, "Thank you, thank you, for finding Molly's killer." She stepped away and started walking toward the terminal, turning to look at him one more time as she walked through the automatic doors.

"You're welcome," Eric replied after she was gone, almost in a whisper.

40

The ITWG met to digest the latest intelligence from Khalid's interrogation, as well as the information Lisa and her NSA colleagues had been able to extract from Vasily's computer. Much to Lisa's chagrin, the encryption key only worked on one computer, the one that contained Vasily's work-related and non-work-related emails, as well as some apparently benign applications; they were still unable to crack his main work computer.

Wardlaw began the meeting. "Sam, bring us up to speed on what we've learned at Guantanamo."

Sam leaned forward slightly and began, "Khalid al-Hassan, who was picked up in Mexico and extradited to the US, is currently detained at Camp Five, where he has been undergoing interrogation. In order to maintain his status for criminal prosecution, he has not, I emphasize not, been subjected to enhanced interrogation techniques. Fortunately, he has apparently started to cooperate." He turned toward a screen where bullet points were visible to most of the room. "First, he claims he planned the attacks with his brother, Hamid, who currently resides in Chechnya."

An analyst on one side of the room interrupted. "Are you saying this was planned in Chechnya or that the brother is currently in Chechnya?"

Sam consulted his notes. "It appears initial discussions began in Syria, Palmyra to be precise, and continued in Chechnya."

Lisa chimed in, "Just a reminder, when my NSA team and I went through everything on the computer we were able to decrypt, we found a series of emails from an individual referenced as Kha. That's the Cyrillic character at the beginning of the Russian spelling of Hamid."

There were grunts of recognition around the room. "Weak confirmation, but confirmatory nevertheless," Wardlaw volunteered and looked at Sam.

Sam continued, "Khalid al-Hassan left Syria about two years ago, entered Mexico legally on a Venezuelan passport, and has traveled illegally between Mexico and the US for much of that time."

"How was he funded?' someone in the back asked.

"He carried cash into the country from Mexico. Incremental funds were transferred to him via Western Union." Several people in the room made notes to themselves to try to trace those transfers. "Most of the money was US dollars. It was smuggled into Mexico from, we believe, Venezuela."

"How did the money get to Venezuela? Or are they involved?"

"We don't think Venezuela is officially involved as a matter of policy, too dangerous, although as with other smuggling activities, it's likely high government officials were involved. We think the money originated in Iran as part of their smuggling of munitions and other items into the Western Hemisphere through Venezuela."

"Please proceed with what we're learning at Gitmo," Wardlaw ordered to get the discussion off this tangent.

"Ok, where were we ... yes ... the attack was planned in Chechnya."

"You told us that," Wardlaw admonished impatiently.

"Sorry." He looked through his notes. "Al-Hassan was assisted by men provided to him in Mexico. We believe they were also smuggled in through Venezuela."

"Iranians?" someone asked.

"How would that work with a Sunni terrorist?" someone else questioned.

"No, we don't think they were Iranians. Itinerant Sunnis, either Palestinian or Iraqi, Al-Hassan told us, guessing by their accents," Sam replied.

"He didn't know?"

"He apparently never asked. He was impressed with their skills and they kept to themselves. And he kept to himself," Sam answered.

"I find that hard to believe," a senior expert in the area opined.

Sam continued, "He did intimate that they seemed somewhat mercenary. That is, they seemed conflicted, committed to the cause, but they also wanted to get paid."

"Do we know what the entire budget was?" someone asked.

"Al-Hassan said he handled about a million six hundred thousand."

"Phew," came a voice from the back of the room. "That's a good chunk of change."

"But they got results," someone else said to grunts of agreement. "At this point the impact of the attacks on the US GDP is estimated at more than seventy-five billion."

"Sourcing of the drones?" Wardlaw asked.

"Here. Multiple online retailers and camera shops, delivered to a box at a UPS store and paid for with stolen credit cards." When no one commented, Sam went on, "According to al-Hassan, the men who joined him in Mexico had skills in bombmaking and electronics. It is believed they reentered Mexico after the attacks."

"Where did they acquire those skills?" Wardlaw interrupted.

"Building ANFO bombs is a pretty standard jihadi skillset," Sam answered confidently.

"But what about the triggering of the bombs? And the guidance for the drones?"

The next several minutes were spent answering those questions. They touched on a new area of development in terrorist skills. Exploitation of the electronic components and assemblies in the Phoenix warehouse had revealed that the trigger boards had been programmed to use GPS location and precision time to trigger the containers near the fiber-optic regeneration locations. Experts had discovered the terrorists had programmed a time window in the code as well, so that the first container to pass a regeneration building would not necessarily detonate, allowing more container-laden trains to follow it along the track, all working their way west. Additional evidence came from piecing together fragments from the explosion sites, where FBI and ATF agents discovered the remains of the GPS antennas and the bombs' penetrations through steel container walls. There was grudging admiration for not only designing such a complex system but for making it work on the first try.

The drones were a different matter. They appeared to have mainly been launched from elevated parking structures so as not to attract attention from the ground. So it was likely that the drones had been programmed to fly waypoints to a precise GPS location and, when that location was attained, detonate their explosive payloads. But how had they been so accurate? Internet mapping programs would not provide the necessary accuracy. A location would have to have been referenced to a GPS location that was scouted with precision. And surveillance camera videos, where available near the substations, did show suspicious-looking men walking, pausing, and continuing while holding what could have been handheld GPS devices. Again, the care the terrorists took in execution and the sophisticated planning that preceded it were extraordinary.

One of the analysts who had been studying the technology volunteered an answer. "Our liaison with Mexico has turned up examples of cartel smugglers flying drones across the border, as well as attempting armed drone attacks on Mexican military and law enforcement. That may be the basis for the technology used in the Eight-twenty attacks. The Mexican technology was believed to be home grown, but there may be some cross fertilization with Iranian or other Middle East expertise that's been supporting the cartels. *That*, we just don't know. Regarding the triggers for the container bombs, the FBI didn't recover any computers at the crime scenes, so we don't have any evidence that the code was written here in the US, but it could have been. The components were based on the Raspberry Pi processor, which is very commonly used around the world. It has good programming infrastructure and lots of peripheral components, including GPS, so that is not dispositive. The Raspberry Pi and its components are almost exclusively China sourced, and we've been unable to trace the specific sourcing of the components recovered at the crime scene."

"They used Python?" an analyst asked, referring to the software used on the Raspberry Pi processor.

"Yes."

"What distribution?"

"Python Three. All that means is the code is less than ten years old."

"Any idea where they got the package?" someone asked, referring to the raw Python programming environment.

"Looks like Piwheels."

"Well, that fixes it within a few years of present."

Wardlaw interrupted the nerd dialog. "We're getting way down in the weeds here. Anything else, Sam? Anything about why al-Hassan was back in Mexico and what he was planning?"

Sam cleared his throat and resumed, "Al-Hassan says he was supposed to be exfiltrated from Mexico, but the smugglers or traffickers held him, he thought, for ransom. His plans were to make his way back to Chechnya and his brother."

"Exfilled? I thought he entered legally?" someone asked.

"He apparently did. We were able to trace it back through Mexican immigration."

"Something's not adding up here," a Russian expert spoke up. "Chechens go to Syria or elsewhere in the Levant. Syrians don't go to Chechnya. This guy is dark, he'd stand out like crazy among Russians, and he's a lot darker than your typical Chechen. You really think the Russians would let this guy in and let him make his way to Chechnya, where the Russians are sensitive enough about Chechen Islamists, much less foreign fighters? Doesn't add up."

The comments generated conversations all around the room, which Wardlaw let proceed for a few minutes, himself confused by the notion of a Syrian freely entering, leaving, and expecting to re-enter

Chechnya. Finally, he motioned for quiet and asked, "What's all this telling us?"

One of the senior Russian analysts began, "Look, we know the Russians have a couple hundred, maybe a thousand Chechens and Ingush in Syria, some of whom have Spetznaz training. Maybe the al-Hassan brothers have some connection to these Chechens? And the Chechens are playing a double game with the Russians, playing both sides, killing ISIS jihadists for Moscow while hitting Muslim-oppressors in the West at the same time."

The room took a moment to digest that thesis. "The scary thing," Wardlaw said, "is that Moscow benefits both ways."

41

B oris Levertov slouched in the back of his chauffeured, black BMW as it raced around the Moscow Ring Road. He was returning to his Kremlin office, and the flashing blue light on the roof advertised his permission to travel in the special express lanes reserved for high government officials, oligarchs, and other favored persons. Otherwise, the "race" on the heavily trafficked highway would have been at approximately the pace of a crawling tortoise. Levertov was responding to a phone call he had received an hour earlier from the representative of a US luxury-goods importer, telling him that the exclusive handbags and purses he had inquired about were in her shop.

The BMW slowed as it left the Ring Road for the heavier traffic of Kutuzovsky Avenue, which would become New Arbat Avenue on the other side of the Moskva River. After less than a mile, his driver would enter the restricted boundaries of Red Square and would dutifully deposit Boris in front of the former GUM Department Store, ironically located across the square from the familiar, red-brick tomb of the founder of the Soviet Union, Vladimir Ilyich Ulyanov, better known as Vladimir Ilyich Lenin.

During the days of the USSR, the enormous GUM had been filled with shoppers who would line up across Red Square to shop at the one store in the vast Soviet Union that was not short of everything Soviet citizens wanted to buy. The irony was that today, in post-Soviet Russia, the GUM was a mall dedicated to conspicuous consumption, featuring luxury products and fashions that few contemporary Russians, much less their Soviet forebears, could afford.

Boris stepped from the car and walked to the arched stone entrance of the mall. Mixing with the crowd under the glass-and-cast-iron roof, he climbed the stairs to the second floor and walked almost to the end, where he found a small, elegant boutique that carried leather goods, watches, cigar cases, silk scarves for men and women, and a variety of other products, none of which cost less than an average worker's monthly salary. Inside the brightly lit room, he saw Liz Sanders and another woman, a lanky Russian he did not know.

Liz smiled when she saw him and called in Russian, "Welcome, Boris. Shall I show you those articles you requested? They just arrived."

"Yes, thank you," he replied.

Liz stepped behind a curtain at the back of the store and emerged with two large handbags, one a pebbled brown leather, the other a smooth aubergine. She placed them on a large table in the middle of the room, its Florentine "Pietra Dura" marble top artfully covered with silk scarves and ties. Boris made a show of inspecting them, stroking their sides, gently sniffing the leather, lifting them to feel their heft. The bags had an almost imperceptible extra heft, perhaps half a pound, because each bag contained 100,000 Euros, in purple, 500-Euro notes, hidden under the crumpled golden crepe paper that filled the bags almost to the handles.

Boris smiled and said, "Very good, can you charge them to my account?"

His smile deflated just slightly when Liz, herself smiling radiantly, replied, "I would prefer if we charged your credit card while you're here." Boris took this as a little game they played, Liz and the government she represented trying to recover a small amount of the treasure they provided their spy. For Liz and her handlers, it was nothing of the sort; the credit card receipt was just one more piece of leverage to keep Boris from straying. That and the fact that Boris' son, a student at a well-known college in Cambridge, Massachusetts, had been arrested with two kilos of cocaine the year before, and Liz's colleagues had negotiated with the US Attorney to suspend prosecution as long as Boris cooperated.

Liz ran Boris' card, which was approved for the charge, and produced two white-and-gold shopping bags, one for each of the handbags. "Let me carry these out for you," she gently entreated, and Boris gallantly stepped aside to let her go first.

Once outside they stood at the rear of the BMW, Boris motioning for the driver to release the trunk lid. Once the lid was opened and the driver could not see them, Liz slipped the bags into the trunk and handed Boris a small, folded paper. "I need this by tomorrow. Call my shop and tell my assistant that there's a defect with one of the bags and I'll meet you at the shop. Apologetically, of course." She smiled at him.

Boris slipped the paper into his pocket, slammed the trunk lid, nodded to Liz, and stepped around and into the BMW, which sped away.

42

Eric had returned to Mexico City to work with Inspector Ruiz, trying to trace the route of the other men involved in the attacks. Now he stood on the curb, waiting, on a bright morning, the smog barely noticeable. The inspector had texted that he and his driver were stuck in traffic, and Eric knew he was reluctant to use his emergency lights and siren to carve a path through it. He smiled as he pictured Inspector Ruiz telling his driver, "Norte Americanos are important but not *that* important."

Eric liked Ruiz. He was smart, professional, and seemed honest, something not to be taken for granted in law enforcement organizations between the US border and the Tropic of Capricorn. Eric reflected that, as an FBI agent, he was immersed in a culture largely free of corruption. In the history of the bureau, agents had almost never betrayed an investigation or a witness. That was not who they were. If they strayed, they strayed big time, like Robert Philip Hansen, who had betrayed a whole generation of intelligence agents in the US and Russia to the Soviet Union. Thankfully, Hansen was an outlier.

Eric was broken from his reverie by the approach of a black Tahoe featuring a smiling Inspector Ruiz in the passenger seat. Ruiz stepped out and gave Eric a hug. "Welcome to Mexico, my favorite gringo."

Eric smiled. "I would call you my favorite Mexican, but I don't want it to get back to Montez." They both laughed as they climbed into the SUV.

On the way back into Mexico City, wading through the traffic, the stink of older, poorly tuned cars almost making them gag, they made small talk, covering baseball, the President of the United States, and the upcoming inauguration of the newly elected Mexican president. "Do you think he's in the pocket of the Venezuelans?" Eric asked, confident enough in their friendship that he did not worry about offending Ruiz.

"No, I think he shares many of the same ideas, but he is more a populist and less an ideologue. And Venezuela is, for anyone who really cares about the people, a cautionary tale. I do not think anyone can look at a country that has so much more oil than we have and believe that we should follow all the policies that led them to ruin."

"My, Ralph, you are a Fox News conservative," Eric said, and they both laughed.

The Tahoe pulled up in front of the federal police headquarters, and as they stepped onto the pavement, Eric and his host felt free for the first time to speak openly about the case. "Any lead on them?" Eric asked.

"It is difficult because we do not know who the 'them' are. Did they come in as a group? From the same country or different. On what dates?"

Eric understood the complexity. Mexico received about 40 million visitors each year, mostly tourists, but some businessmen as well. The US had provided a batch of fingerprints and whatever images of the known terrorists they could find, but that was pretty slim information to find seven men out of 40 million. Hence, the assistance of Inspector Ruiz's intelligence unit. "Have you been able to run the passenger lists on the flights from Latin American countries?" Eric asked, knowing Khalid had entered Mexico with a Venezuelan passport and on a Venezuelan flight.

"Working on it. Ecuador, Bolivia, Cuba, or Venezuela, most likely.

Do you know if your man was the ringleader or if someone else was pulling the strings?" Inspector Ruiz asked.

"That's getting into CIA territory, so I don't really know. But given the sophistication of the attacks, I think there must be some larger organization involved. Hard to figure out who or what's behind an organization we hadn't heard of before a few months ago."

Ruiz grunted his assent.

ONCE UPSTAIRS in Inspector Ruiz's office, Ruiz and Eric spent a few hours staring at hundreds of images of arriving and departing passengers and the fuzzy digitizations of their passports. Since they knew neither the fake nor the real names of the terrorists, they had to rely on matching their appearances against whatever surveillance-camera videos they had, and what they had was not great. They were hoping the terrorists had been a little sloppy and entered as a group. If they were able to match multiple passengers on the same flight, they would have a higher confidence that they had the right men. Of course it was always possible the men had arrived illegally by boat or small plane, in which case they had little chance of finding them.

By 2 P.M., Eric and his host were worn out and famished, so they decided to walk to a local *parillada*, a restaurant serving grilled meats and vegetables, "Mexico City style." On the way they discussed the case, their respective supervisors, and their respective personal relationships. By the time they were seated, the conversation had circled back to the case.

"Do you have any intelligence assets who can tell us if they came by boat?" Eric asked, reflecting on the apparent fruitlessness of their morning review of the legal entrance records.

"If they came from the Western Caribbean or the Eastern Pacific, you know, Guatemala or El Salvador, Belize, Honduras, they could have taken a boat small enough to land on a beach. It would be very hard, and we would have to be very lucky, to pick that up. More distant, say Venezuela, and they would need a port. Then we get back to the question of which cartel, if any, was helping them. West Coast would be the Jalisco-New Generation Cartel, while the Sinaloa or the Gulf Cartel would be the most likely for the East Coast," Ruiz replied and took a long pull of a Victoria beer.

"If they came by boat from Venezuela, we had discussed possible assistance by the Gulf Cartel, right?"

"Yes, they have the strongest connection with the Venezuelans. But you must remember, these relationships are changing all the time, with power struggles, new circumstances," Ruiz reminded him.

"Any suggestions on how we run this to ground?" Eric asked, his gaze direct on his colleague.

Inspector Ruiz looked into the distance over Eric's shoulder for a few moments. "I have an idea," he said. "But you cannot be involved."

Eric looked at him quizzically but said nothing.

AFTER THEY FINISHED THEIR MEAL, they walked back to the office, again making small talk. At the entrance Inspector Ruiz turned to Eric and said, "I need to make some calls. You should go back to your hotel or do some sightseeing. Have you seen the Shrine of Our Lady of Guadalupe in Tepeyac, on the north side of the city? It is very moving. It will explain a lot about Mexicans."

Eric was at once amused about the notion of "explaining a lot about Mexicans" and curious about why he was being brushed off. It was possible Ruiz did have to make some calls, but why not let him stay in his office, in the spare office Eric was using, or in a conference room? He didn't voice any of this, simply replying, "I might do that. We see a lot of Our Lady of Guadalupe in Tucson." He shook Ruiz's hand, turned, and walked away in the direction of his hotel.

AS ERIC WALKED he turned to look over his shoulder and saw Inspector Ruiz had not entered the building but in fact was walking in the opposite direction. Eric stepped into an entranceway in case Ruiz turned around. He was beginning to lose sight of him in the crowd, but in a split second he decided he was not in the mood to be a tourist, and he started walking in the inspector's direction. He kept his distance, using other pedestrians as cover without even thinking about it, his FBI training in tailing suspects making it second nature. He felt fortunate there were just the right number of people on the street: too many and he would lose him, too few and it would be hard not to be seen. He was randomly ducking behind a tall woman with shopping bags when he caught a glimpse of Inspector Ruiz turning on his heel—obviously checking to see if he could catch a glimpse of any pursuer. Eric was confident he had not been seen when Ruiz turned back and continued walking, more slowly now, withdrawing his phone from his pocket, keying in a number, and raising the phone to his ear. After about 30 seconds he replaced the phone in his pocket.

Twenty minutes later they turned onto the broad Paseo de la Reforma, and it became more difficult to tail Ruiz without being spotted. Eric dropped back a little more but could still see Ruiz walking purposefully toward a broad expanse of green in the distance, the Chapultepec Park. A few more minutes and the inspector entered the park where the Paseo crossed its northern third. Just as Eric was wondering how long this sojourn would last, he saw Ruiz turn left into the park proper. From the distance he could not discern Ruiz's destination, but as he reached the spot where Ruiz had turned, Eric saw him climbing the steps of a low, modern building of glass and steel. As he came closer, he saw that it was, in fact, modern: the Museum of Modern Art.

Eric stopped on the pavement 50 yards from the entrance. There was no way not to be seen if he went in. He was tired and willing to admit defeat. He suspected his friend had not gone to look at abstract paintings but, instead, was meeting someone and did not want to be seen doing so.

~

As it happened, the person who did not want to be seen was not Inspector Ruiz, but the man he was meeting, the Second Counselor at the Cuban Embassy in Mexico City, Ernesto Corrales. Señor Corrales was still 20 minutes from the museum, so Inspector Ruiz took his time, slowly pacing from picture to sculpture until he reached *La Dos Fridas*, a dual self-portrait by Frida Kahlo. He sat on a bench opposite the painting, happy to be off his feet. In what seemed like only a moment later, he was joined by the Cuban.

"*Buenas tardes*, Ernesto," Inspector Ruiz greeted him, still staring at the painting.

"Buenas tardes, Raphael," Ernesto replied and, continuing in Spanish, asked, "What can I do for you?"

"I have a problem of some bad people coming into Mexico and making trouble in El Norte. I know you have nothing to do with it, but I need your help to find if they arrived here how I think they arrived here, and if they are now back where they came from," Inspector Ruiz told him.

Second Counselor Corrales paused for a moment, looking in the same direction as the inspector—at the image of the two Frida Kahlos, their anatomically correct hearts superimposed over their bodies, the hearts joined by a single blood vessel across the space between them. "What do you think Señorita Frida was trying to tell us with her painting?"

Inspector Ruiz was puzzled. He knew the message of the picture related to Frida's marital problems with Diego Rivera. But what was Corrales asking? Why did spies relish speaking in riddles? "We all have two natures, but you can only love one of them?" he volunteered in response.

Corrales chuckled. "Yes, I think you are right. Our friends in Caracas, we love them because they are socialist and they make trouble for the *Yanquis*, but they are not too smart. I will see what I can find out— for you, not for the Yanquis." Corrales leaned forward and pulled himself up, stretched his back, and walked back through the museum the way he had come.

43

The phone call came as Liz had expected, Boris Levertov explaining to her assistant, "Please tell Ms. Sanders there is a defect in one of the bags that I bought. I would like to return it this afternoon. I will require another bag like it." Her assistant confirmed the appointment for 4 P.M. and called Liz, who was walking back from a lunch at the Ritz Carlton with a Saudi diplomat. Boris's statement that he would "require another bag like it" meant that he wanted another 100,000 Euros for the information.

Liz chewed absently on her lower lip, a habit she fought, as she thought about the implications. For 300,000 Euros, the information better be good. She pulled her phone from her Hermes bag and updated her Facebook page with a remark about the excellent herring she had just enjoyed at the Ritz. The post would alert her embassy contact that she needed an urgent meeting at a pre-determined location, Restaurant Karamzin on Leningradskiy Avenue. The meeting would be at 8 P.M., so Boris could arrive late to the boutique and she could still make the restaurant.

Liz took a short detour to her apartment. After checking her makeup and replacing her pantyhose, which had a small run, she opened a small cupboard in her bedroom closet that contained a safe.

She opened the safe, and under various jewelry boxes found a small box containing 500-Euro notes, strapped in 100-bill packages. As Liz withdrew two packs—100,000 Euros—she chuckled to herself. When the European Union completed withdrawing the 500-Euro notes from circulation, she was going to need a bigger safe to accommodate the equivalent 200-Euro or 100-Euro notes. At least the fine leather bags she would use to transfer them were big enough.

Back at her boutique in the GUM building, she readied the replacement handbag, complete with the small stack of bills at the bottom, and waited for Boris to arrive. He was remarkably punctual, but his expression was pained and Liz was suddenly on guard. She looked past Boris to the hallway of the mall, but no one was standing behind him. As she approached him in greeting, she looked down the hall, but nothing seemed unusual, no one standing close by or looking in their direction. She hugged him and whispered in his ear, "Are you OK?"

"Fine, fine," he whispered back then, at a normal volume, continued, "I was very disappointed to find that this handbag, which I paid much money for, was defective. But thank you for replacing it so promptly."

"I am very sorry. The defect is inexcusable. Please inspect the new bag to make sure it meets your standards," Liz responded.

Boris moved to the table where the replacement bag sat. He held it up, rotated it, felt the sides and then felt the inside. When his hand got to the bottom and touched the bundle, Liz thought she saw his expression brighten slightly.

Maybe he's just nervous, she thought.

"This will be quite satisfactory," Boris said, noticeably more relaxed.

Liz felt her tension ease as she wrapped the bag and inserted it into her trademark, white-and-gold shopping bag, "Please allow me to carry this out for you," she said and took his arm with one hand, the other carrying the bag. When they were in the hall, which was sparsely populated this late afternoon between the luncheon and after-work rushes, she asked him in a low voice, "What did you learn." She felt Boris jerk slightly, as if he were taking a great gulp of air.

"You must promise me that no one will know the source of this information. If it becomes known, I guarantee I will end up in basement of Lefortovo," he began, invoking the name of the infamous KGB prison, now under the control of the FSB, where many a spy had met his or her end with a bullet behind the ear.

"No one even knows who I am," Liz replied, squeezing his arm and smiling at him. Her confidence was sincere, as only Liz and one person in Langley knew Boris' identity. "So...?" She let the question hang as they passed a couple of shoppers.

"It was an initiative of the GU. They are sucking up to Popov, trying to make the FSB and SVR look bad. Popov was not briefed on it before it was initiated, but he was told once it was in place and gave his approval. Now Popov is ecstatic that so much damage was done without pointing back to Russia. He sees it as honest, you would say 'payback,' for US sanctions and pushing down oil prices." Boris looked from side to side and licked his dry lips.

"What about the Chechen connection?"

"The GU used the Chechens to turn the Syrian, who was paid many rubles, maybe Euros, to plan the execution of the action, using his brother's help."

"Did they provide other personnel for the project?"

"I do not know, but I do not think so. That would make a connection to the GU."

They had reached the doors of the GUM that opened onto Red Square and the Kremlin walls beyond. The irony of conducting their conversation with that view in the background amused Liz, and she smiled slightly. She leaned into Boris and kissed him on the cheek. As she handed him the shopping bag, she whispered, "Keep in touch. I always have more handbags for you."

Boris smiled uncomfortably, nodded to her, and turned toward his waiting car.

∽

LIZ PRACTICED her usual tradecraft to try to detect any watchers, and if she found them, throw them off her trail. She observed no one, but she still made several changes in her route that were designed to be abrupt enough to throw off pursuers but not so abrupt as to confirm she was using spy techniques rather than unplanned detours into shops or a step off the street to make a call. On one "call" she switched her phone to video. As she turned her head with the phone to her ear, she leaned out of the doorway and recorded who was behind her and what they were looking at, all without ever turning around. She briefly reviewed the video while ostensibly in the act of terminating the call and saw nothing suspicious. She repeated the act twice more during her journey to the restaurant.

Her contact presumably exercised the same caution but with more vigor, since the Russians presumably knew or at least suspected he was a spy. Liz and her contact both knew that, as with their meeting outside the Izmailovo Market, a dead drop or one of the many electronic means of conveying information was much safer for both of them. But Liz was in a unique position, a sole operator without any day-to-day support, and it was better for her to spend even a little time with someone who knew her secrets, in whom she could confide, than always to live her double life alone. As a precaution any face-to-face meeting was in a location unlikely to be visited by her well-healed customers and contacts.

When Liz arrived at the restaurant, she saw that John was already seated. She looked around, walked to his table, and greeted him.

"How are you?" he asked.

"Good, business is good."

Even though their conversation would be inaudible in the crowded restaurant, John habitually looked around and moved in closer before he spoke again. They both were speaking Russian so that even if their words could not be heard, the jarring dissonance of a foreign language in a place where only the mother tongue was ever heard would not attract attention. He took Liz's hand in his, both as a cover and as a sincere gesture of affection, as he asked, "What did you find out?"

"Group two planned it to make group one look bad in front of the boss. The boss didn't know it was planned and initiated but gave the go-ahead when presented with the plan in place. The boss is pleased." Liz used euphemisms for the GU, FSB, and Popov. "The southerners under the control of group two used the Easterner to work out the details with his brother. It doesn't appear that the group gave any assistance, other than money, so they could maintain deniability."

John leaned back in his chair as the waiter came with bottles of water and vodka and a platter of smoked fish. Liz suddenly realized she was famished and served herself pieces of fish, several dollops of sour cream, and a large piece of black bread. "Anything else?" John asked.

Liz chewed more slowly, looking into the distance behind John. She swallowed, shook her head no and said, "You know how sensitive this is. My source would be liquidated if he gets fingered." Unspoken was the trouble Liz would be in.

"That shouldn't be a problem. The bigger issue is that, now that you've corroborated the earlier information, what are the policymakers going to do with it?"

44

A day later, Inspector Ruiz was seated in front of another painting in the Museum of Modern Art, this time Luis Arenal's *La Muerte de Zapata*, or *The Death of Zapata*. The inspector wondered if there was some meaning to the Cuban asking to meet in front of a somber portrait of peasant women viewing the dead revolutionary in his casket. He did not have to wait long for Second Counselor Corrales to join him on the bench. "Buenas tardes, Ernesto," he greeted the man.

"Buenas tardes, Rafael," replied the counselor, who got right to the point. "I do not wish you to share this information with the Norte Americanos, but I know you will." He paused for a moment before continuing, "The men you are seeking are back in Venezuela. They worked for al-Qaeda in Iraq before becoming, you might say, free-lancers, jihadists with a taste for money. They have worked for other revolutionary groups, which in some cases also had significant commercial interests with groups in your country. The Venezuelans will protect them, and the Yanquis will not be able to get their hands on them."

"How did they enter and leave Mexico?" Inspector Ruiz asked.

"On a boat carrying product from Colombia via Puerto Cabello to Altamira."

Inspector Ruiz silently cursed the Mexican Marines, who were supposed to be securing Mexican ports and preventing this kind of smuggling. "I appreciate it, my friend. Anything else I should know?"

"Just that neither the Cuban nor the Venezuelan governments knew anything about what these men were going to do."

Ruiz thought about that statement. Was it pro forma or true? As he thought about it, staring at the image of a dead revolutionary, he decided it made sense. As much as both governments hated the Estados Unidos de América, neither would want the wrath that such a major terrorist attack would loose on them. "Gracias," he said as he stood and walked away, stealing a last glance at the lifeless Zapata.

BACK IN THE OFFICE, Ruiz found Eric waiting for him.

"I'll be leaving tomorrow. The bureau wants me back in Tucson. Anything else I should know?" Eric asked expectantly.

Inspector Ruiz smiled, playing with his friend. "Why do you ask?"

"Call it my FBI intuition."

Ruiz walked around his desk to reach his chair then waved for Eric to sit down. "I have spoken with a source that is in position to know much of what happens in Venezuela. He has some political differences with the US, so I thought it better if I spoke with him alone."

"Fair enough. He's *your* source," Eric responded.

"OK, well our guys did come in by boat from Venezuela, without the knowledge or support of the Venezuelan government. They are jihadi freelancers from Iraq, former al-Qaeda. They entered and left Mexico via the Port of Altamira. They are back in Venezuela, and the Venezuelans are not likely to give them up."

"Is there a cartel connection?" Eric asked.

"I think it is indirect. These men work for the cartels, but the cartels do not have an interest in provoking the US government, so I think it is safe that they were not directly involved beyond helping smuggle these men in and out of Mexico and the US"

"Can I report this back with high confidence?" Eric asked.

"*Si,*" said Inspector Ruiz.

"*Che bueno,*" replied Eric.

45

The briefing for the president was conducted in the White House Situation Room with only senior advisors to the president in attendance, no staffs. The director of the CIA and the director of national intelligence wanted to absolutely minimize the chances of a leak to the press. The CIA director started the briefing, "Mr. President, let me summarize what we know. The August twentieth attacks were perpetrated by a group of Middle Eastern terrorists led by one Khalid al-Hassan, whom we now have in custody in Guantanamo."

"Like I said, I'm glad I didn't close it," the President interjected.

"Yes, sir. Al-Hassan was operating under the direction of his brother, Hamid al-Hassan, who is in Chechnya. Khalid al-Hassan was assisted in the planning and execution of the attacks by what we now believe was sort of a pick-up group of Iraqi jihadist mercenaries who joined him in Mexico."

"I understand the Mexican drug cartels were involved?" the president half stated, half asked.

"We believe a cartel was involved in smuggling the men into Mexico and then into the US, but we do not believe the cartels were involved in planning the attacks. And we believe they did not know the specifics of the men's mission."

The president frowned, but said nothing, simply nodded.

Director Haller continued, "All of the terrorists entered Mexico from Venezuela. Again, we do not think the government of Venezuela was involved, except indirectly by permitting these men to enter their country and operate therein." She paused but the president did not react, so she continued, "This is where the case becomes," she paused for a second, "extremely sensitive. By tracing the flow of money and using very highly placed sources in and around the government of the Russian Federation, we now believe with high confidence that the Glavnoje Upravlenije, that is the GU, or the Main Directorate of the General Staff of the Armed Forces of the Russian Federation, planned and funded the August twentieth attacks. *With* the permission of the president of the Russian Federation."

The president frowned again, and the director was not sure if it were due to the tongue-twisting Russian name she had just effort-lessly spoken or the implications of her statement. There was silence in the room as everyone absorbed the finality of an idea that had been rumored among the highest intelligence and national security circles for the past few weeks.

The chief of staff broke the silence, asking, "What's your confidence level in all that?"

The CIA director took just a moment to consider the question. "Ninety percent." Someone in the room softly whistled.

The National Security Advisor leaned forward in his chair, asking in an adversarial tone, "Let me get this straight. You're saying Popov approved this?"

Haller straightened and responded, "The information we have is that the GU planned the operation and put it in place before notifying President Popov, but that Popov approved the final execution of the plan, the attacks themselves, and is pleased with the result."

Secretary Martin looked pained. "Let's parse this. What kind of confirmation do you have indicating the GU planned the attacks?"

"We have two intelligence sources plus the flow of the money to the hacker who executed the SCADA attacks on the electrical substations. We also have the very suspicious circumstances under which the Syrians Hamid and Khalid al-Hassan made their way to Chechnya and lived there unmolested for several years."

"OK, what about the Popov angle?" he asked.

Haller paused. "We have two independent high-level sources," she began then realized there was really only one source that mentioned Popov. "Correction, we have a senior source in the office of the president of the Russian Federation that provided the intelligence that Popov approved the operation."

"So you really only have one source asserting Popov's involvement," Martin asserted.

"That is correct, Mr. Secretary, although the GU operates under direct control of the president of the Russian Federation," she replied.

"Certainly, but there's always the chance of a rogue element in the GU launching this operation. I would certainly want a lot stronger confirmation before I risked a shooting war with the Russians," Martin responded.

The president pursed his lips and nodded. "Go back and see what else you can find," he ordered, and looking around the room, he added, "I want some options for us if this thing is true."

46

B ack at CIA headquarters Haller gathered her senior staff to discuss the question of Russian presidential involvement. "Do we have any other supporting information? Or opposing?" she asked.

One of her staff asserted, "Popov is bold but not reckless. This seems a bridge too far for me, even for him." That started a free conversation around the table that went on for several minutes.

Finally, Haller said, "But back to the thesis. What if he thought he would have perfect deniability?"

"There is no such thing as perfect deniability. Secrets always leak eventually," one senior staffer said.

"I don't know, we still have a few." This from another staff member. Soft laughter followed that comment, even from the director.

"We currently don't have anyone inside the GU, just on the periphery, right?" Haller asked and received nods to the affirmative.

Another of the staff, a hardened veteran of the Cold War, remarked, "In the old days we used to use newspaper articles and photographs to figure out who was in and who was out. What do we have in the way of information on recent awards, promotions, et cetera, for senior GRU officers?" He used the earlier—and some minds, still current—term for the spy agency. "For that matter, even for GRU staff? Is there anything we can correlate with the attacks?"

One of the director's staff called down to his department and asked for a particular analyst to come up to the conference room. When the analyst arrived after a few moments, the director asked, "What do we know about recent changes, awards, promotions in the GU hierarchy?"

The analyst, with obvious confidence, quickly began, "One big item is the director. For about twenty years the new director of the GU has been a promotion from Strategic Intelligence. Korobov, Shlyakhturov, Igor Sergun, were all deputy directors for Strategic Intelligence. That's the department charged with running illegals, et cetera. Then along comes Kolmogorov. You will remember he gave a very aggressive, anti-Western speech at the Moscow Conference on International Security back in April. That speech was certainly sanctioned by the office of the president of the Russian Federation. He's an admiral in a world of generals, land and air, Korobov was in the Air Force. So the news is that Kolmogorov just leap-frogged Suslov, the head of Strategic Intelligence, to become the new director."

"What does that mean?" asked the director, aware that the promotion broke precedent but unsure how far to take it.

"The implication is that Kolmogorov is now Popov's favorite."

"What was the date on the promotion?"

"It was announced on August twenty-fourth."

The room took that in. "Implication is a very weak standard in intelligence. We need something more," the director decreed. "What was Kolmogorov responsible for in the GU?"

"Well, normally, as a vice admiral, he would be Director of Fleet Intelligence. But at Popov's request he was dual-hatted as head of the Second Directorate, which is responsible for intelligence on potential adversaries in the Western Hemisphere."

"So that's an intelligence-gathering responsibility, not operational?" Haller asked, seeking clarification.

"Well, actually, the Second Directorate includes a department, the Second Direction, that is responsible for developing agent networks near and behind potential enemy lines for intelligence gathering, sabotage, et cetera. Sabotage is a major responsibility of the Second Direction."

Several people around the table jerked slightly at the mention of sabotage.

"Anything else you see as relevant to Kolmogorov's ascension to the head of the GU?"

"Well, he's known to hate the SVR, but then all of those GU guys do. Sometimes, it seems the GU will do things just to stick it to the FSB, as when they implicated the FSB in the Shaltai-Boltai Ring," the analyst said, alluding to a Russian cyber-crime group whose name in English meant Humpty-Dumpty. "Popov is giving the GU a very long leash because they're succeeding where the FSB and SVR are failing."

"In your estimation, is Popov aware of all major GU operations?" Haller asked.

"Popov's a spook, he loves this stuff, the Skripal assassination attempt in the UK, cyber-attacks on Ukraine and the US Some of us think he actually gets involved in operational details just to keep his hand in things. Who's going to tell him no?"

Haller leaned back in her chair, rocked a few shallow rocks, and asked, "Does anyone else have any questions?" No one spoke up, so she thanked the analyst and he excused himself. "So where does that leave us?" she asked those remaining.

"In a sense no closer to a definitive Popov connection, but all circumstantial evidence points to it," one of the staff volunteered.

"The evidence is very strong, I would say indisputable if I were to go out on a limb, that the GRU was behind the attacks, and I would find it very hard to imagine that either: a) Kolmogorov did not tell Popov before the actual attacks proceeded or that; b) Kolmogorov did not tell Popov after the fact and he was rewarded for their success," the old Soviet hand opined. The room nodded affirmatively.

The director leaned forward in her chair. "Well, I think we tell the president that we're certain Popov either gave the go-ahead before the attacks or rewarded the perpetrator after the fact. Either way we're certain the president of the Russian Federation supported the August twentieth attacks on our homeland."

47

T he next morning Haller had just finished presenting the CIA assessment and was pleasantly surprised at the reception. What had changed? Probably the acceptance that whether the Russian president had been involved in the planning or not, he had not distanced himself and his government from what was undeniably an activity perpetrated under Russian sponsorship. "Whether we are punishing Popov or the GU, we need to make this action very costly for Russia," said National Security Advisor Keeler. "A démarche won't do," he emphasized, using the diplomatic term for a protest lodged with another government.

"Where are my options?" the president asked.

The secretary of state took the floor first. "If you would like to take the diplomatic route, I would recommend we take our evidence to the Security Council, the UN, and call for international sanctions. While we're waiting for UN action, we can apply unilateral sanctions on Russian financial transactions."

The president frowned. "Too weak."

Haller, Martin and their staffs had already met before the meeting with the president. Martin began, "Mr. President, DoD and the intelligence community have been discussing potential actions that hit the

Russians where it hurts but not to the point that we start an armed conflict or have to involve out NATO partners."

"What good is NATO if they won't help us when we need them?" the president asked.

"Well, in this case, I don't think we need NATO, and we're not proposing military action, per se. We would propose that we give the Russians a taste of their own medicine." The president did not respond, so Martin continued. "We would propose that the Global Warriors of Jihad and Righteousness, the Sons of Khalid ibn al-Walid strike natural gas distribution facilities within the Russian Federation."

"Wait a minute, that group doesn't exist!" Keeler protested, his face turning a shade of pink, his mustache flopping.

"We know that and the highest levels of the Kremlin know that. That's exactly the point. They will know that we know what they did, and that there are consequences. But we have as much public deniability as they do," Martin finished.

"If we do it right. Just who are you going to infiltrate into Russian territory who won't give the game away if they're caught?" the secretary of state asked.

"We have an operational concept that will provide the required isolation between the US and the actors in theater. I don't think we want to go into more detail at this time," Martin replied. The president's eyebrows lifted but he did not respond.

"What is the scope of the attacks you're proposing, and what would the impact be on the economies of our allies in Europe?" asked the president's chief of staff. "They rely heavily on Russian natural gas."

The secretary of defense looked to Haller, who began, "First, the Europeans and the Ukraine have storage reserves, and we can supply Europe through existing LNG terminals in the Netherlands. Second, our emphasis will be on transmission capacity in eastern Siberia that is primarily serving or intended to serve the new export market to China. We want to hit the components that, like the substation transformers damaged or destroyed in the August twentieth attacks, will take the longest time to repair or replace. Russia exports about forty billion dollars' worth of natural gas per year, so the goal would be to make a major dent in that export income commensurate with the damage they did to our economy. Keep in mind that the US GDP is about ten times that of Russia, so a ten- or twenty-billion-dollar decrement is a much bigger hit for them versus the seventy-five-billion-dollar hit we took."

The president nodded. "I want to know how you're going to do this without getting Russia to know it's us and respond."

"Mr. President, the right people will know it's us, just as the right people in this country know it was them. President Popov and the military intelligence community will know that we've used the same subterfuge, the same false flag, to attack them that they used to attack us. But their people won't know it was us, so they won't feel compelled to retaliate overtly. Our recommendation," he paused and looked at the director of the CIA before continuing, "after our successful retaliation under the guise of the Global Warriors, would be to communicate with President Popov and tell him, subtly, that we know his government was behind the Eight-twenty attacks, and the attacks on their natural gas infrastructure was the price they paid."

"So I call him *after* our attacks?" the President asked, his brow slightly furrowed.

Before Martin could answer, the secretary of state held his hand up. "I think we need to think through how we confirm to them what we think they will guess from the Global Warriors' claim of responsibility. Maybe we keep our powder dry unless they ask or accuse."

Looking at Haller, the chief of staff asked, "Do you think they would stay quiet or try to escalate, publicly or in private?"

The director took a moment. "I think Popov will swallow this one, blame it on Islamists in Chechnya, Ingushetia, or on some other North Caucuses people. Or he could blame it on the Syrians he's bombing. That seems more probable, although it suggests similar criticisms of his administration's internal security competence. Hopefully, he won't use it to commit another atrocity," he added, referring to

Russia's heavy hand in the Chechen wars and against civilian-filled rebel enclaves in Syria.

The National Security Advisor turned to the president and said, "Mr. President, I would recommend that you have more detail before you approve this course of action."

"That makes sense," the president responded. "Get to it, but quickly. I want to get this message to the people who have to have it."

"Yes, Mr. President," Martin and Haller replied in unison. The director asked, "Do we have your approval to perform some initial assessments in-country, not operational, just intelligence gathering?"

"You going to send some people in?" the president asked.

"No, we'll use someone who's already there," Haller answered.

AFTER THE BRIEFING, Martin and Haller walked side by side from the Situation Room. "How are we going to proceed?" the secretary asked.

"Who do you want to be point for this? SOCOM?" the director asked in reply.

"I think that makes the most sense."

"OK, I'll send a team down to MacDill, and they can start working the scenarios," Haller replied, referring to MacDill Air Force Base in Tampa, Florida, where USSOCOM, the US Special Operations Command, was based. "What do you see as a timeline?" Haller asked.

The secretary thought for a minute and responded as they entered the elevator that would take them from the White House basement, where the Situation Room was located, to the building's main floor. An aid held the elevator door for them as the secretary politely stepped aside so the director could enter the elevator before him. "I think it will take a while to plan this mission and train the execution. I'll leave that to USSOCOM—they're the experts, after all—but I'd hate to have a team in-country during the winter. Too many things to go wrong and too many footprints left."

The director grunted her affirmation as the door closed.

48

Since few alleged terrorists are captured alive, each time it actually happens the question of how to prosecute and punish them animates Washington's political and legal discourse for months. Senators and Congressmen opine gravely on cable news. Legal experts discuss "enemy combatants," "habeas corpus," "the Hamdan decision," "Supermax," and all the considerations at play with a dangerous criminal with dangerous friends for whom the normal rules of evidence may prevent a successful prosecution in Federal court.

The current crisis was no different. Legislators from hard-hit California, the epicenter of the terrorist attacks, screamed, at least figuratively, for blood. That only one man had been arrested for the attacks made the decisions all the more difficult. So, after much consultation inside the Administration, the Justice Department decided to punt on the terrorism prosecution for the time being and, instead, focus on Khalid al-Hassan's role in the murder of a federal officer.

KHALID HAD ONLY SPENT a few months as a guest of the detention facility at Guantanamo's Camp Delta when he was flown back to Tucson for his arraignment for the murder of Border Patrol Officer Margaret Walsh. Dressed in his usual orange jumpsuit, and manacled at wrists and ankles, he and his security detail boarded a Navy C-40—the military version of a 737-700—at sunrise and flew from Cuba to Naval Air Station Corpus Christi, Texas. Since the Cuban government would not allow the flight to pass over the island, the aircraft first flew south toward Haiti, then west past the Cayman Islands and almost to the Yucatan peninsula before turning northwest toward the US mainland.

The January air in Texas was crisp, a welcome change from the humidity that drenched the Gulf Coast most of the year, and Guantanamo all of the year. The new arrivals drew in great breaths of cool air as they descended a ladder onto the tarmac. Khalid, escorted by his six-member Naval security escort and the airplane crew, shuffled into a white Navy van for the ride to the brig, where he was locked in a small cell and provided a light Halal lunch of pita bread, lamb, and couscous. The rest of the party retired to the enlisted dining facility, where they enjoyed hamburgers and French fries.

After a two-hour stop to eat and refuel, the security detail returned to Khalid's cell in the brig. He had finished his meal and was kneeling on the floor, apparently praying in what he believed to be an easterly direction. One member of the security detail wondered silently how Khalid knew which direction faced Mecca, since there were no windows in the cell and no marker on the floor of the cell, as there were at Guantanamo. Another sailor unlocked the door, and as two members of the detail entered the cell, Khalid opened his eyes and turned toward the group. The two sailors with him gently grabbed his upper arms and helped him to his feet.

"Time to go?" he asked and the men nodded.

Once they were outside the cell, Khalid noticed the group had expanded by three men and a woman. They were wearing blue nylon windbreakers with "US MARSHAL" in yellow block letters on the back, badges hanging from shiny beaded chains around their necks.

The woman looked at him intently and said, "Khalid al-Hassan, I am
Deputy US Marshal Renee Wexford. My colleagues and I are taking
you into custody for arraignment in Federal Court for the murder of
US Border Patrol Agent Margaret Walsh. Your Navy security detail will
accompany us. Will you come with me, please?"

One of the sailors smirked slightly as he considered whether
Deputy Marshal Wexford's polite request could actually be refused.
Khalid did not react to what she said and looked away from the
woman, turning to one of the sailors. "I need to go to the bathroom,"
he told the man. The head of the security detail looked at the
marshals, who nodded and, accompanied by one of the marshals,
Khalid was led to a nearby men's room.

Once they were inside the men's room, Khalid stopped in front of
a stall and stretched out his arms in front of the chief petty officer
leading the security detail. The chief withdrew the key for the manacles from a chest pocket of his uniform blouse, and as he did, Khalid
ducked down and tried to pull the chief's M-9 pistol from its mid-
thigh holster. The abrupt motion surprised the detail, including the
chief, but, after a second, the group coalesced into a ball of men
pulling at Khalid's arms, two sailors attempting to draw their
weapons.

The marshal who had accompanied the detail into the bathroom
had apprehended and transported hundreds of fugitives, some armed
and dangerous, and he hesitated less than the Navy men. Within a
second and a half he had drawn his Glock 17 and pointed it at Khalid's
face, yelling over the din created by the security detail's shouts and
grunts. "Khalid al-Hassan, stop what you are doing and step back with
your hands empty or I will shoot you in the head."

That got Khalid's attention, as well as that of his combatants, and
they all stepped away, Khalid more slowly and deliberately than the
sailors, his hands, indeed, empty. The sailors collected themselves and
grabbed his arms, pushing him angrily against the toilet stalls, one of
them muttering, "Fucker." Khalid's faced showed equal parts hatred,
pride, and disappointment, and he stood perfectly still, staring at the
marshal covering him with the Glock.

The marshal made eye contact with the chief, who nodded, and he slowly replaced his weapon in its holster, shifting sideways to lean against a sink just as the three remaining marshals burst through the bathroom door, hands on their weapons.

"Everything OK in here?" Deputy Marshal Wexford asked as she and her colleagues tried to size up the situation. She eyed the men grouped tightly around Khalid, their faces all showing a combination of anger and embarrassment.

"Yes, ma'am," the chief replied with a strong Georgia or Alabama accent, his brow damp from adrenaline.

After a moment, Wexford turned and left the men's room, leaving the rest to decide if Khalid should be allowed to defecate.

ABOUT THE SAME time as the confrontation in the Texas men's room, Eric was driving to the Tucson International Airport to pick up Caitlin, who had insisted on taking a redeye from Anchorage by way of Seattle to attend the arraignment. Much as he wanted to see her, he had tried to dissuade her from coming, not wanting both their emotions to resurface. Since Caitlin had returned to Anchorage two months ago, they had texted daily, talked frequently, skyped weekly, but had not seen each other in person.

Eric parked in the short-term lot in front of the terminal and started walking toward the building. His phone beeped and he read the text: Caitlin telling him she had landed. He crossed the roadway and entered the terminal at the Arrivals level, watching the monitor that showed arriving passengers as they were perhaps 30 seconds from descending from the secure area into the Arrivals lobby. He stood staring at the display, wondering if she would ever appear, and then there she was, her coat over one arm and a rolling suitcase trailing the other. A smile on his face, he thought about walking closer but then decided he wanted to take her in as she closed the distance.

Caitlin was glancing from side to side, obviously looking for him and then seeing him as she reached the bottom of the escalator. She looked down at her suitcase and then back at him, a smile spreading across her face, her green eyes sparkling.

Eric's smile widened and he started walking toward her, reaching for her coat as he enveloped her in an embrace before he even kissed her. "It's really good to see you," he whispered slowly, his lips next to her ear. He kissed her neck and then relaxed his grip to face her.

"Me, too," she said, and then, realizing her non sequitur, said, "It's really good to be here," and kissed him warmly.

They broke and Eric reached for her bag. "How was your flight?"

"Uneventful, which is always good."

"Hungry?"

"Actually, yes."

"Mexican?" he asked.

"Sure."

They were quiet the rest of the walk and as they drove to a restaurant on the south side of town. Caitlin watched the unfamiliar yet familiar landscape pass by. "You had rain," she said.

"Yes, about three days ago. If it keeps up, we'll have a good wild-flower bloom in the spring."

"Is he here yet?" she asked, as if she had not heard him and they were having a completely different conversation.

Eric turned to look at her. He knew exactly whom she meant. "I think he gets here later today."

She turned to look at him, her expression blank. He knew her well enough to know her emotions were boiling inside but she did not want to share them. "You don't have to go if you don't want to," he said and immediately regretted it. He turned to her and her eyes were like green flames, her jaw clenched.

"You know I have to," she whispered, her lips tight.

"Sorry. I know." They were at a light now and he stared at her sympathetically. She smiled slightly and turned back toward the passenger window.

The light changed and he turned away.

49

Tampa was also enjoying a dry January when the CIA team arrived at MacDill a day or so after Khalid and Caitlin arrived within a few hours of each other in Tucson. The team cleared security and were driven to one of the many SCIFs on the base. The SCIF in this case was a nondescript brown-and-tan block building behind a razor-wire fence on a facility that was already highly secure. They were escorted past the security guards and into the building, where they passed through a cypher-locked door into a vestibule blocked by a combination-locked door like that on a bank vault. That inner door was ajar, and when their escorts pulled it open, they entered an enormous room filled with cubicles, conference tables, monitors, safes, padlocked cabinets, paper maps on rolling boards, etc.

They were joined by a US Army colonel and a US Navy captain bearing the insignia of Delta and SEALs, respectively. Each man was accompanied by a half dozen additional officers and senior enlisted men. They did not wear ribbons or other decorations on their camouflage utility or working uniforms, but the CIA contingent could tell by their bearing that many of them had been in very dangerous places doing very risky things. Some of the CIA agents had done the same. One of the CIA men nodded to a SEAL senior chief with whom he had worked in Afghanistan. The senior chief smiled tightly and nodded back, a recognition of what both had seen "downrange."

The group sat around a large table, plastic bottles of water at each place. A small pile of file folders marked "Top Secret," with a series of code words associated with special-access programs, was stacked at the end where the senior USSOCOM members sat.

The leader of the CIA delegation was a tall, graying man in late 40s or early 50s who introduced himself as "John Farmer." Farmer began, "Gentlemen, we have tasking from POTUS to develop an actionable plan for a series of covertly executed, coordinated, retaliatory strikes against Russian gas production facilities."

Among a group that had heard it all and rarely reacted to words, the mention of "Russian" provoked visible but silent response among the service members. For all of their adult lives they had been either spectators or participants in proxy wars between the US and Russia: Vietnam, Afghanistan, Grenada, Iraq, now, Syria. Removing the proxy, the buffer between the countries, was deadly serious.

"I presume this is related to the Eight-twenty attacks?" the colonel asked.

"Yes. We have established the attacks were instigated by elements of the GU with at least the tacit agreement of the highest Russian leadership." Farmer let that sink in, then continued, "The goal here is to walk the fine line between overt state-on-state attack and inexplicability. We want the Russians to understand this was a consequence of their actions but not have their public loss of face require further escalation on their part."

"Plausible deniability?" one of the Delta operators asked.

"In effect, yes," Farmer replied.

"So, what are you thinking?" asked the senior SEAL.

Farmer reached next to his chair and withdrew a thin file covered in classification markings from his briefcase. "We're proposing targeting three locations. This gives us some significant impact on their gas production and infrastructure and mirrors the sophistication of the multiple-location attacks perpetrated on us. As with the power substations and the fiber optic regen stations they targeted, we're going for infrastructure that's expensive and time consuming to replace. We want this to hurt for a long time." He handed a USB thumb drive down the table and asked one of the Delta operators closest to a computer to insert it and open a file labeled "Target Overheads." At the same time, he passed out hard copies. When everyone had a set of papers in front of them, Farmer began again, "These are the three prospective targets-slash-locations. Let's work through whether, in your estimation, they're viable."

The first slide opened, displaying an overhead image and a summary of the target, heavy with classification markings. "That's the Amur Gas Processing Station. It's a critical location on a new pipeline Gazprom is building from Siberia into northern China. It's a few klicks south of the city of Svobodny on the Zeya River, and about fifty kilometers north of the Chinese border at Blagoveshchensk." He waited while the group read and considered the slide.

"That's a huge facility. What, exactly, are we targeting and with what ordnance?" one of the SEALs asked.

Farmer pointed to a spot on the image. "We're suggesting these large towers, which are used for separating helium from the feed gas. Like most of the major components of the plant, they have a multi-year lead time and have to be transported by barge. Destruction of them would set the Russians back a few years. We'll let you figure out what you need for the job."

"Presumably, they would still be able to sell gas, just not helium. Isn't there something more crucial to the whole capability of the plant?" asked the same SEAL.

Farmer looked to his team. "We'll have to get some more information and circle back on that."

"And another thing," the SEAL added. "If those are pressure vessels, they'll have heavy steel walls. Anything we can transport on our backs will only make big dents or tiny holes, if we can even infiltrate the site and place the demo charges. I don't see how we're going to do enough damage to take the plant out of service for any length of time."

"If we can infiltrate, maybe we can cut the supports or struts and let gravity collapse them. That would do the job," another SEAL opined to mutters of approval. "I'm going to assume you can get us drawings of those towers or whatever you think we should kill," he continued.

"We can provide them to you now," Farmer assured him.

"If this is a construction site, are they working twenty-four hours a day?" a Delta operator asked.

Farmer looked at his team. "Yes, at least on part of it, based on what components are available."

"The whole site is already graded and prepared, so there isn't activity across the entire site," one of the CIA analysts added.

"Lights?"

"Some."

"Guards?"

That last question was on everyone's mind. Each Special Warfare professional immediately started processing the likely infiltration, operating, and exfiltration environment for Russia, based on training and not a little on stereotypes. Would they encounter drunken, apathetic guards who could easily be avoided during reconnaissance of the targets and avoided or non-lethally neutralized during the operation? Or would they be highly trained and motivated like the "Little Green Men," Russian Special Forces without names, rank, or unit insignia on their uniforms, who had quickly and skillfully overwhelmed Ukrainian forces and seized the Crimea?

Any assault team already had to consider how to avoid or, worst case, react to, local police, the *militsiya*—the term still used for the National Police—as well as border guards, regular Russian military, curious citizens—the whole spectrum of human interactions that could compromise the operation and get them taken prisoner or killed.

Farmer looked to his team.

"Yes, there are some guards, mainly to prevent theft of vehicles, tools, and materials," one of the analysts admitted.

"Quality?

Slight hesitation. "Since this is a Gazprom project with foreign investors, we'll assume they're better than the average within the Russian Federation." the same analyst replied.

The Delta and SEAL operators talked among themselves about the implications. "What kind of cover is on the periphery?" a Delta operator asked.

"Conifer forest, patchy, unclear what the immediate periphery looks like at ground level. We're in the process of getting some ground-level reconnaissance in the very near future."

"This is winter, and it will stay winter there for a while. The cover will look completely different in the spring or summer, if we're waiting that long to execute this mission" a Delta master sergeant replied, concern in his voice.

"Every one of these targets will have challenges. Let's get through the target list, and then we can sort through what's viable and what's non-viable," the SEAL captain ordered.

Farmer called for the next slide and passed out another set of heavily marked hard copies. "Tyumen Compressor Station, ten klicks northwest of the city of Tyumen, not far from the Tura River and about two hundred and eighty kilometers from the border with Kazakhstan. We picked this because of the proximity to a republic with a predominantly Muslim population and because it's a critical junction in the southern pipeline network."

"I don't like it," a SEAL lieutenant commander, who had a Master in International Relations, spoke up quickly. "First, Kazakhstan is one of the least radicalized in the former Soviet Union. The government regularly cracks down on Salafists. It's been tough for them to get a foothold. What does that do for the cover story?"

"We thought the repression would be a useful component to the statement taking credit for the attacks," an analyst who had accompanied Farmer volunteered.

"Well, I don't like it either," another SEAL commented, pointing at the computer display. "What you don't see is that Tyumen isn't too far from Chelyabinsk and Chelyabinsk-Six-Five." He was referring to the capital of the region and the nearby "secret city" for nuclear research that was now known as Ozersk. "That area has to be crawling with FSB and other spooks. Not the best place for infiltration."

"Russia's a big damn country. No place is going to be easy to infiltrate," one of the Delta operators commented. "And that looks like more than three hundred kilometers from Chelyabinsk or Ozersk."

"About three hundred and forty klicks to either," one of Farmer's team commented, which seemed to satisfy them that the proximity to Chelyabinsk would be among the least of their problems.

"What's the specific target?" one of the SEALs asked.

"The actual compressor stations, which are these buildings with the exhaust stacks," Farmer said, using a laser pointer to circle the target on the display. "This should be easier than Amur, since the lines are pressurized, and if you hit the line close to the output of the compressor, we believe either the resulting explosion or the ingestion of excess gas into the engine, the prime mover for the compressor, will destroy it through an over-speed." His audience nodded affirmatively.

"How thick is the pipe?" one of the Delta operators asked.

"Less than an inch," Farmer replied.

"That can be punctured with a Mk-thirteen," one of the SEALs replied, alluding to their standard sniper rifle firing a potent .300 Winchester Magnum round.

"A little hole won't get us the effects Farmer's suggesting," one of the Delta's corrected, and the SEAL nodded.

"So, we need a big hole. How big?" another Delta operator asked.

Farmer looked to his team and pursed his lips. "Maybe a good part of the diameter of the pipe? About half a meter?"

"Shouldn't be too hard to do if we can place charges. If we have to do it remotely, it'll be harder." That statement brought general agreement around the table, with some teasing of the Delta for making such a trivial statement.

"Sapper heaven is unimpeded access to place a demolition charge on a target," one of the SEALs intoned to more laughter.

"Do we need to demo each compressor output line, or will one take them all out?" another SEAL asked.

"Let's just do 'em all to be safe," a third SEAL answered,

"Moving on to the next target," Farmer said and asked for the last images to be selected. "The last target group is the Severo-Stavropol-skye Gas Storage Facility, located fourteen kilometers north of the city of Stavropol. That's three hundred and forty kilometers east of the Sea of Azov, three hundred and eighty west of the Caspian Sea, and three hundred and fifty north of Grozny, Chechnya. It's the largest gas storage facility in the world and has a capacity to store about one-point-six trillion cubic feet of gas." Pointing to a row of 16 small buildings, he added, "There are multiple compressor sites, but we consider this the main one we'd like hit."

"Are there valves that will prevent all that gas from venting to the atmosphere?" one of the Delta operators asked, remembering the environmental disaster when Saddam Hussein set fire to nearly 700 oil wells in northern Kuwait to punish the Kuwaitis as his army retreated.

"There are, and we *don't* want to cause an environmental disaster," Farmer responded. "But we want that gas to stay in the ground for a while."

Conversation continued for the next hour on the sizes of the teams for each target set, potential infiltration routes, cover stories and CIA support while downrange, sabotage tactics for each site, and exfiltration options. Farmer and his analysts fielded numerous questions. Did they want small teams, easier to infiltrate, hide, and exfiltrate? Or larger teams, more robust if something went wrong? The consensus was smaller. What about the ordnance or explosive charges for each target? That would require more research.

"We have to balance effectiveness against the targets with survivability for the teams," the colonel remarked. "We aren't sending our guys there just to get captured or killed. That's bad for them and completely compromises the mission. I don't know about the SEALs, but I have very few guys who could pass for Islamic terrorists, even if they could speak Arabic or Chechen or Russian."

"I've got a few guys who can speak Arabic, but they're all blond," the SEAL captain said to chuckles.

"That does highlight one of the major risks," the SEAL lieutenant commander commented. "The attribution to the known but non-existent terrorist organization relies on no one being captured or really even observed. I've been to Russia. They know an outsider when they see one, and they're very suspicious of them."

Farmer allowed a slight grin as he said, "A few of us have been there too. Most of the time we try to exploit inefficiency or apathy, but there's always that one person who actually tries to do his or her job. You know, the one who doesn't go along with the old joke from Soviet days, 'we pretend to work and they pretend to pay us.' The Agency will work with you on clothing, cover stories, whatever we can to get you what you need for the mission. But you guys have to tell us if you can do it, and what you need."

50

T he arraignment of Khalid al-Hassan for the murder of US Border Patrol Officer Margaret Walsh was held at 10 A.M. in Courtroom 3-B of the Evo A. DeConcini Federal Courthouse before US District Court Judge the Honorable Wendy R. Gorman. The midmorning hearing gave plenty of time for US and international news agencies to set up their satellite-feed trucks. The murder of the border patrol agent was, frankly, not very interesting to most of the press outside Southern Arizona or conservative outlets like Fox News. But since the defendant was also suspected of leading the most successful terrorist attack against the US homeland since 9/11, CNN, MSNBC, ABC, CBS, NBC, BBC, DW, AFP, RT, NHK and CCTV were joining their local and regional brethren on the sidewalk outside the courthouse.

The timing of the arraignment had allowed most of the press to gather after rush hour, but their trucks parked along Broadway Blvd., a major thoroughfare into downtown Tucson from the Interstate, had already caused traffic backups and harsh words. The US Marshals Service, which provides security for US District Courthouses, had already swept the satellite trucks for bombs and weapons with the

FBI's assistance. FBI snipers had also taken up positions on the court-house roof and the roofs of adjacent buildings in case any al-Hassan sympathizers tried to rush the courthouse and rescue al-Hassan. Or for that matter, try to kill him.

Since his flight from Cuba by way of Texas, Khalid had been ensconced in a cell in the courthouse's basement lockup, the only pris-oner so fortunate, the rest having been moved to the Pima County Jail. The courthouse was fairly new and the lockup had none of the prison funk of the old brig in Corpus Christi. This morning Khalid had already enjoyed a shower and a change of clothes, although the latter was just another orange jumpsuit. Khalid had always thought of himself as a snappy dresser, so the jumpsuit was just another indignity that gnawed at him.

The courtroom, located on the six-story building's third floor, was already almost full with press when Eric arrived with Caitlin that morning around 9:30. He was wearing a dark suit, white shirt, and dark tie, she a somber blue dress that reached to her knees and opened just below her neck. Eric walked her to the front of the observer section of the courtroom, a row of blond, wooden benches, and sat beside her in the front row when the bailiff, knowing who Eric was, and suspecting who Caitlin was, asked a reporter and a sketch artist to give up their seats. Court staff busied themselves around the judge's raised bench, carrying file folders, glasses of water, and the general accoutrements needed for a day in court. Normally, Khalid would already have appeared before a magistrate for his initial appear-ance, but the terrorism investigation took temporary priority, and in this case the US Government broadly interpreted the "without unnec-essary delay" clause of Title II Rule 5 of the *Federal Rules of Criminal Procedure*.

A few minutes before 10 A.M. a door next to the bench opened and into the courtroom shuffled Khalid al-Hassan, escorted by five deputy US marshals. This was the first time Caitlin had seen him in person, and even after having seen dozens of online, TV, and newspaper images, she was startled by his sudden reality. Eric turned to look at her, and saw her face blanch then her cheeks grow pink with suppressed rage. Caitlin looked at him, knowing what he was think-ing, and mouthed, "I'm all right," as Khalid took his seat at the defen-dants table just a few feet away. Perhaps he could feel her stare, because he turned to look behind him and locked eyes with her. *How could he know who I am?* Caitlin wondered. Then she realized he did not know, he was frozen by the anger in her eyes, which he saw nowhere else in the room.

After a few seconds Caitlin broke her stare with Khalid and turned toward a second door behind the bench where Judge Gorman emerged from her chambers. The bailiff called, "All rise," paused slightly and continued, "The US District Court for the State of Arizona is now in session, the Honorable Wendy Gorman, presiding."

The judge took her seat and the rest of the court joined her. She looked down at her papers for a moment then, peering over her glasses, asked, "Counsel?"

Two men at opposite tables stood. "Richard C. Worth, your honor, appearing for the United States," the first man said.

"Jonathan Barkhausen, your honor, appearing for the accused," the second man quickly added.

"Very good. Bailiff, would you read the charges to the defendant?" the judge asked.

The bailiff rose. "That on the twenty-fourth of July, two thousand eighteen, the defendant did commit the premeditated murder of United State Border Patrol Agent Margaret Walsh in the city of Nogales, the county of Santa Cruz, the state of Arizona, and that this murder of a United States officer during the performance of her offi-cial duties did violate Title eighteen Section eleven fourteen of the United States Code 'Protection of Officers and Employees of the United States', as amended in two thousand two, which states that 'whoever kills or attempts to kill any officer or employee of the United States or of any agency in any branch of the United States Government—including any member of the uniformed services—while such an officer or employee is engaged in or on account of the performance of official duties, or any person assisting such an officer or employee in the performance of such duties or on account of that assistance, shall be punished in the case of murder under Section eleven eleven.

"United States Code Title eighteen Section eleven eleven, as amended in two thousand three, states, 'Whoever is guilty of murder in the first degree shall be punished by death or by imprisonment for life.'" The bailiff sat down.

The judge had been watching the defendant, who was standing expressionless, although Caitlin liked to think he shuddered slightly at the word "death." Now the judge addressed him, "Defense has already waived the reading of the affidavit of one Capitan José-Antonio Garcia of the Municipal Police, Nogales, Sonora, Mexico, describing the capture of Mr. al-Hassan in Mexico and the retrieval of certain evidence associated with the murder. Mr. al-Hassan, do you under-stand the charges against you and the penalty if convicted?" When Khalid remained silent, the judge looked to his public defender. "Mr. Barkhausen, does your client understand the chargers against him and the penalty if convicted?"

"He does, your honor."

"Then why is he not addressing the court? Is his hearing damaged?"

"No, your honor."

"Mr. al-Hassan, I will ask you again. Do you understand the charges against you and the penalty if convicted? You need to answer the court. The court is more than me. I am just a representative of the US Government."

Khalid's lawyer leaned over to him and whispered in his ear and, barely audible, Khalid finally muttered, "Yes."

"That was a yes, Mr. Barkhausen?" the judge asked.

"Yes, your honor."

"All right. Mr. Worth, the government's position on bail, as if I didn't have a suspicion what that might be."

The assistant district attorney smiled and said, "Your honor, Khalid al-Hassan is a significant flight risk. He has no known family or connections in the United States, his only brother is in Chechnya in the Russian Federation, and he entered and left this country illegally multiple times. The government requests that Mr. al-Hassan be held in detention, either under the custody of US marshals or under Department of Defense jurisdiction. I would request that further discussion of the latter be outside of open court."

The judge nodded. "Mr. Barkhausen?"

"Your honor, we strongly object to housing Mr. al-Hassan anywhere other than the US federal prison system and associated pretrial detention facilities. Any other site, particularly outside the Continental US, would be deleterious to the preparation of my client's defense."

"You don't like to travel to sunny Caribbean islands, Mr. Barkhausen?" That caused light laughter in the court. "OK, I don't blame you. Khalid al-Hassan will remain in the custody of the US Marshals Service pending a hearing where the United States Government will provide cause for holding him at another location. This court is dismissed." The judge rose and the rest of the room joined her at the bailiff's order.

"So that's it?" Caitlin asked Eric as they stood watching the judge, and then the defendant, leave the courtroom. They remained in place as the press rushed to report their stories.

"It is for now. This was just an initial appearance, a procedural thing. He enters a plea during the preliminary hearing," Eric answered, his arm around her chastely.

"When will that be?"

"Not scheduled yet. Normally, they would schedule that today, but I think the intelligence agencies aren't done with him yet and they want him back down in Gitmo."

"So, what was the purpose of today?"

Eric paused, smiling weakly. "This was what we call a 'dog and pony show.' It was a way for the government to look like it's doing something without actually doing something."

They were walking out now, slowly shuffling at the back of a line of press, their feet sliding on the polished floor. "Why aren't they doing something?" Caitlin asked, less emotionally than Eric expected.

"I suspect there are still major elements of the terrorism investigation they're still sorting out, and they don't want him out of pocket for long."

Caitlin thought about that. As they reached the stairs to descend to the lobby, she said, "I don't have a problem with that. As long as he does end up being prosecuted for Molly's murder."

"He will be, he will," Eric replied and took her hand.

51

Russia is a huge country, spanning 11 time zones over its 5,000 mile east-west expanse. Crossing that chunk of Eurasia were a couple, Georgi and Katya Volkov, who had just started a journey in St. Petersburg, in Russia's far west, that would take them to Svobodny, in Russia's far east. The drive would need perhaps 10 days to cover the distance, assuming no extended stops, bad weather, or accidents. Stops the couple could control, but bad weather was a given in January and accidents highly possible, given weather, poor roads, and vodka. An accident could lead to unnecessary contact with the authorities, which the couple wanted to avoid at all cost since they were CIA agents operating under non-official cover. Georgi and Katya had many skills: covert surveillance, covert entry, recruiting sources. Indeed, Georgi was the man who had entered Vasily's apartment twice and Katya was the woman who had delayed Vasily in the club. But their most important skill was their success in blending in and not attracting attention.

At the moment the Volkovs were driving towards Stavropol. It would have been much faster to fly or take the train, but buying tickets leaves traces for authorities to follow, so they were cruising down a secondary highway north of Smolensk in a *bukhanka*, or "loaf of bread," the venerable UAZ-452 4-wheel-drive van that the Ulyanovsk Automotive Plant has manufactured since 1965. Simple, rugged and capable of burning low-octane gasoline, the bukhanka gave the couple plenty of room to transport the handmade wooden toys they carried in the rear cargo compartment and still have space for an impromptu kitchen and sleeping area behind the front seats. The partition between the cargo compartment and the passenger compartment was a sheet of steel, painted olive-drab like the rest of the vehicle. This particular bukhanka had an extra olive-drab layer that provided a secret compartment of a few inches to conceal some items the Volkovs might need but would not want discovered during a casual search of the vehicle.

The bukhanka swayed down the 2-lane highway. The road surface was largely clear of snow, but the drifts on either side were a few feet high, and there were spots where the snow had been blown onto the surface of the road. These were not much of a problem for the Volkovs, since one benefit of driving the bukhanka was that they were not very fast, and no one expected them to set the pace on the highway. But the cars that passed them at high speed were a hazard, particularly when they seemed to ignore oncoming traffic, which, thankfully, was sparse. Georgi was driving, Katya dozing in the passenger seat. The most direct route from their home in St. Petersburg to Stavropol would have lead them through Moscow, but they were happy to take the longer, western route to avoid the Russian capital and the high density of traffic, police, and counterintelligence agents there.

After a few more hours, the bukhanka pulled into the yard of a small house outside of Smolensk, where the couple would stay for the night. The owner was a friend of a friend and rented a spare room to truck drivers and other travelers to earn extra income. Georgi stepped out and stretched, Katya joining him in the motion. Georgi walked around to the double doors on the right side of the van that opened to the passenger compartment behind the front seats and picked up two small bags, which he carried to the front door, Katya following close behind. He knocked and after a moment the door opened and a tall, unshaven man in a stretched pullover sweater greeted the Volkovs.

Inside, the man led them to the kitchen, where the obligatory shot of vodka was poured and drunk. After a few moments of small talk, he led the couple to their room and bid them good night. The next morning they shared a breakfast of farm cheese, black bread, and bad coffee with their host and then started on their way again. Two more days and they would arrive in Stavropol.

The Stavropol region gave to the Soviet Union General Secretary Yuri Andropov, his successor, Mikhail Gorbachev, and their antagonist, dissident Alexander Solzhenitsyn, but it was the oil and gas reserves below the surface that had powered the nation's development in war and peace. Those depleted gas wells now provided the massive volume needed to store more than a trillion cubic feet of gas produced in the still-productive fields in Siberia and the Caspian Sea. The storage wells spanned hundreds of square miles, and the Volkovs had no hope of reconnoitering the whole area, just as the Special Warfare teams had no chance of damaging it all; hence, their instructions to focus on a central location that could disable the pipeline network, stranding the gas in the ground.

Like many Russian drivers, the Volkovs had a small digital video camera mounted on the dashboard of the car that recorded 4K video onto an SD card. The ostensible purpose in most Russian vehicles was to capture the malfeasance of other drivers when an accident occurred, with the unintended benefit of providing hours of amusement to viewers of YouTube. In the Volkovs' case, they had two cameras on the dashboard, along with one in each of the side windows and two in the rear windows of the cargo compartment. The data would be encrypted on Katya's laptop, along with metadata containing the time, date, and GPS location in such a way that a casual user or even a competent intelligence agency would see only blank sectors on the SD cards in between pictures of the Volkovs with their wares at various craft fairs.

After a few highway passes, the Volkovs stopped at a pullout a mile from their target. Katya stepped out, walked back to the double doors on the passenger side, and pulled a small black box from under one of the seats. She opened the box, withdrew the contents, and turned to Georgi. "Do you think we're clear?" she asked.

"I think we are. I didn't see any fresh tire tracks at the gate. Let's go with it."

Katya nodded and switched on the UAV. While it wasn't invisible, it was considerably quieter than a typical consumer UAV, thanks to the shape and size of its propellers and their slower speed. It also had four, small, 4K cameras. The UAV rose above the treetops and started its path toward the target.

Georgi remained in the van, viewing a low-resolution feed on his cell phone as the UAV flew over the fir trees and then into a clearing containing a series of low buildings with large pipes entering and leaving. He watched as it flew over each building, then as the UAV flew in between them, perhaps six feet off the ground, to show what it would look like to a human observer. Georgi relaxed as he saw there were no people on the site but then tensed as he noticed surveillance cameras pointing from the buildings. His mind raced with questions: *Where is the guard station? Is anyone watching the cameras?* He hadn't seen any cameras facing the road.

When he told Katya what he had seen, she wasn't surprised, but she also started to think about what their alibi would be and how they would explain the UAV if Gazprom security or the militsiya accosted them. But even after the 20 minutes it took for the UAV to complete the mission and return, they had seen only a few farm vehicles pass by, and as Katya withdrew the SD cards from the cameras and returned the UAV to its box and the box to its resting place under the seat, they were able to relax.

Georgi looked through the windshield and in his mirrors at the highway and saw no traffic, so he lifted a small box from between the bukhanka's front seats and stepped from the vehicle. Across the road from the pullout, he strapped a small camera to a tree as unobtrusively as possible. The camera would watch the traffic patterns on the road and the pullout, but he would have to come back in a few weeks to retrieve it and its data. He walked back across the highway, climbed into the bukhanka, and started the engine with a clatter and a puff of blue smoke from the exhaust. They pulled back onto the highway and started their way north toward Tyumen.

52

Less than two weeks after their meeting with Farmer's team, USSOCOM received the initial reconnaissance that the Volkovs had developed near Stavropol and Tyumen and that another CIA asset had developed near Svobodny. The SD cards arrived in Washington via diplomatic pouch following a series of dead-drops by the reconnoiterers and pickups by CIA couriers. Farmer's team reviewed the raw video feeds and provided SOCOM with highlights of the targets, as well as the entire video for their use.

After a week the team returned to SOCOM to discuss the mission. This time, as word of the mission and its risks had diffused up the chain of command, the entire SOCOM senior leadership attended, including the commanding general, the deputy commander, and the vice commander, along with the senior enlisted leader, a command sergeant major. Before the meeting the commanding general met privately with Farmer. "I confirmed with my chain of command that, subject to final approval by the president, this mission is going forward. But I am very uncomfortable with the parameters. The risk of exposure is enormous and the repercussions of having one of my teams captured or killed on Russian soil are unacceptable," the general stated emphatically. "I argued this should be operationally back in CIA's tent."

"I understand your concern, General, but we simply don't have enough trained operatives to accomplish the president's objectives," Farmer replied.

"Objectives you people put in his head," the general spat. The general had seen more than his share of combat over nearly 40 years in uniform, and his eyes burned warrior-hot at Farmer.

"Well, actually, it's my understanding that the director and SECDEF together thought this up," Farmer replied evenly.

"Sure, sure, and I will salute and say, 'yes, sir,' but I'm not happy about the risk to benefit ratio, and I'll do everything in my power to mitigate it."

"Have you already been briefed on the latest CONOPS for this mission?" Farmer asked, referring to the Concept of Operations, or how SOCOM capabilities would be used to accomplish the mission's goals.

"No."

"Well, sir, neither have I. I suggest we go in and hear what they have to say."

The general stared at Farmer, then turned on his heels and walked into the SCIF.

THE BRIEFER WAS a SEAL lieutenant commander who, over the last ten years, had served with teams in Iraq, Afghanistan, and Africa. Like many SEALs he was not very tall but rather compact and muscular and, in any kind of fight, full of confidence out of all proportion to his physical stature. He began at a lectern, a laser pointer in his hand, before a large video display which showed the "Tip of the Spear" emblem of USSOCOM until it was replaced with a map of Russia with the three target locations highlighted, empty spaces around the perimeter of the slide filled with classification markings.

"We have been working these target missions with four considerations in mind," he began. "The first three are the ones we always have: getting in, killing the target; and getting out. We added a fourth one, which is, 'How do we support the cover story that well-trained but non-state terrorists are killing the targets, rather than steely-eyed, US Government snake eaters like us?'"

That caused general laughter in the room and even a tense smile from the general.

"All humor aside, infiltrating the interior of the Russian Federation in three locations is going to be very challenging. We can't HALO in," the briefer said, referring to the high-altitude/low-opening parachute technique. "Too much air defense. We aren't going to fly in over hundreds of kilometers at low altitude in helos or fixed wing, and each location is way too far from water to come in over the beach. And we absolutely, positively, need to have these strikes executed at the same time, preferably down to minutes, so there is no time for security to alert other Gazprom sites. So we're going to have to rely on our Agency friends to smuggle us in so the teams can emplace their munitions at more or less the same time—just a few hours, at most— before the targets go kinetic. Details to be worked out. That, Mr. Farmer, is going to be your problem as well as our problem."

Farmer nodded. "We have some ideas."

"Care to elaborate?"

"Not at this time."

The briefer continued with a new chart, "In terms of ordnance or munitions, we considered the location of cover and hardness of the respective targets. For the two sites that are operational, that is, that have gas flowing through them under pressure, we like the idea of using UAVs with EFPs like those used on the Eight-twenty attacks, in keeping with the cover story, et cetera. Remember the fourth consideration. One question is can we get them accurate enough just with GPS to target a pipe that's only a meter or so wide. The CONOPS doesn't have us standing around waiting for this thing to go up. We want to be far away from the big boom, and I mean past-the-roadblocks far away. Hundreds of kilometers, preferably out of the country." He let that sink in.

The USSOCOM commander was rubbing his chin with concern, but when he did not comment, the briefer continued, "So we need to deploy them in a camouflaged container, we call it a "duck blind," that we can leave at the edge of the cover and which will be programmed to open and deploy the UAVs at the right time." He flipped to a slide that showed the "duck blind" concept. "Also, we want them all to detonate at the same time, to within a hundred milliseconds of each other, so that an incidental explosion on one line doesn't blow the others off target."

He flipped to another slide. "Natural gas, it's mostly methane at these sites, is flammable or explosive at a concentration by volume of between five and fifteen percent in air. A couple of us went out to Eglin … That's Eglin Air Force Base, on the Gulf Coast of Florida for those of you who might not know …" He paused while laughter again rang out. It was a safe bet everyone in the room knew exactly where Eglin Air Force Base was. "… and did a few tests with EFPs on gas cylinders, you know, like you'd use for a barbecue, as proxies for the pipeline. It was hit or miss whether the venting gas detonated. The SOCOM science geeks told us that it really depends on what's happening at the interface between the venting gas, which carries off a lot of heat, and the atmosphere. What we'd really like is rapid venting of all the lines and then detonate the cloud of gas, making a thermobaric weapon out of it. So we'll have one UAV that drops flares at a to-be-determined distance—the SOCOM science geeks are going to help us with that, too—and hopefully, that'll blow the whole thing at once. Make a nice, big, boom."

"I never want to hear 'hopefully' in a briefing," growled the deputy commander, a SEAL vice admiral.

"I understand, sir. My point was that we're proposing a CONOPS that still requires some refinement."

"Fair enough." The deputy looked at his boss, who nodded. "Proceed."

"Yes, sir. We propose to use the same tactics at Tyumen, albeit on a smaller scale."

"How many UAVs are we talking about?" one of Farmer's team asked.

"Twenty-five for Stavropol, Thirteen for Tyumen."

"And we are providing them?" the CIA man asked.

"That was the understanding."

The CIA team looked at each other and Farmer shrugged. "Subject to the outcome of this meeting, we'll start sourcing the same components the Eight-twenty team used."

"Where are you going to have them delivered?" one of the Deltas asked.

"That's a good question. I really don't think we have time to set up a front in Chechnya or Syria, and I really don't want that complication. We'll just make sure there are no serial numbers or anything recognizable that would allow the FSB to trace them anywhere other than back to China. We want them to find UAV parts. That all fits the cover."

"What about the EFPs?" the Delta asked.

"We have an inventory we can use, which I think some of you SOCOM guys seized in Basra a few years ago. We might modify them slightly for greater effect against the pipe, that is, so they'll make a bigger hole. Again, we'll obliterate the markings. At best all they'll trace back to is Iran." The room seemed satisfied.

The briefer took a drink of water and flipped up his next chart. "As requested, we have targeted these fractioning towers using demolition charges to collapse the towers at the base. We'll position the demo charges here"—he used the laser pointer to identify specific locations —"so they'll collapse transversely and maximize collateral damage on the site, this piping, these valves, this machinery, et cetera. Let gravity do the work. Now that means we actually have to infiltrate the site. The recon team got us imagery that suggests there are regular security patrols, and most of the site is well lighted, with construction going on twenty-four seven. Fortunately, since these towers are the largest single components on the site and were installed first, the area of the site where they are is not as well-lit. We plan to infil from this cover here"—he pointed again—"which makes it about five hundred meters on open ground to get to the first tower."

"How much C-four is that going to take? That steel must be awfully thick," the deputy commander commented.

"You're right, sir, a hundred pounds of C-four on that wall would barely dent it. Courtesy of the Agency, we have the construction drawings and details of the mounting at ground level. Samson?" He looked to a SEAL lieutenant, who stood and addressed the admiral.

"Sir, the base has to be designed to withstand the massive compression load of all that weight, about four hundred tons fully assembled, but still be able to absorb expansion and contraction without cracking the concrete foundation. There are bolts and fasteners down there that we'll cut with cutting charges, first on one side, the side we want it to fall, the direction we want it to fall, and then, after a delay to give the structure time to start sagging that way, we'll cut the other side to let it topple." The SEAL paused, waiting for questions.

"You can time it that closely on this type of detonation? Won't you blow the fuse wire for the others with the first charges that close?" the deputy commander asked.

"Wireless, sir."

"What does that do to our deniability if pieces of those fuses are recovered?"

The lieutenant paused. There was some discussion around the room until, finally, a SEAL commander stood and said, "Sir, these fuses are designed to look like cell phones so if they're recovered in pieces or intact, they'll look like standard jihadi kit. The Russians would have to hack deep into the phone. A casual hack will look just like a regular cell phone, complete with a few Chechen and Syrian phone numbers."

The deputy commander smiled. "I like it. Where will you stage? That road looks awfully close, and if there's construction activity twenty-four seven, there'll be traffic on that road."

"Sir, we have a location over here, this distant corner, where we can exit our transportation and hump to the opposite side through cover to this location closest to the towers," the briefer said, highlighting each location with a swirl from his laser pointer. "The team that kills this target won't have to hump the weight the other teams will.

"Transport?"

"TBD from the CIA, sir."

"That's a big TBD. Your thoughts, Mr. Farmer?"

"We have some ideas, sir, but nothing I can commit to at this time. I can assure you that we'll get your men to and from the targets with the highest possible probability of success," Farmer replied.

The deputy commander harrumphed but said nothing. SOCOM worked with the CIA all the time, but they hated relying on any agency outside their command for something as critical as infiltration and exfiltration. Navy submarines and Air Force and Army Special Operations helicopter squadrons normally fulfilled those roles, but not here.

FOR THE NEXT hour there was give and take among the special operators about the size of each team, their composition, training timelines, etc. The commanding general had left the room for most of that time and returned just as they were finishing, hopefully to give his blessing. "Gentlemen," he began. There were two CIA women in the room, but the Special Warfare community is so male heavy that he could almost always say that with impunity. "I think you have a reasonable plan, subject to how the CIA comes through on the infil and exfil plans ..." He looked at Farmer. "... and the rest of their deliverables. I need to brief the chairman tomorrow on our progress." He was referring to the chairman of the Joint Chiefs of Staff, the nation's most senior military officer. "What's your timeline? I know the president wanted this done yesterday."

The O-6s—Navy captains and Army colonels—looked at each other and nodded and a Delta colonel stood. "Sir, we're looking at a four-week training timeline just for the targets themselves, simulated layouts, et cetera. We don't have an infil or exfil plan from the CIA yet, and we're going to want two to three weeks to train on that. On top of that, the CIA's telling us we're six to eight weeks out on having fully programmed UAVs."

Several of the military in the room glanced at the CIA contingent without judgment, but without much affection either.

"I know the National Command Authority wants this done ASAP, but we have to be two hundred percent ready for this one." He paused but no one spoke. "I think realistically we're looking at ten to twelve weeks, best case. That's assuming the CIA's able to keep to their schedule, everything they build is tested and works, and we can build, test, and verify the duck blind. That puts us ..." he paused again, "... ready to execute to go in-country around mid- to late April."

One SEAL whispered to another, "Hit 'em on May Day, the drunkest day in Russia."

"And that's sayin' something," the other replied.

The commanding general looked around the room and said, "I don't know if I'll get pushback from the chairman, but that's the message I'll give him. In the meantime, do whatever you can to make this mission a success. I want all of you back here when I pin on the non-existent medals."

The room laughed and rose as one as the general left his seat.

FARMER MADE a beeline to catch the general as he made his way to the door with his staff. "General, if I could have a word with you in private."

The general looked at him quizzically but nodded, asking, "Subject?"

"There's an additional element to this mission I think we should consider," Farmer replied as they passed through the doors and into a corner where they could talk.

53

The general's briefing with the chairman of the Joint Chiefs of Staff was unremarkable. The chairman sympathized with the practical limitations of executing such a complex and high-risk plan, but he knew the president would be unhappy with what he and his advisors would perceive as glacially slow retaliation. He warned the general to expect pressure from the White House.

The chairman and Secretary Martin joined the director of national intelligence and CIA Director Haller to brief the president and his closest advisors. Given the massive damage a leak would cause, the broader national security and diplomatic team had been kept "out of the loop" and, hopefully, would remain so. Even the president, given to intemperate musings on social and broadcast media, understood the stakes: best case, universal condemnation and ridicule; worst case, hot war. Since anyone who worked in Washington understood the probability of keeping a secret is inversely proportional to how long it is kept and how many have to keep it, that alone compelled the decision-makers to favor the fastest possible execution of the plan.

The black Suburban carrying the secretary and the chairman pulled into the heavily guarded driveway between the White House and the Eisenhower Old Executive Office Building, and the two men and their aides stepped out and strode into the White House under a cold, gray sky. A Secret Service agent escorted them down a hallway to an elevator that would take them to the basement and the Situation Room. The men were startled when they entered and the president was already seated. "I'm sorry, Mr. President, are we late?" the secretary asked.

"No, no, I just thought I'd come down a little early. The CIA is telling me about these UAVs they're making, the copies of the ones from California, that we're going to use in Russia."

The chairman and the secretary relaxed, seeing that the president was in a good mood, the CIA director apparently breaking the ice. "Yes, sir," the secretary responded, and they took their places at the table.

"So where are we on this thing?" the president asked.

The secretary looked to the chairman, who began, "Mr. President, SOCOM and the CIA have developed what the SOCOM leadership and we consider to be a workable plan for executing covert retaliation against the Russian Federation. They have developed robust targeting packages for each of three target sites: the first one is a gas storage facility near Stavropol. That's in the North Caucasus, east of the Sea of Azov and west of the Caspian Sea,"

"Azov, that's where there was that trouble between the Ukrainians and Russians?" the president interjected.

"Yes, sir. The second location is a gas compressor station near Tyumen, in central Russia north of Kazakhstan. And the third is a gas processing station in eastern Russia near Svobodny, just north of the Chinese border. SOCOM and the CIA are working on all of the details. Infiltration is a primary issue since we cannot, practically, introduce special operators into these parts of Russia using our usual techniques —off a submarine or flown in with helicopters,"

"Too far?" the president volunteered, his arms crossed over his chest.

"Yes, sir. We don't want our soldiers hiking through three hundred miles of Russian territory with their weapons and backpacks."

"And we don't have any stealth aircraft that can carry them?"

"No, sir, we have no operational, stealth, fixed-wing aircraft that can carry personnel and gear, and our helos have only a very limited, low-observable or stealth component. They don't have the range and would likely be picked up, either on Russian air-defense radar or seen or heard by ordinary citizens."

"So how are you going to get them in?" the president asked.

The chairman looked in the direction of the intelligence professionals, "The CIA is going to help us with that."

The president turned in their direction and asked, "How are you getting them in?"

"Mr. President, at this time we don't have all of the details," Haller began. "But we have some assets in the area we can use for smuggling people and materials around the country. We'll likely bring them in through a third country and then transport them by road."

"By road?" The president's eyes widened.

"That seems to be the best technique."

The president seemed satisfied. "Well, keep me posted. When are we going to do this?"

The chairman looked at the president and said, "Mr. President, our teams need ten to twelve weeks to make this all work. That puts the operation around the beginning of May,"

If the chairman had been expecting a volcanic reaction, he did not get it. The president merely rose from his seat and said, "Thank you,"

The meeting was over.

AS THEY WALKED BACK toward their waiting SUV, Martin turned to the chairman and said, "You didn't include that additional element the CIA suggested. Are we going to request authorization?"

The chairman looked straight ahead, "I'm not sure how I feel about it. I think it works, but I don't like the idea."

"I know what you mean. But one man? And he has a lot to answer for." The two walked pensively out of the building and into the back seats of the Suburban.

54

The winter rains that swept in from California turned Tucson gray and misty, a scene that disappointed visitors but thrilled locals, for they knew it promised benefits both visible and invisible: spring wildflowers and a higher water table. By now Caitlin had spent enough time in the Sonoran Desert to prize water like the Sonorans on both sides of the border, so as Eric drove them south on I-17, she rolled down the window and, braving the cool roar, held her arm in the slipstream and felt the rain. Eric smiled, watching her, not minding the draft or the noise. Every so often the windshield wipers would sweep an extra splash of water over the A pillar of the car onto Caitlin's arm and inside onto her shoulder and the seat, but she didn't complain nor did Eric when he received the occasional ricochet. The highway gently climbed as they passed Tubac and the rain became heavier. Caitlin closed the window and used her fleece to dry her arm and hand. She turned to Eric and smiled, asking, "How much farther?"

"Maybe twenty miles," he replied, turning to her as he did. "Sure you want to go?"

"Yes. Definitely. It's part of closure." Eric nodded and turned his attention back to the road.

Not long afterward the car turned onto West International Drive, just on the north side of the border fence and, a street later, to the house. Eric was driving slowly, more slowly than the street required, but he did not know how she would react to seeing the site of her sister's death. He made one more turn and then there it was. The yellow police tape long gone, the only color on the brown-buff scene was a vase of drying flowers and a deflated balloon placed by a Border Patrol colleague on the walkway leading to the front door. It was more than six months since the Nogales Fire Department had washed the blood from the cracked concrete.

Caitlin softly sucked in her breath when she saw the house, then slowly, silently exhaled. She looked at Eric as they parked and she nodded, her lips tight. Eric exited the car and walked around to her door, opened it, and helped her out. Caitlin seemed slightly unsteady, but she smoothed the front of her dress and stood with her back straight, already starting to walk in front of him to the spot where the flowers were placed.

As she stepped from the street onto the sandy, sparse lawn, she turned slightly and asked him softly, pointing at the flowers, "Is that where she was?"

"Yes."

"What part of her was there? I want to visualize how she was lying."

Eric winced. He really did not want to go into that much detail, although Caitlin had already seen the worst when identifying the body of her sister in the Santa Cruz County Morgue. "That's about where her shoulder blades were. She was lying almost straight down the sidewalk."

"Did she look peaceful?"

With anyone but Caitlin he would have laughed sarcastically and said, "Of course not, she was shot in the face," but he lied and simply said, "Yes." In addition to the blood and the entrance wound, he could not forget the expression on Molly's face. Pain from the first few shots into her vest? Surprise?

Caitlin turned to him and smiled weakly, "I know you're lying. But

I understand." Eric relaxed a little, and she moved right to the vase and sat, yoga style, on the wet pavement. She touched the spot where her sister had last breathed, bent over it, and silently sobbed. Eric's eyes welled with tears too, and he did not know whether to touch her or leave her alone. He elected to leave her to her grief just a little longer. After a minute Caitlin lifted her hand and moved her upper body away from the spot as if her hand were now very heavy and she needed all of her strength to lift it. Eric took that as a cue to help her, and he gently touched her shoulders then slipped his hands under her arms to help her to her feet. She did not resist, and when she was standing, she took a deep breath, paused, then turned away from the house and walked with him back to the car.

FOUR HUNDRED MILES to the northeast it was cloudy but not yet raining at the White Sands Missile Range, 3,200 square miles of high desert extending north from above El Paso a hundred miles up the Tularosa Valley. A contingent of CIA technical personnel operating under the cover of the US Army Aberdeen Proving Ground were testing the latest software load on one of the few UAVs they had to work with. The agency was still waiting for delivery of the large purchase they had elected to make using front companies in Moldova.

In their isolated corner of the range, the CIA personnel had set up targets of the size and shape the SOCOM teams would encounter and were evaluating the accuracy with which the UAVs could guide themselves to a vulnerable location. As part of their survey of the sites in Russia, the Volkovs and the other CIA asset had used UAVs with GPS guidance. The GPS location was recorded with the imagery, and the agency had used that data, compared with overhead imagery, to establish there was no GPS "spoofing" or other interference that would, at least in theory, prevent the UAVs from being guided to their targets.

The CIA team was aware that Russian reconnaissance satellites likely watched White Sands as they made their passes over New Mexico, home to US nuclear-weapons research at the Los Alamos and

Sandia National Labs, so they had painted the targets to blend with the background to make them less likely to be detected by high-flying cameras but still be visible to their much closer UAV cameras. And, to prevent Russian radar-surveillance satellites from seeing them, the targets were made from heavy cardboard rather than metal.

When Khalid's team had planned the Eight-twenty attacks, with whatever help was provided by Russian intelligence, they had been faced with a problem: how do you position a UAV carrying an explosive payload over a target that is a meter wide when the UAV's GPS was only accurate to five or ten meters? All evidence, including Khalid's own statements, and the fact that there were more UAVs used than terrorists to steer them, indicated that the UAVs used in the Eight-twenty attacks had flown autonomously. Evidence recovered at the Phoenix warehouse, and fragments recovered at the substations, suggested that the standard GPS receivers on the UAVs had been replaced with a more sophisticated unit that exploited an additional GPS satellite signal to improve their positional accuracy to perhaps a third of a meter. The UAVs flying at White Sands included the more sophisticated GPS receivers and, so far, most of the trial flights had resulted in a UAV hovering over a "lethal" spot on the target.

55

Georgi Volkov stepped out of his dented Lada sedan in front of a wide, wooden double door set into a tall, masonry wall. Dark green paint peeled from the door to complement the dirty yellow paint shedding from the stucco nearby. He knocked on a human-sized door set into one of the larger doors, and after a few moments it opened wide enough for a large, unshaven man to inspect the visitor and then open the door to admit him into a yard filled with old cars and trucks in various states of disassembly. Off to one side of the yard was a tank trailer, the front of which had been neatly cut from the rest of the trailer with an oxy-acetylene torch and set on the ground. Another man was grinding the cut edges smooth, the sparks flying from his grinding wheel scaring a mangy dog who repeatedly slinked up to the man, then fled panicked when the sparks came his way. Georgi watched this sequence occur half a dozen times as he followed the man closer to the trailer, slowly shaking his head at the dog's stupidity.

"Is this what you want?" the man who had answered the door asked, pointing through the opening into the inside of the trailer.

"Let me see," Georgi replied, climbing the short ladder leaning against the opening and crawling inside. "Torch?" he asked, and he was handed a flashlight.

Georgi bent low and walked back along the tank's floor. Midway down the tank was a broad steel cylinder welded to the top and bottom of the tank, and he had to twist around it to continue his journey. A pipe ran from the side of the cylinder facing the rear of the trailer, ending in the back wall. Along the floor about every seven feet were low bulkheads welded to the bottom with flat plates welded between, and at many locations large steel hooks were welded to the sides. Georgi turned and walked back the length of the trailer toward the opening and climbed down. "Yes, it looks good. How will you seal the door?"

The man looked over to the wall of the tank where the end had been cut off. "We will weld on a flange and install a gasket. The handle that latches it will look like a grab-handle. We will put one on the hinge side so it does not look out of place."

"Power?"

"We will tap into the lighting cable underneath and run it into the tank."

"Air?"

"Same thing. We will tap the brake line and bleed in air through a filter. It won't smell great but it will do what is needed. We can fit a few cylinders underneath in case the tractor needs to be separated." The man had worked with many smugglers over the years, and he never said more than he needed to about another man's business.

"What about the tractor?"

"We have one over there that will work. I will go over the engine and transmission to make sure you will not have any problems."

Georgi looked around the cluttered yard. "I think this will be satisfactory. Now, can you make two more?"

56

The city of Grozny rests in a broad plain at the foot of the northern Caucasus mountains where the border between Georgia and the Chechen Republic runs through mountain peaks that rise more than 16,000 feet above sea level. To the east and south, the restive Republic of Dagestan continues to the Caspian Sea, while to the west lie the sliver republics of Ingushetia and North Ossetia, and more fragments of the former Soviet Union until Russia-proper resumes as the land reaches toward Sochi and the Black Sea.

The sixth day of March was a new moon, and the sky over the mountains was clear and star-filled but devoid of moonlight, the air cold but above freezing. In a clearing in the foothills above Grozny, a noisy shadow momentarily blocked the stars as an unmarked Russian Mi-8 helicopter dropped into the field, disgorged its black-clad passengers, and rose back into the sky, flying to a small airfield outside the city to refuel. The six men who had crouched on the ground as the helo ascended now ran to the tree line and stopped ten yards in, listening for any sound besides the now retreating "putt-putt-putt" of their transportation. After five minutes of silence, they started on their path down the hill through the trees.

The men made their way silently through the forest, constantly turning to their sides, searching for any signs of movement other than their own. Every five or ten minutes the leader would raise his arm and the men stop as one, squatting in place and listening. After a moment or two the leader would rise, and the men would continue soundlessly on their way. They repeated the cycle a dozen times before they reached the edge of a clearing where they paused and spoke their first words since jumping from the cabin of the helicopter.

"*Tsel v pole zreniya,*" the leader spoke into his radio softly. "Target is in sight." The man at the rear of the formation clicked his radio twice in confirmation.

As the group arrayed itself at the edge of the woods, the leader scanned the target with a small pair of binoculars in front of his night-vision goggles. He saw two men with automatic weapons on their side of the target, both apparently dozing. The range was no more than 50 yards, an easy shot. The men looked at their leader, and he signaled with both hands for two men to move through the woods around the side of the target and assess the conditions there. They immediately started moving in that direction, one on each side of the clearing.

After a few minutes the men heard, "*Odin plyus odin.*" One plus one: the same configuration of guards as the rear of the target.

"*Kaznit' za tridtstat', moy znak,*" the leader broadcast. "Execute in thirty, my mark."

One man on each side of the target aimed his rifle at one of the dozing guards, as the two in front were doing unseen. Their breathing slowed, fingers lightly pressing triggers as they waited for the command. As the radio squelched, they were already starting to exhale and squeeze, the 5.54 mm bullets striking their targets before the leader had finished pronouncing the word. Four "pops" blended with four wet "thwacks" and four men crumpled onto the muddy turf without a further sound.

The team waited ten seconds, watching for any movement inside the target. No lights came on, no door opened. "*Prodolzhit,*" the leader whispered into his radio. "Proceed."

The four men at the rear and the two at the front trotted forward, the two converging at the front door of the house taking positions on either side. Their primary job was to stop "squirters," anyone who might try to escape. Their secondary mission was to breach the door and flank any defenders who might take the primary assault team under fire. But there was no motion in front, only thumps and clunks from inside, no pops from their team's suppressed weapons nor the deafening "clack-clack-clack" of unsuppressed fire. They waited, listening, and then heard, *"Vo vladneii"*—"In possession"—over their radios, and the two men started back toward the rear of the building. There they met not four but five men, the fifth standing a little dazed with duct tape over his mouth and his wrists zip-tied behind his back. His ankles were joined with a loose band of nylon webbing to allow him to walk but to keep him from running, and he was wearing worn, green, Russian-issued BDUs with no insignia, contrasting with the black the others wore.

A man on either side grasped the man's upper arm and started marching him toward the tree line, their rifles slung over their outside shoulders. The other four took up security positions around the trio, scanning the perimeter for any movement.

AFTER CLOSE TO two hours passage through the forest, the leader radioed, *"Izvleka'"*—"Extract"—and the pilot of the refueled helicopter clicked his push-to-talk switch twice in confirmation. He reached up and started one engine then the other, the rotor above his head starting to turn as the engines came up to speed. He watched his gauges as the engines warmed and the oil temperatures rose into the green band. After a few minutes he rotated the throttle on his collective lever and pulled it up, the helicopter breaking free of the pavement and rising into the still-dark sky. The pilot turned the helo toward the clearing it had left a few hours before.

IT WAS DAYLIGHT, a slightly foggy morning when the helicopter descended into a camp in northern Turkey near the Georgian border, having crossed the latter nation just a few hundred feet above the terrain without a radio call or challenge. All of the men on board were tired, and with the fortunate exception of the pilots, they had taken turns dozing, their prisoner safely zip-tied to a cargo tie-down at the center of the helo. As the rotor blades spun down, one of the men extracted a long knife from a pocket along his trouser leg and cut the zip ties that held the prisoner to the helicopter. "Welcome to Turkey, Hamid," the man said in Texas-accented English, and he pushed Hamid toward the door and onto the hard soil below.

57

F armer and three other CIA agents showed their credentials at
the main gate to MacDill. They maneuvered around the jersey
barriers to join the broad boulevards that ran into the base,
around its perimeter, and then into the USSOCOM headquarters. This
was getting to be almost as familiar a route for Farmer as his commute
to Langley, albeit with less traffic. As important as this mission was,
he could not understand why he and his team were not issued an
agency jet, fast and anonymous, to get from DC to Tampa, rather than
having to fly commercial, rent a car, etc. At least they were able to stay
at the bachelor officers quarters on base, no fancier than a Marriott
Courtyard but a lot more convenient. Even though it was on base, the
rooms had little red and white signs reminding guests not to discuss
classified information.

Gathered inside the SCIF today was almost the same group that
had gathered two months earlier. The commanding general was at the
Pentagon, and a few of the special warfare operators were busy, but
the deputy commander and the rest of the senior staff anxiously
waited for a status update. One of Farmer's staff stood at the lectern,
the USSOCOM arrowhead from last time replaced by a CIA eagle-and-

shield logo. The room quieted as the aide began. "I want to bring you up to speed on three aspects of SMELOST," he said, using the code-name that had been assigned to the operation, the English phonetics of a Russian word meaning courage, audacity, and daring. "We have good news on the drone, uh, the UAV trials at White Sands. The combination of the latest guidance software load and the enhanced GPS receiver has been scoring what count as direct hits on the target locations. We have refined the target locations based on the combination of the overheads and the recon on site, and we think we have a solid set of target coordinates accurate enough to achieve effects."

"Do you have any backup on effects?" the deputy commander asked.

"Admiral, we haven't done any testing ourselves. We've relied on industry experts to assess effects."

"Confidence level?" the admiral asked.

The briefer paused and gathered his thoughts. "I don't have a numerical for that, sir. The industry experts have told us that a massive leak of un-ignited gas will cause over-speed or other damage to the compressors. A massive blast will cause ballistic damage, which may or may not be as difficult to repair." The admiral nodded and the briefer continued, "We will have the complete inventory of UAVs ready for the operation next week, including GPS mods and software loads, plus additional vehicles for training."

"Warheads?" a Delta asked.

"More than enough. We have verified the arming and detonation, but we'll send you additional for familiarization."

"Good. When will we have them?"

"We'll have a plane down here by Tuesday."

The deputy turned to one of his aides and said, "Coordinate with Base Ops that we'll be receiving a priority flight that includes munitions. I don't want anyone surprised." Turning to the briefer, he asked, "What color will the plane be?" meaning would it be gray, Air Force, or white, CIA.

"White, sir."

"OK, all the more reason to make sure we're in sync on this one," he replied to the attention of the whole room.

The briefer continued, "Thank you, sir. The second aspect of the op is the infiltration and exfiltration." The screen showed a map of Russia and its environs, arrows originating from locations outside the border and landing at points inside, then replaced by different colored arrows following what appeared to be roads to the target locations. "Let's start with Amur, the target near Svobodny. The team will join a special-warfare-capable submarine in Japan. I understand SOCOM has been in contact with CINCPAC for coordination." Noting the nods around the room, he continued, "The sub will transit submerged to a location here," his laser pointed to a position in the sea between the Sakhalin peninsula and the Russian mainland. "The sub will be met by a helicopter, Russian helicopter, that will pick up the team and transport them at low altitude to a location here," another point of the laser, "outside of Khabarovsk, where they will be met by covert ground transport."

He selected the next slide, which showed the outside and three pictures from inside a tank trailer. "We have constructed three of these trailers, one for each team. Access is through a hidden hatch in the front of the trailer. The trailer has a small tank in the center connected to the main drain valve and the filling hatch at the top that will contain a dummy cargo of diesel fuel so it will pass inspection if stopped."

The faces in the room carried expressions ranging from approval to mild skepticism.

"We've tried to make the interior as habitable as possible. There are eight foam mattresses, you can see them on the bottom of the tank, here and here, for example." The laser played over one of the images. "Hooks for hanging weapons, backpacks, vests, et cetera. self-contained portable toilets, water, MREs. Extra foam to keep things from banging on the side. Power and air supply from the tractor. The charges will already be on board; we'll smuggle them in, so you'll just have your normal going-to-war gear from the sub to the helo and into the truck."

"How long are we going to be in that can?" one of the SEALs asked.

"That's no can, that's a Russian Winnebago," a SEAL quipped. Scattered laughter met the comment.

"The trip by road from Khabarovsk to the target is about nine hours sustained. You guys will refine the timeline with us and the Navy, but we should see the rendezvous with the sub at zero-two hundred local time; that's twelve hundred Zulu," he replied, using the military designation for Greenwich Mean Time. "Rendezvous with ground transport about zero-three hundred local, thirteen hundred Zulu. About eight hundred kilometers driving, make it a leisurely twelve hours with fuel stops or traffic. The target is in the next time zone, so we'll drop an hour local time. We have a safe house midway, a warehouse building with an enclosed yard to give the team the opportunity to stretch out, exercise, whatever you guys need to keep sharp short of firing weapons."

"Damn," someone cracked, and even the admiral chuckled.

"Yeah," the briefer smiled and continued. "We'll have the tires on the trailer partially deflated to give it the illusion of being full, as well as to make the ride a little softer for you guys, but I know you don't like being out of view of what's happening."

"The driver is one of your guys?" a SEAL asked.

"Yes."

"Will we have comms with him?"

"Right now, all we can promise is a signaling system through the electric line. You know, flash the lights in some sequence. We've provided a way for the driver to see your response through a light on the dash of the truck," the briefer responded.

"That works," the SEAL said. "Anything that makes it harder for the militsiya or whoever to guess there's someone in there."

"Amen, brother," the wise-cracking SEAL volunteered.

"OK, we have a leisurely jaunt across the Russian countryside. What's zero hour at the target?" another SEAL asked.

"That's the tough part. These targets are spread across six time zones. Since we want all of the kinetics at the same time, that means we're driven by sunrise in the eastern-most target, Stavropol. The good news is that, since the duck blind seems to be workable and, indeed, working, those teams can emplace them earlier than the Amur team. We just don't want to blow Amur while there are a lot of workers on site, particularly Germans and Swiss working on the fractioning tower. So you guys go in at zero-two hundred local, eleven hundred Zulu. Transport drops you off at the location, you hump about half an hour, an hour for emplacement, half an hour back, extract at zero-four hundred local time. Blow at zero-six hundred, so you're two hundred kilometers away."

"That seems to be cutting it pretty close," the admiral commented.

"You can pull forward to zero-one hundred if you want."

"What's the traffic like at that time?"

"Light, except for the south end of the construction site."

"Won't that make our truck stand out?"

"No, there will be lots of fuel trucks in the area. Since they're working twenty-four seven, at least on that part, there will be similar traffic."

The admiral's expression was pained, but after looking at the members of his command, as well as the CIA contingent, he said, "You guys still have a lot to work out. I want to see another pass on this before we ask for final approval from the chairman. What about the other targets?"

"Yes, sir. Tyumen. We have the team traveling under cover as engineers for a joint US-Kazakh gas exploration team working in western Kazakhstan. You'll fly commercial into Almaty, then charter using a reliable Kazakh, uh, charter, to the exploration site. A day or two there and you'll be flown ostensibly to another exploration site, but really to Astana, which is about three hundred klicks from the border with Russia. We can travel entirely on land, about twelve to fourteen hours, or we can arrange a helo to get you guys closer to the border and cover the balance by truck. Same accommodations on the truck as the others. We made three trailers."

"Let's talk about that offline and make the decision," the Delta lieutenant colonel who would be leading that team decreed.

"So how many days before H-hour are we arriving in Kazakhstan?" a Delta asked.

"Again, we still have time to refine details, but we would recommend five to seven days, minimum."

"Weapons?"

"We'll smuggle them in and they'll join up with you in the truck."

"Can we carry sidearms before that?"

"I wouldn't recommend that. The Kazakhs are pretty strict about firearms, and it won't fit with your cover."

"So what are our ROEs on this op?" a SEAL asked, looking for clarification about the rules of engagement, how and when deadly force could be used.

The admiral leaned forward in his chair. "If you can believe it, that's still a matter of discussion between the secretary and POTUS. And the director."

"No point in having weapons if we can't use them," someone muttered.

"It will be addressed," the admiral said, meaning that discussion was over for now. "Third target?"

"Yes sir, for the gas storage site in Stavropol we have the team flying AMC, the Air Force's Air Mobility Command, into their base at Incirlik, Turkey, Then via covert helicopter into a camp in northern Georgia, where you'll meet the ground transport. Tank truck again. That flight's about thirteen hundred kilometers, but we have two mandatory refueling stops, the second in northeastern Turkey, near Ezurum, so you can stretch your legs."

"Covert helicopter?" someone asked.

"Russian Mi-eight, generic paint job. We've used it before."

"Not the same helo in all three locations?"

"No."

"I assume you're using smuggling routes in and out of Kazakhstan and Georgia. Can these be trusted?" a Delta asked. "The security of the routes and the locals guarding them?"

"Money talks, and we've used these routes before. Our people have ongoing relationships with the smugglers that are mutually beneficial."

"Timeline for this target?"

"This is a highly populous area, and we don't have a safe house that can accommodate the trailer, so we'll need to cover the six hundred kilometers in a continuous evolution. That's eight to ten hours. Sunset in Stavropol will be nineteen twenty-one local, twenty-two twenty-one Zulu, so allowing for delays en route, we leave the camp in Georgia around fourteen hundred Zulu for arrival at the target around twenty-one hundred local time."

"That seems too early. I think we want to be emplacing around zero-two hundred," the Delta colonel said.

"We'll work out the zero hour on target with you and then work backwards for the rest of the timeline. The traffic data our agents developed show very light travel most of the day, occasional traffic except for their nominal rush hours in the morning and evening. Perhaps one car per hour after twenty-three hundred local time. Same with the Tyumen site. Amur will be busier."

"Yeah, we know," the wisecracking SEAL commented, drawing a slight scowl from the admiral. An all-Delta team would take Stavropol, a mixed Delta-SEAL team would take Tyumen, but because of the seaborne insertion, the Amur op would be all SEAL.

The briefer continued, "Obviously, you and the agency still have a lot to definitize, but I would like to move to our last item, if I may."

"Proceed," the admiral decreed.

"Thank you, sir. Our tech people have been working with your tech people and operators to refine the 'duck blind,' the structure that lets us emplace the UAVs and depart the site before they operate. I think the original concept was called the 'duck blind' because it was a tall, camouflaged box at the end of a clearing. All of this is driven by the imperative that the attacks proceed simultaneously but across six time zones, with the one in the latest time zone, Amur, occurring before daylight. Given the challenges we're having getting the teams onto the targets, we had to limit the size and weight of the duck blinds, since they will be man-carried. Each UAV and payload will weigh about ten kilos. We have twenty-five programmed for Stavropol and thirteen for Tyumen, so that's a lot of weight and volume to carry. Assuming an eight-man team for Stavropol and a six-man team for Tyumen, that's twenty or thirty kilos per man, plus all the rest of your gear. So the duck blind can't be heavy, and it can't take up much volume."

"We won't be going far with it, but we appreciate your concern," one of the SEALs commented.

"We want it to be light, but it can't be too high-tech, in keeping with our non-state cover." The briefer pointed to a slide showing a frame with camouflage fabric over it. "So we came up with a fabric-covered plastic frame that will be easy to carry—well, relatively easy to carry—and can be assembled in a few minutes. The UAVs will be unfolded, the warheads attached mechanically and electrically, and the UAVs set in the frame." He pointed to another slide. "Each duck blind will hold four UAVs."

"What have you done for safing and arming? I don't want to plug that EFP in there just to have it blow up in my face," commented a Delta assigned to Tyumen.

"Good concern. SOCOM designed a simple, spring-wound timer, based on a kitchen timer, that will start when you pull this pin here." He called up another slide and pointed at the top of the UAV with his laser. "It grounds the connector to the warhead and electrically isolates it on the UAV side for an hour, so you have that much time before, worst case, the warhead blows."

The Delta smiled. "Good. Seems well thought out. But that does set an hour as the shortest time between emplacement and kinetics."

"That's correct, but your timeline has several hours between nominal emplacement and kinetics" the briefer replied. The Delta nodded.

THE ROOM FILLED with chatter among groups of SEALs, Deltas, support staff, and intelligence agents. Farmer rose from his seat and walked over to the Navy commander who would be leading the SEALs in the Amur operation. "Commander Harrison, could I talk with you a second?" he asked.

"Sure, what's up?"

"I'm not sure if your chain of command has discussed this yet, but there will be one more element to your mission."

58

The chairman of the Joint Chiefs of Staff had completed his briefing to the president, which had gone well. The president had asked few questions and had essentially approved the mission. "The last subject we need to discuss, Mr. President, is rules of engagement. We need your approval for the conditions under which deadly force can be used by our men on the ground."

The president looked at the chairman, his arms folded, and asked, "What do you want it to be?"

"Mr. President, for the purposes of this operation, you have approved the temporary transfer of these soldiers and sailors to the CIA. They will not be wearing their normal uniforms. I don't want them taken alive, so I would recommend that as soon as the operation commences, they have the freedom to defend themselves. Using deadly force, if necessary."

The president turned to the secretary of defense, "What do you think?"

"Mr. President, the chairman and I are in full agreement. This is a deadly dangerous situation. We temporarily transferred these men to the CIA because, if things went badly, we did not want this portrayed as a military operation against the Russian homeland, something

Popov could use effectively for propaganda purposes. Frankly, if things turn kinetic, it fits our terrorist cover better if our men return fire. If our men are killed, eventually, the Russians may be able to identify them, but it will be a lot tougher if they're not captured alive. To the best of our knowledge, none of these men have fingerprints in Interpol or any other international database. They're using gear that's either Russian or available on the open market, Russian firearms, nothing that would identify them as Americans per se. If we tell these men, 'Don't be taken alive,' they won't be."

The president leaned back slightly in his chair and looked at the ceiling above him for a moment. "I approve," he said, and the briefing was over.

59

T he month of May was opening cool and wet in the Caucasus. Katya Volkov stared through the rain-spattered windshield of a battered KAMAZ tractor pulling a tank trailer over a gravel road. They were near Mount Elbrus, on the Russian side of the mountains, or more precisely, in the Republic of Kabardino-Balkaria of the Russian Federation. As she expected, there were no FSB border guards on this remote crossing from Georgia, since few smugglers even took the trouble to come this way.

Georgi was dozing in the seat next to Katya, and as he bounced awake from a particularly nasty bump, he pitied the men in the trailer. All three of the trucks had a man and a woman in the cab, the presence of a woman being a distraction to any police or militsiya who might stop them, putting them at ease compared to an encounter with a single male. Whatever feminism there was in Russia lost to the prejudice that a woman was less likely to be committing a crime than a man.

About two hours later, as they approached the border between the Kabardino-Balkaria and Russia proper, Katya saw a checkpoint, not FSB but militsiya. Katya didn't smoke, but she pulled a full, already-opened pack of Marlboro cigarettes from the dashboard and lit one.

"Pretend you are sleeping," she said to Georgi, which he did. They came to a stop at the back of a line of five cars and one truck. After a few minutes it was their turn for scrutiny.

A militsiya officer walked up and lazily knocked on the window. "Papers," he demanded, looking largely disinterested. Katya handed her papers down, the registration for the truck, and Georgi's for good measure. The officer looked through them, and after he got to Georgi's, who was still pretending to sleep, he glanced again at Katya and looked far longer than needed just for identification. Katya was an attractive woman, not young but also not soft and bulky like many Russian women her age. The officer asked more forcefully than before, "What are you carrying?"

Katya took the cigarette from her mouth, and as the officer's eye followed it, she answered, "Diesel fuel for his father's farm in Kaskadnyy." She reached for the pack of Marlboros and handed them down to the officer.

The officer looked at her, took a cigarette and placed it in his mouth, then took the pack and placed it in his shirt pocket. He handed the papers back to Katya and commanded, "Go on." Katya was enough of a pro not to have gotten too tense about the checkpoint, but there was no question she relaxed as they drove on.

FIVE THOUSAND MILES to the east a trailer containing six SEALs had completed its rest stop and was on its way toward Svobodny. The transfer from submarine at sea to the hovering helicopter had proceeded without much complication, even though one member of the group had never done such a transfer before. He had never been on a submarine before. Indeed, he had never been at sea before. The six SEALs that made up the team on its way to Amur had been joined by Hamid al-Hassan.

Since Hamid's capture by a CIA operational team made up of contracted former SEALs and Deltas, he had been interrogated by a group of Turks who had honed their skills on captured members of the Kurdish PKK militia. Nothing Hamid said would have been admissible in court, nor would it ever end up in court, but it did fill in the blanks in the story of the Global Warriors of Jihad and Right-eousness.

As the CIA had suspected, Hamid and Khalid were, in fact, coopted by the Chechen "brothers" working for the Russians in Syria, who told Khalid they were deserting the Russian army and returning to Chechnya to wage jihad. Tired of the hardships of the Syrian war, Khalid and Hamid were happy to try their hands in Chechnya. The Chechens smuggled them through Turkey into Armenia and though Armenia into Chechnya. As they traveled with the Chechens, they had long discussions on the theology of jihad, the now distant but glorious history of Islamic military successes, and the craft of 21st-century jihad: bomb-making, suicide bombing, the use of explosives, and chemical, biological, and nuclear agents for mass casualties. The al-Hassan brothers spoke with irony and anger that, even as there were more Muslims than ever on Earth, they were ever more the underdogs.

When the Chechens introduced them to a Russian known as Gregor, they were immediately suspicious, but when Gregor asked them if they were interested in jihad against the Americans, their fears were dispelled. The Americans supported the Zionists who were killing their brothers in Syria—never mind that the Russians were too —and were killing their brothers in Iraq and Somalia and Afghanistan and everywhere else, the Muslim world chafed against the infidel power structure of western liberal culture.

Hamid and Khalid formed the Warriors of Jihad and Right-eousness, and Gregor regularly visited them in the house on the mountain outside Grozny. A group of Chechens "protected" them, and if Khalid, who was more worldly than Hamid but equally committed, at least to the theory of jihad, chafed at the restriction against trav-eling without an escort, he never told Hamid. Khalid idolized his older brother. He saw Hamid in his glory, a new Sheik bin-Laden, a new Sheik al-Baghdadi, a true "son of al-Walid." Even when Hamid met privately with Gregor, and it bothered Khalid just a little that he was excluded, he knew that their work together was for the glory of Allah. He kept to his study and did as he was asked.

Hamid never left the house except to walk in the woods nearby, always with two Chechens. Khalid often accompanied another one of the Chechens, Daud, a half mile into the woods to shoot targets with their AK rifles and Makarov and Sig-Sauer pistols. Khalid liked Daud, who teased him that he would find Khalid a Chechen wife. Khalid would have liked that. Despite the proximity to his brother, Khalid was lonely. And as the months passed, he sensed a distance from Hamid. What Khalid did not realize was that the distance was despair. Hamid had realized that he and Khalid were now tools of the Russians and there was nothing he could do about it.

THE SEALs in the trailer rested quietly, trying to expend as little energy as possible. Even though they were lying down on the foam mattresses, they involuntarily used their core muscles to keep from moving with the motion of the truck, and they had to fight that urge to keep their strength for the mission. This was not a foreign problem for SEALs, who frequently preceded a mission with an hour or more of bone-jarring motion breaking waves in a small, fast boat.

Hamid, on the other hand, was not SEAL trained. Occupying one of the mattresses, disconsolate, partially sedated, and zip-tied to the side, he moved freely with the motion of the trailer, occasionally bouncing against its hard steel wall.

The driver, an older, gray-haired, Russian man, was accompanied by a stocky woman with bright blonde hair. As they approached Svobodny, he toggled a switch that flashed the lights inside the trailer in a pattern that meant, "Thirty minutes." The SEALs roused themselves, checked their gear, and sat as best they could on their mattresses, lightly swaying as the trailer bounced. Each man was an island of concentration. Staring, they saw nothing but the mission, replaying their parts over and over. They had trained for weeks at MacDill, at Eglin, and at White Sands. They had gone over the mission again at their rest stop just a few hours ago. Every man was confident, but every man also believed the aphorism attributed to the 19th-century Prussian General Helmuth von Moltke which, paraphrased, said, "No plan survives contact with the enemy." In this operation the key was to avoid that contact.

THE LIGHT FLASHED THE "FIVE MINUTES" signal and the SEALs became more animated. They gathered their gear and turned reflexively toward the front of the trailer where the door would open. One of the SEALs used his knife to cut the zip-ties holding Hamid in custody and, stowing his knife, roused him to a sitting position. Hamid was groggy, but the SEAL did not know how much was an act, so he left the nylon band on his ankles and the zip-ties on his wrists. The trailer slowed and they felt a slow turn and then a stop, the air brakes making a final "shurrrrh."

"NVGs," the SEAL commander ordered, and just as he did, the lights went out as the driver turned off the headlights and marker lights on the exterior of the truck. It was truly pitch black, so the night-vision goggles had nothing to amplify except noise, each SEAL seeing only a formless sky of star-like speckles flashing in the goggles' eyepieces. Then they heard a metallic scrape, the door swung open, and they saw the interior of the trailer in ghostly outlines, the opening a brighter, contrasting oval. They slowly moved toward the opening and carefully jumped down, one of the SEALs roughly handing Hamid down to a SEAL on the ground.

The night of the mission had been chosen for its new moon, and the sky was indeed moonless, and also overcast. The only light by which the NVGs would work would normally have been the dim, muffled starlight, but the lights of the nearby construction site and the city of Svobodny reflected off the bottom of the clouds, and the SEALs could see clearly. They silently followed a path into the trees and started making their way to the opposite end of the site.

Hamid was escorted in the middle of the group by two SEALs, his mouth duct-taped so he could not call out. He had already been told what would happen if he made a sound. Even compliant, he was a burden because he could not see in the dark and could not walk well with the band between his ankles. Every few steps he would stumble, causing the SEALs holding him to struggle as well. Finally, one of them muttered, "Fuck this," and cut the band at each ankle, picking it up and putting it in his pocket so he would not leave a clue. The march got easier.

They reached the edge of the forest closest to their target, the fractioning towers, and paused to assess the situation in front of them. They had a chain-link fence and perhaps 50 meters of open terrain before they could use the cover of the enormous pipes that crisscrossed the site to work their way across. At the far corner of their end of site, they could see a vehicle, presumably security guards. No other vehicles or people were visible. But someone was probably there. You could count on that.

The leader gave the signal to proceed. One of the SEALs crouched forward with a small bolt-cutter and started cutting the fence close to a post so they could unobtrusively re-close it when they left. After he had cut about man-height above the ground, he stowed the cutters in a pocket on his lower pants leg and spread the fence, stepping inside and holding it for the rest of the group. After the last man entered the site, he pulled the fence back to the post and temporarily wired it closed.

The SEALs purposefully crossed the site, two SEALs stopping at each tower. The two SEALs with Hamid stopped at the middle tower, the farthest from the ostensible perimeter patrol of the security guards. Hamid's sedative had largely worn off, and his eyes were wide with curiosity and fear. They zip-tied him to a bolt on one side of the tower and set to work placing the charges on either side. They worked carefully, positioning the cutting charges for maximum effect. Since the towers had been made in Switzerland and Germany, Teutonic efficiency meant the mechanical details exactly matched the drawings they had been given. Explosives placed, they checked the cell phone

timers for proper function before connecting the wires to the detonators. One SEAL whispered to another, "This is too easy."

Not three seconds later they heard the familiar, mechanical "pop"
of a suppressed weapon. They crouched and looked in the direction
from which it had come, the tower farthest from where they had
entered the site, and looked for movement. They saw none. Unlike the
operation to snatch Hamid in Chechnya, where the operatives had not
trusted their encrypted radios and thus chose to speak Russian over an
open radio channel, the SEALs heard a crisp voice command in
English through their earpieces, "No further contact." They relaxed
and went back to completing the emplacement of the explosives.

As they finished, the two SEALs from the farthest tower
approached, supporting a limp figure in a Gazprom security uniform.
"What happened?" one of the SEALs asked.

"This guy started walking on our side and turned toward us," one
of the SEALs carrying the dead man replied. "He stopped, squinted a
little then started walking faster, reaching for his radio. He didn't get a
chance to key it."

"Do you think he has a partner?"

"Didn't see one. Hopefully, they'll just think he's sleeping somewhere. Gonna leave him outside the fence in the forest." the first
SEAL replied as he and his partner passed them, dragging the man.
One of the SEALs at the middle tower looked down to see if the man
being dragged was leaving a trail, but the tips of his shoes just
bounced along the gravel, leaving nothing detectable. When investigators found him tomorrow or the next day, the medical examiner would
find a Russian-made bullet in his head.

When all of the explosives were in place, the wiring double
checked, and the cell phones apparently working, the SEALs turned to
Hamid, who seemed to sense what was coming. He started to squirm
and kick, his untethered legs dangerous to the lower regions of the
SEALs' bodies. One of them hit Hamid in the forehead with the butt
of his rifle and his squirming stopped. Blood oozed from a wound on
his forehead.

The SEAL who hit Hamid stepped back, Hamid tried to focus his eyes, then he heard someone behind him whisper, "Sorry, Hamid," and his eyes grew wide again as he felt a palm on his bleeding forehead and a knife slice neatly through his neck. He started to struggle again, but his life was ebbing in spurts of red, and within a few seconds he was still, his eyes lifelessly staring at the sky.

The SEAL behind him brushed the blade of the knife on Hamid's tunic to clean it and re-sheathed it, while the other carefully stripped off the duct tape from Hamid's mouth and cut the zip ties from his wrists and the remnants of the nylon webbing from his ankles. The two men laid him on the ground behind the group of explosive charges timed to fire after the first one.

They took a final look around the base of the tower, rechecked their handiwork, and carefully made their way to the fence being held open by a SEAL. Once through, the SEAL rewired the fence, and they made their way quickly, quietly, through the forest.

60

When they returned to the rendezvous point, the truck was nowhere in sight. For the first minute or two they were unconcerned. They were running a few minutes ahead of schedule, and the plan was for the truck to park away from the site so as not to draw suspicion. But after five minutes, they were getting antsy, even though they were out of sight in the trees. Commander Harrison checked his watch. Still not late. But another ten minutes passed and now the truck *was* late. "When do we go to Plan B, skipper?" one of the SEALs whispered.

"Give it another ten."

"Wish they'd given us a cell phone. Could've called for an Uber," one of the SEALs cracked. A few of the others smiled, but they didn't laugh.

Thirty minutes later they saw headlights coming from the direction of Svobodny, and they started to relax. But the relaxation was short lived when the lights got closer and they recognized not a tractor pulling a tank trailer, but a KAMAZ dump truck. "Plan B," Harrison whispered. "Balaclavas." The SEALs pulled out black balaclavas that matched their uniforms and covered their faces except their eyes.

"Lawrence, can you drive a six by six?" Harrison asked a chief petty officer.

"Yes, sir."

"OK, you're in front with me. You drive. Samson, bind, blindfold, and gag the driver and put him in back with the rest of you. Hopefully, it's not full of mud or garbage," Harrison finished with a grin. "And by the way, no English in front of this guy."

Harrison timed their approach until the truck could not turn around but still had time to stop. He, Samson, and Lawrence stepped in front, the latter pointing their weapons at the driver, who was startled to see the black-clad figures appear out of the forest. The commander held up his hand in the universal gesture for "Stop." The driver complied and held up his hands. Harrison walked to the driver's door, opened it, and asked in unaccented Russian, "Where are you going?"

"Zavitinsk," the driver replied anxiously.

Harrison did not know how far that was, so he asked, "How much fuel do you have? How many kilometers?"

The driver looked puzzled. He thought for a minute. "I think half a tank. About three hundred kilometers."

That was not going to be enough.

"Thank you. Now go with this man. He will not hurt you, praise be to Allah."

The driver stepped down from the cab, obviously trying not to make any threatening gestures. Samson blindfolded and gagged him and helped him into the bed of the truck which, fortunately, was empty save for a few small rocks and clods of dirt. He fell heavily into the bed and groaned but sat up. Samson jumped in after him and bound his wrists with zip-ties. The rest of the team sat with their backs against the sides of the dump bed.

61

The North American Air Defense Command, or NORAD, headquarters is located deep inside a mountain near Colorado Springs, Colorado. Charged with protecting US and Canadian airspace, particularly from airborne and ballistic missile nuclear attack, NORAD has an array of sophisticated space-based sensors for detecting high-energy events anywhere on the globe, particularly, ballistic missile launches. At 1504 Zulu time on May 5th, an infrared sensor on a geostationary Space-Based Infrared System (SBIRS) satellite detected a bright flash followed by persistent infrared (heat) emission in the vicinity of Stavropol Krai, Russia. The data caused an alarm to sound inside Cheyenne Mountain.

The senior officer in the operations center at that moment, a Canadian brigadier general, saw the alarm and ordered more detail shown on one of the 12 enormous displays at the front of the room. One showed the estimated trajectory; after a few moments it was clearly static. Not a missile launch, at least not a successful one. At that moment another alert, a bright flash followed by an enormous heat signature, pulsed near Tyumen. "What the hell is going on?" the brigadier asked no one in particular.

The operations center watched anxiously as this one also flared brilliantly in place. At one of the consoles, a master sergeant who had decorated his station with a tiny sombrero for Cinco de Mayo muttered, "Sweet mother of Jesus."

The general reached for a telephone and called the Pentagon operations center. The duty officer responded that she would notify the joint staff. She called the office of the Joint Chiefs of Staff and told the duty officer, who said he would notify the chairman's chief of staff. After the call from the duty officer, the chief of staff called the chairman and relayed the information.

The chairman, as it happened, was already in the White House Situation Room with the president, the vice president, the secretary of defense, the director of the CIA, the secretary of state, and the national security advisor. The men and women in the Situation Room were watching screens showing overhead imagery of the Amur Gas Processing Station, along with news-feeds from CNN, BBC, and Russia Television. All three networks, along with Agence France Presse, Deutsche Welle, China TV, and Reuters, had just received an email statement claiming credit for terrorist attacks the press did not yet know had occurred. It read, in part:

We, the Global Warriors of Jihad and Righteousness, the Sons of Khalid ibn al-Walid

Celebrate a new victory over the infidels, the apostates, the Byzantines and the Jews.

The Umah will crush them all until all know Allah and his prophet, Mohammed,

Blessed be His name. Allahu Akbar, Allahu Akbar, Allahu Akbar.

Noteworthy was the reference to "Byzantines," rather than "Romans."

An additional screen showed a feed from the Operations Center at NORAD. They could easily see the alerts from the massive gas explosions and had just watched two of the three towers topple in Amur. While the networks had not yet reported what had occurred, CNN already had a crawler at the bottom of the page that reported the terrorists' claims.

"Well, it looks like they did it," the president said.

"Yes, sir, it does," the secretary of defense replied wistfully, thinking about the risks the men now faced escaping from the country. He had already received word that two of the teams had safely left Russian territory by the time of the explosions. That left one team still "downrange."

AT THE MOMENT of the secretary's concern, the SEALs and their guest were driving on a highway through Zavitinsk, about 230 kilometers from where they had stolen the truck. So far they had not attracted any undue attention. The two men in the cab had stripped off their tunics and tactical vests and were wearing only unobtrusive black T-shirts.

Commander Harrison was getting nervous about the range of the truck. The driver had been vague about the amount of fuel he carried and the distance he could travel. Chief Lawrence, who was now driving, had been watching the fuel gauge and had concluded it did not actually work, since it still showed half full after more than two hours of driving. They were both relieved to see a modern station with multiple pumps appear ahead of them, and Harrison pointed. "Pull in there. Pick the outside diesel pump."

Lawrence pulled up to the pump and set the brakes, then looked at his boss with a sheepish grin. "Other side," he said and smiled. He released the brakes and maneuvered the truck so that the pump was on the same side as the fuel tank.

"I don't know what the protocol is here, but get ready to fill and I'll go inside and pay." Harrison donned the driver's reflective jacket and climbed down from the passenger side of the truck. He walked toward the brightly lit convenience store and stepped inside. He waited in line for the cashier, careful not to smile, which would have marked him as either a foreigner or an idiot. As he waited he calculated how much he should offer, again to avoid suspicion. Diesel was 46 rubles per liter, the tank was probably 300 or 400 liters, say 16,000 rubles. He pulled out 20,000, pointed at the truck, and handed it to the cashier, who stared at him dully and took the money, pushing a button on a control panel as he placed the currency on top. Lawrence was watching him, so he walked to the door and nodded, and he could see Lawrence start the process of filling the tank.

Harrison turned back to the store and, picking up a basket, started loading it with bottled water, energy bars, chocolate, and then, almost as an afterthought, a half-liter of vodka in a plastic bottle. After a few minutes of paging through Russian hot rod and porno magazines, he saw that Lawrence was finished. He walked back to the cashier and unloaded the food and drink he had gathered and pointed to a prepaid cell phone on the wall behind the counter. The cashier retrieved it, rang it all up, and gave him his change. Harrison nodded, gathered his bags, and walked back outside.

When he reached the truck, he stepped to the side opposite the convenience store and started knocking on the side of the dump bed in Morse code. "Tossing food n water stop make driver drink vodka ar." The last two letters meant "end of transmission."

He listened and heard reply taps. "Interrogative none for us."

He chuckled, knowing the sender meant vodka, and tapped "Soon." Harrison started tossing the contents of his bags, aiming for the middle of the truck to avoid hitting his men, all the while trying not to attract attention. Finished, he walked around to the cab, climbed in and handed Lawrence a water bottle and an energy bar. "Home, James." Lawrence was young enough that he didn't get the joke, so Harrison looked at him, smiled, and said, "Let's go."

As they started back onto the highway, Harrison tore open the box holding the phone, praying that the battery was charged. He inserted the SIM card and turned on the phone. It greeted him happily, making chirpy noises and displaying four bars of signal and three bars of battery life. Good. He dialed a number and after a few rings heard a voice answer, "Da."

"Hello, Dimitri, my mother cannot go to Kiev after all. She is thinking about somewhere closer to home," the commander said in Russian.

"Let me think about that and I will call you back. At this number?" the speaker asked.

"Da," Harrison answered and hung up. Kiev was the code word for Khabarovsk, and he had just told the CIA asset on the other end that they could not make the pickup. Brevity is highly valued in all covert communications, but he wished there had been time to ask what had happened to their transportation. Screw-up? Mechanical trouble? Or were they compromised? He had to assume the latter and act accordingly. Plus, by now Russian authorities would be aware of the attacks against three Gazprom facilities and would be tightening security. It would not take long for roadblocks and checkpoints to develop.

ANOTHER 140 KILOMETERS down the highway and the phone rang. "My travel agent has some suggestions for your mother." The voice on the other end of the phone proceeded to give a ten-digit phone number starting with a Moscow area code. "If that doesn't work, try this number," and he gave him another ten-digit number.

The commander wrote them both down before asking, "What time do you think I should call?"

The voice on the other end answered, "He works late, try him at nineteen hundred local time."

"He does air and rail?" Harrison asked.

"He will probably recommend air."

"Thanks," Harrison replied. He turned off the phone, removed the battery, tore it in half, and tossed the two pieces along the side of the rode a kilometer apart.

62

T
he Amur Gas Processing Station was filling with uniforms: Svobodny police, militsiya, Gazprom private security, and FSB. Svobodny was a small, unimportant city except for the gas plant and the city's proximity to the Chinese border, so the local FSB contingent was quite a bit sharper than might be predicted by its population of less than 100,000.

The FSB colonel who commanded the force had just arrived and was starting to turn a bright shade of pink. "Get these idiots out of my crime scene," he raged to deputies on either side, and they scurried off to tell uniformed FSB officers to clear out anyone with the wrong uniform. A few moments later his principal deputy, an FSB major, returned to his side, and as they approached the destruction, they started talking about the case. "Witnesses?" the colonel asked.

"None yet, sir. One of the security guards is missing."

"Hmph," the colonel grunted. "Evidence?"

"So far, sir, there are some wires, probably from the detonators. The ground here is gravel, so we will need to shovel and sift to find anything smaller. There also appear to be human remains. Oh, and a metal detector found a spent cartridge case over there," he pointed to the tower still barely standing, "Five point four by thirty-nine." That made it Russian issue or one of the millions made elsewhere for Russian rifles and their derivatives.

"Shit," the colonel spat. "Show me the remains." They walked closer to one of the collapsed towers. Its destruction had also destroyed piping, compressors, and valves in a one hundred meter by twenty meter area. The collapse of the other tower had done the same. The third tower was tilting precariously. Gazprom was anxious to bring in a crane in an attempt to steady it, but that would be at least another day, and no one knew if it would fall in the meantime.

They reached an area 10 to 20 meters from the base of one of the collapsed towers. Here the tan gravel was accented with color—a patch of green here, a little red there. As they came closer, they could see, farthest from the blast, a hand and arm in a green sleeve, then a damaged head with an arm and an upper torso attached, then closer yet, a lower abdomen with legs akimbo, intestines sneaking from under the clothing like a mass of red and white snakes. The colonel had never seen a suicide bomber in person, but this looked like the pictures he had seen in training.

The two men continued to the base of the ruined tower. The colonel examined the neat cuts through the massive steel, like the proverbial hot knife through butter. "Cutting charges," he remarked. On the opposite side he could see that the steel had bent before being cut. "They knew what they were doing. Cut that side, let the structure sag that way, then cut the steel holding it in place," he said, gesturing with his hands the flow of destruction. They walked back toward the human remains. The colonel slipped on a pair of rubber gloves from his pocket and reached down to turn the head to see the dark face. "I don't think his skin is dark from burns. He's not from around here," he remarked. "Circulate pictures of his face. Clean him up first." Then he looked closer and saw the knife wound at the neck. "Curious. Curious," he commented, mainly to himself. He stood up. "I want fingerprints, DNA, photographs. This man was killed before the explosions and left here. Why?"

The deputy stopped. "A message?"

"Perhaps, but to whom?"

63

L
awrence looked over as Harrison scribbled additional numbers on the paper below where had recorded the phone numbers. The caller had not given him actual phone numbers; rather, they were latitudes and longitudes in a simple code: ignore the first three numbers (the area code); add two to the first; subtract two from the second; add two to the third; ignore the fourth; subtract two from the fifth; etc. The first group gave the latitude and the second, the longitude.

When Harrison completed the calculations, he pulled a commercial, pocket GPS unit from one of his pockets and plugged in the numbers. When he saw the result, he said, "Shit, we're almost there." Ahead he saw a disused gravel side road. "Turn there and park about two hundred meters down."

Lawrence did as instructed. A few hundred yards down the road there was a slight bend that masked view of the truck from the main highway. Lawrence brought the truck to a stop and killed the motor. Both he and Harrison opened their doors and listened. Silence. Harrison climbed out of his door and levered himself up to see over the side of the dump bed. His men smiled up at him.

"Our buddy's passed out," one of them volunteered, poking the man as a demonstration.

"Good. Let's get him out and back in the driver's seat with his bottle." He looked down at the now depleted vodka bottle. "Geez, he did drink a lot. You guys help him?" They laughed. "OK, here's the good news. We have a new rendezvous, about three hundred klicks from the original location, so we have a good chance of not being pinched if our driver gets turned. The bad news is it's about thirty-five klicks through this forest to the clearing where the helo's supposed to land. We have ..." He looked at his watch, as much out of habit as out of need, since he knew what time it was. "Thirteen hours to get there." The substitution code had extended to the time. The commander had added six hours to 1900 and obtained 0100 for the rendezvous.

LESS THAN THREE kilometers per hour may sound leisurely, but trudging through a forest with unknown undergrowth meant a challenging hike. So they did not dawdle. They cleared the dump bed of any debris they might have left, wiped down the cab for fingerprints, and deposited the driver, neatly passed out, behind the steering wheel. Then they continued a mile down the road, no civilization in sight, before they cut into the forest.

Harrison did not know how strong the signal would be under the canopy of fir trees, so before they stepped into the forest, he took a GPS reading and determined the compass direction they needed to follow to the rendezvous site. He held out his arm and told his men, "This way to salvation, boys."

64

The president of the Russian Federation was in a foul mood when he was informed of the three apparent terrorist attacks against Russian natural gas infrastructure. He shared his foul mood by calling the chairman of Gazprom and savaging him for poor security at his company's facilities, the crown jewel of one of Russia's most important export sectors and a major source of its foreign currency. After he hung up with Gazprom, he ordered the heads of his intelligence services to be in his office in two hours with whatever information they could provide.

THE FSB DEPUTY in Svobodny had been unusually efficient in attempting to trace the dead terrorist's identity, having his picture taken and circulated through the FSB's networks within half an hour of the colonel's order. The result was a color print shoved into the hands of the directors of the GU and the FSB as they left their respective offices for the short, police-escorted limousine ride behind the Kremlin walls. To the director of the FSB, the face looked vaguely familiar, but the head of the GU blanched when he recognized Hamid al-Hassan, one of his most important assets.

Curious why he looked so familiar, the FSB head called his office and was informed that the description matched that of a man who had been reported kidnapped from Chechnya a few months previously. The GU desperately wanted him found. No fingerprints or DNA match yet, the latter not likely for a few weeks. *Interesting,* the FSB director thought. *What is the GU's interest in this man?*

THE LIMOUSINES ARRIVED ALMOST SIMULTANEOUSLY, the two men emerging, saluting each other, and striding into the double doors held open for them by uniformed guards. "Anything interesting to report?" the director of the FSB asked his colleague and rival.

"Only very preliminary," the director of the GU replied.

The head of FSB smiled slightly to himself and thought, *Always keep your powder dry.*

The two men were led into the president's office. Popov pointed them to chairs at the short table extending from his desk and motioned for them to begin. He looked at one man, then the other, saying nothing.

The director of the FSB started, "Mr. President, the FSB has taken control of the investigations at the three sites. It appears explosives were used in each terrorist attack. Preliminary results are that airborne explosives were used in the Stavropol and Tyumen attacks, while metal-cutting explosives were used in Amur."

Popov's eyebrows rose. "Airborne explosives? What do you mean?"

"Our investigators found some debris consistent with the use of UAVs, such as those used in California."

The president looked at the director of the GU and his eyes narrowed. He turned back to the head of the FSB. "Please, proceed. And what does the use of 'metal-cutting explosives' mean?"

The FSB director continued, "The terrorists used an explosive composition and configuration that was intended to cut the steel at the base of fractioning towers. So they were highly sophisticated," he paused. "Or state sponsored." He let that last statement hang.

Popov looked at the director of the GU while asking the FSB director, "Anything else?"

The director of the FSB had known the question was coming and he relished it. He had to fight from smiling as he drove the dagger into heart of the director of the GU. "We found a body at the scene of the Amur terrorist attacks. His body showed considerable signs of damage from the explosives, so it appears he was in the vicinity of the explosives when they detonated. We think his name is Hamid al-Hassan, who was reported by the GU as missing from Chechnya. He was originally from Syria." He paused, savoring the deliciousness of this moment. "That is all we know at this time, Mr. President."

The president stared at the director of the GU then turned to the head of the FSB. "General," he said evenly, "I need to speak with the director. Would you excuse us, please?"

The director of the FSB could not suppress a slight smile as he stood from his seat. It was a huge grin inside but just a smirk on the surface. "Yes, Mr. President."

65

H arrison motioned quietly for a break, and the men dropped where they could each lean against a tree trunk. The forest was not dense with undergrowth like a jungle, just ferns and small plants starting to grow from the soft floor, but retreating glaciers or some geological phenomenon had created ground that rose and fell a few feet every few yards, and with the soft soil it was very fatiguing. By now the men had not slept in more than 24 hours, and while they were used to this type of deprivation, it wasn't fun.

The commander looked at the GPS, which was having trouble receiving the satellites through the canopy. By a combination of dead reckoning and spotty GPS measurements, he estimated they had about another 20 kilometers to go in seven hours. "Let's shove off," he commanded quietly, and the weary men rose against their trees and started north again.

⌒

THE HIKE so far had been uneventful, but the SEALs were well trained and they knew not to take good luck for granted. They walked quietly, without whistling, coughing, or conversation, knowing how out of place and recognizable those were in the wild. They had gone perhaps another kilometer when the point man held up a fist. In a second they had halted in place and squatted down to lower their profiles against the trees. Harrison slowly made his way to the front, where the point man touched his nose and silently sniffed. The commander sniffed and smelled it as well: cigarette smoke. They carefully looked in the direction of the wind and through the tree trunks saw a figure making his way across their path, more across than toward, but coming dangerously close. He was carrying a double-barreled shotgun in one hand and a hare or rabbit in the other.

The commander cursed the interminable Siberian spring twilight and the black BDUs they wore, which were utterly ineffective at breaking up their outlines compared to camouflage. He would have been happy with desert tan right then. He signaled for the SEALs to go to ground slowly, so the movement would not attract the man's attention. Then they saw it: a dog trotting at the hunter's feet. The wind was blowing perhaps five knots in their direction, and it should keep the dog from smelling them. But would it?

They watched for the next ten minutes as the man, hare, and dog passed in front and to their right. They waited another five, until they could no longer see him, and then another few more to be sure.

Harrison had just motioned for them to rise and resume their passage when he heard the sound he had been dreading; the dog started to bark. Now downwind, it had smelled them. They heard it grow louder, and then they could hear the man asking the dog, "*Chto eto, mal'chick?* What is it, boy?" and then the dog was there, running at them and snarling.

One of the SEALs shot it with his rifle, a "pop" followed by a soft, "eeooo," from the dog. And then the man was there, huffing and yelling, seeing his dog dead and the men in black in front of him. Furious, he dropped the hare and raised his shotgun. Harrison shot him dead.

It all happened so fast, Harrison thought. *When it goes to shit, it really goes to shit fast.*

The SEALs stood for a moment, breathing and listening,

HENRY PHILIPS

processing what had just happened, and then the commander
motioned for them to continue.

Their long, silent walk continued.

66

L iz Sanders stood in one corner of her shop before turning off the lights. Her assistant had already left for the day, and now Liz stepped back into the center of the boutique where her favorite table with her most exclusive products dominated the room. She ran her hand over the silk scarves, stroked the leather handbags, bent low to inhale the aroma of expensive hides. After a moment she straightened, looking around one more time as she walked to the corner and turned off the lights, pulling down the rolling door at the front of the store and locking it as she exited. Langley was undecided about whether or not to pull out agents who did not have diplomatic immunity, particularly NOCs like her. She did not know if she would see her boutique again. It had started as a cover, but it had become her identity.

Liz took the long way home, walking around the river side of the Kremlin and then around the back of the fortress toward Tverskaya Street and her apartment. After some wet weather early in the month, May had turned clear and warm, beautiful walking weather. She felt invigorated by the time she reached her apartment and stepped inside. She stopped at the refrigerator for a Borjomi mineral water and then made a direct line for her bathroom, alternately taking long pulls of the water and shedding articles of clothing until she was naked and could step into the hot shower.

The water soothed and relaxed her, purging her pores like a sauna, and when she was finished and wrapped in her robe, a towel circling her head, she felt ready to check her Facebook page and see what the future held for her. She opened her laptop, carrying it from the desk to her sofa, where she sat with her legs folded under her. She typed the password for the laptop, then opened Facebook and typed her password there. The page populated with several messages from friends, some real, some fake.

One of the fake friends said, "We had flooding this year when the snow melted and the ice built up against the bridge." That was a message to meet under the west side of the Krymsky Bridge in Gorky Park. The usual time was 10 P.M. and the message hinted no differently, so she sighed, closed the laptop, and rose from the couch to get dressed for the meet.

LIZ WALKED from Tverskaya Street to the bridge, taking a route away from the Kremlin since the complex had a large number of surveillance cameras. She wore athletic shoes and a dark warmup suit, easy on her feet and just the right amount of warmth as the night got chilly. She crossed the bridge, descended the steps into the park, and walked away from the bridge, back toward the Kremlin.

She took a seat on a bench where she could enjoy the view across the river. She looked across, then up and down, then across again. After fifteen minutes and a few more observation cycles, she rose from the bench and walked back toward the bridge. It was almost 10 P.M. and she could see a figure standing underneath the bridge. Hopefully, it was John. She walked closer and confirmed it was him.

Liz walked up to John, and uncharacteristically, she lifted herself on her toes while pulling his face down to her and kissing him on the lips. Not with great passion but not purely businesslike either.

"Whoa, what was that?" he asked, smiling.

"I don't know, I guess I'm just giddy tonight. And a little lonely. Doesn't it help our cover?"

He laughed softly. "Yes, it does, but I'm a married man."

Liz frowned slightly. "Sorry, I forgot. Don't want to cause a scandal. So what's up?" she asked, slightly too perkily.

John's face turned serious. "We want you to find out from your friend what the reaction is in the president's office to the terrorist attacks. And based on that, we may want you to pass on a message."

Liz became as serious as John. "So that was us?" she half asked, half stated. John nodded slightly. "OK, I'll try to get him in tomorrow or the next day." She paused and looked away toward the brightly lit walls of the Kremlin, down the river. "Am I staying or going?"

John had known the question was coming. "Depends on the answer you get."

67

It was dark now, very dark. Like the previous night, tonight the sky was overcast with no moon, but now, in nearly unpopulated eastern Russia, there were no streetlights to reflect off the clouds, and their progress was very slow. Occasionally, the SEALs lit infrared chem lights so they had some additional illumination. That helped where the canopy was particularly dense, but it made them very vulnerable to detection by Russians with their own NVGs. Mercifully, they were in such a remote area that it was unlikely they would encounter anyone unless the helicopter had been followed. And that carried all kinds of ramifications Harrison did not want to contemplate.

The commander's best estimate was that they had two kilometers to go. His SEALs were dead tired, but being so close to the rendezvous point gave them a burst of adrenaline and they forged on. As they came closer to the GPS location the commander had recorded, he started to question whether he had made a mistake. It was now 2340, less than an hour and a half until the rendezvous. The commander reached into his pocket and found the crumpled paper on which he had written the numbers. Trying not to trip, he read the numbers by chem light. The alternating view between the paper close up and the more distant terrain was making him dizzy. He confirmed his numbers and slipped the paper back into his pocket.

The SEALs walked on for another half hour until, suddenly, there seemed to be a glow ahead. As a group they doused their chem lights by slipping them into their pockets and let their eyes adjust to the dimmer conditions. Harrison realized they were approaching a clearing, and the light they saw was from stars unblocked by the trees. The sky had cleared. He whispered into his radio, "Hold," and the SEALs immediately stopped in place and squatted. He walked forward another 15 meters to the edge of the clearing and scanned the scene in front of him. As best he could tell, it was an abandoned logging camp. He saw no lights or movement and heard nothing other than the sound of owls and other nocturnal creatures.

"Proceed," he pronounced over the radio, and the team joined him. "Police the LZ for any obstructions, wires, whatever," he told them. "It'd suck to have that helo make it all the way here and then hit something."

The SEALs slowly walked into the clearing and did as he asked. Once they were confident the site was clear, they opened new chem lights and arranged them in a cross pattern in the center of the clearing. Then they waited.

AFTER A HALF HOUR they heard the helo approaching from the east, low to the treetops. It swept past them and then rose slightly and circled back, landing into the light west wind on top of the chem-lit cross. The SEALs ran from the edge of the clearing, the first SEAL pulling the side door open and helping his buddies in. Harrison was last, pushing the SEAL at the door into the helo and then jumping in himself. As he slid the door shut, the helicopter lifted from the clearing and turned back east.

The cabin was crowded with six SEALs removing their helmets and various other pieces of gear, the helicopter's crew chief, and a large wooden crate strapped to the deck in the middle. The crew chief looked over the SEALs, guessed who was in charge, and worked his way across the floor of the helo to Harrison. Over the din created by the engines, transmission, and rotors above their heads, he shouted in Russian into the commander's ear, "We have to stop for fuel in Khabarovsk. You and your men must hide in this crate. The police may be looking for you."

Harrison looked at him and shouted back. "You think that crate will fool them?"

"This helicopter carries equipment for oil and gas exploration all the time. We know the police. As long as it is not some bastards from Vladivostok, we will be fine." He was referring to the nearest big Russian city, about 800 kilometers to the south.

Harrison was too tired to argue. He gave him the thumbs up, which he thought meant the same thing in Russia as in the US Whether it did or not, the crew chief nodded and went back to his station.

AN HOUR and a half after the conversation, the crew chief was back to tell the commander it was time to climb into the crate. It was clearly big enough for six men and their equipment, but whether six tired and smelly men could breathe in there for very long remained to be seen. Harrison explained the plan to Lawrence, who was sitting next to him. Lawrence passed it on, and so it went, SEAL by SEAL, as they watched the crew chief unbolt the side of the crate with a battery-powered impact wrench and slide the heavy wooden wall aside enough that the SEALs could scurry inside. They felt the helicopter slowing and descending as the crew chief slid the side back into place, bolted them in, and stowed the wrench.

After a few minutes the SEALs felt the soft impact of the landing, then the rocking motion of the cabin as the rotor blades slowed and stopped. The engines spooled down, and with the helo now silent, the interior of the crate felt like an anechoic chamber. The men who had easily dealt with so much stress over the last two days now felt disorientation and an unfamiliar panic in the silence and total darkness. Well, not total darkness since, as their eyes adjusted further, they could see little darts of light where the rough boards of the crate did not quite meet. And not total silence either, since they could hear each other's breathing and maybe even heartbeats. They listened as the pilots and crew chief began speaking with someone in authority who, even to the ears of the non-Russian speakers, came across as haughty.

Harrison heard the policeman demand, "Why are you flying at night?"

A voice said, "Because they pay us extra to fly at night."

"What are you carrying?"

"A large valve for a gas pipeline. The one in Sakhalinsk is leaking. You want to tell Popov why his gas is still leaking while you make us wait?"

The policeman laughed and yelled, "Asshole," and the SEALs could hear him walk away.

AFTER A HALF HOUR the SEALs heard one of the helicopter's engines turning and starting, then the other. They felt the helo sway as the main rotor started turning, and after a few minutes they were airborne. The crew chief unbolted the crate and the SEALs sucked in the cabin's "fresh" air, even though it smelled strongly of kerosene. It was good to be alive. Within five minutes of takeoff, the vibration of the helo and their exhaustion sent all six SEALs into a deep slumber.

IT SEEMED to the SEALs as if they had just fallen asleep when they were shaking each other awake as the helicopter entered a hover over the surfaced submarine, black and invisible except for a small red light shining on the top of the hull. The sight brought each man instantly alert, and they gathered up their gear as the crew chief slung a thick rope out the helicopter door. A sailor in a survival suit and harness grabbed the rope with a grounded hook and held it to the deck as the first SEAL slid down, followed by four more and, finally, the commander.

As his men passed through a hatch to go below, an officer approached, saluted Harrison, and said, "Welcome back to the Jimmy Carter, sir"

Harrison returned the salute. "Nice to be back," he said before he went below to shower and crash in his rack for as long as chain of command allowed. The helicopter was already gone, and the sub was submerged and heading back to Bangor before he reached his cabin.

68

The sub was well into the Sea of Japan when Liz made a call to Boris the next morning. "I have that briefcase you wanted to see in the boutique. Can you come by today?"

"No, no, I am too busy?"

"Tomorrow then?"

"No, I will be too busy then, too."

Odd. Was Boris getting skittish? Or Greedy? "Well, that is a shame. I have another client who is interested and might buy it before you come in. The briefcase is much nicer than you might expect," she coaxed, meaning the payoff would be bigger. "I would hate to lose you as a customer," She knew Boris would understand that last comment to suggest she had another potential source and might not need him anymore.

There was a pause on the phone, "OK, I am looking at my calendar, I have fifteen minutes at three. I will see you then."

LIZ LEFT the shop for lunch and walked back to her apartment to retrieve the money for Boris. It was a little drizzly but still not unpleasant. She stepped into her apartment and kicked off her shoes before walking into her bedroom closet to open the safe in the cupboard. She removed the last six stacks of 500-Euro notes, 300,000 Euros. *If I stay I'll need that bigger safe.* She replaced her jewelry and closed the safe, checking her makeup in the bathroom mirror before walking back into the living room, slipping on her shoes, and starting her walk back to the boutique.

Boris was punctual as usual, Liz waiting in the vestibule of the GUM as his driver parked in front. She stepped out as he emerged from the car, and he seemed startled to see her. "I knew you were in a hurry, so I came out to meet you." She held out the white-and-gold bag in front of her. "Here's the briefcase. If you decide you don't want it, bring it back." She walked around to the back of the car where the trunk lid was swinging open. Boris joined her. "I need to know what the president has been told about the terrorist attacks and how he is reacting."

Boris blanched even paler than his normal complexion. "He thinks the Americans did it, but there is also some connection with the GU, so he is very angry at them."

"How will he react?" she asked evenly.

Boris looked away from her toward the Kremlin then after a moment back to her. "Popov is a former Chekist. He respects an intelligence operation carried out well, and he understands the message from the Chechen you left." Liz's expression was steady, not betraying the fact she had no idea what he was referring to. "If everyone is quiet, in private he will accept it as a proportional measure, retaliation, and in public blame it on the terrorist group, which he knows does not exist. He'll make some noise, make a few raids, bomb someone in Syria. Then it will go away." Boris shut the trunk and started walking back to the rear door of the BMW, but he stopped and turned back to her. "But it must stop. This thing. And you and me." He looked at her a moment, then looking down, he opened the door and got in, the BMW speeding away as soon as the door closed.

THAT NIGHT LIZ sat in her robe on her couch, her legs beneath her, a glass cup of tea in her hand. The national news on Russia TV was leading with a story about how Russian Special Forces had killed Hamid al-Hassan, the terrorist leader of the Sons of Ibn al-Walid, at his hideout in Chechnya. Al-Hassan's terrorist group had committed the atrocious acts of destruction that damaged three Gazprom sites and killed four Russians. The hunt would continue for other members of the terrorist group. Liz smiled. "I guess I'm going to stay," she said out loud.

POSTSCRIPT

Eric West wore a small smile as he walked through the doors of his new office, a low, red-brick federal building in the largest city in the state. In the banker's box in his arms, he carried a few personal items, a reference book or two, and a framed picture of a pretty, green-eyed woman standing in front of a saguaro cactus, her red hair glowing in the light from the sunset she faced. Eric found his desk, placed the box to one side, and started emptying it, starting with the picture. He moved his computer monitor to the right and placed the picture square in the center of the open space. He finished unpacking the box and slipped it under his desk. Then he glanced over his shoulder and walked to a glass-walled office at the end of the room to introduce himself to the SAC.

AFTER A HALF HOUR or so with the SAC, whom Eric appreciated for his courtesy and thoroughness, Eric was dismissed and he walked back to his desk. He noticed the time, smiled, and pulled out his cell phone. When the voice on the other end answered, he smiled even more and asked, "Hi, neighbor. Got time for lunch?" He listened. "OK, I'll see you then." An hour to kill.

He kept busy by introducing himself to the other agents he had not yet met, finding the canteen, learning what other offices were in the building, even getting recommendations for hikes nearby. When the hour had passed, he grabbed a light jacket that thankfully did not say "FBI" on the back and strode across Sixth Avenue to the Anchorage Museum. He was having lunch with the woman in the picture.

ABOUT THE AUTHOR

Henry Philips is the pseudonym of a successful international business-man. Mr. Philips has traveled widely throughout Europe, Eurasia and Asia, and chose to write under a pen name to avoid potential problems with hostile foreign government officials.

CPSIA information can be obtained
at www.ICGtesting.com
Printed in the USA
BVHW071037211220
596167BV00001B/63